Agravain's Escape
The Return of King Arthur

Jacob Sannox

Copyright © 2020 Alan O'Donoghue
All rights reserved.

Terms and Conditions:
The purchaser of this book is subject to the condition that he/she shall in no way resell it, nor any part of it, by any method, nor make copies of it, nor any part of it, to distribute freely.

This book is a work of fiction. However, some of the characters from the historical chapters are based on real people, including some of the police officers, the Ripper victims and the Marquess of Waterford etcetera. These chapters contain a fictionalised representation based on a combination of research and imagination. I do not suggest that any of the deeds in this book were actually carried out by the historical characters. The remainder of the characters are entirely fictional, and any similarity between the characters and situations within the book's pages and places or persons, living or dead, is unintentional and coincidental.

Cover by BetiBup33 - https://twitter.com/BetiBup33

Typeset by Polgarus Studio – www.polgarusstudio.com

The moral rights of the author have been asserted.

Agravain's Escape is the second book in my
Return of King Arthur series.
If you haven't read the first book, The Ravenmaster's
Revenge, I'd recommend that you do before you get started
on Agravain's Escape, as it's a continuing story.

Jacob Sannox

Acknowledgements

Thank you to my first readers;
Anna, Zoe, Sami, Ben and my parents.

I could not have done it without you.

Anna - My emotional barometer. I love her reactions!

Zoe - Helped kick Nimuë into shape.

Sami - Wants to be a raven familiar, I suspect.

Ben - Who goes above and beyond. Every time.

Mum - Who does not like that Agravain makes tea while wearing dirty gloves. Brilliant.

Dad - Who may throttle me if I write 'onto' or use 'which' instead of 'that' one more time.

Chapter One

Padstow, Cornwall
November 2019

Nimuë felt Merlin's absence. After all the long centuries, despite all that had happened between them, it seemed their connection had never been severed. She stood on the beach before dawn, her eyes glazed and her border collie whining and nosing a chewed-up tennis ball towards her, drawing a shallow groove in the sand.

Nimuë felt Merlin die. Felt a sudden void within her being.

She shuddered and dropped to her knees in the sand, her hands trembling and her hair whipping against her face.

Her consciousness drifted out of her body and hung in the air about her like a mist until the dog began furiously licking her face. The wet tongue on her skin brought her back round, and her spirit re-entered her body.

'He's finally gone,' said Nimuë, fussing the animal. 'Perhaps it's nearly time.'

With the sound of waves lapping at the shore, she picked up the ball and threw it into the water. The collie went haring after it, and she stood, not bothering to brush the sand from her skirt. Nimuë walked barefoot to the water's edge until the shallows washed her toes. She looked left, up the dark beach, then right, back towards Padstow.

Nobody in sight.

Nimuë checked behind her and then, slowly, she walked into the surf until the water covered first her ankles, then her knees, and her hips. She did not stop walking when the waves lapped against her breasts, nor did she tilt her head up as her chin sank below the surface. She walked on until she had disappeared from view, breathing deep and taking the salt water into her lungs.

She closed her eyes and her consciousness ran upriver and down, out to sea. She rose as vapour and fell as rain upon the land that had been her home when King Arthur had still ruled, and Merlin gave counsel.

She sought them out, all of them, Arthur and his knights, but one in particular.

She sought news of Agravain.

⁂

Sometime later, when the sun was up, Nimuë's head once again broke the surface of the water, like that of a seal keeping a cautious watch. Her dog waited with his head upon his paws and a doleful expression. He perked up, however, as he saw his mistress stride back up the sand. His tail wagged cautiously, once in each direction, but he did not hold on to his grudge at being abandoned.

She crouched beside him and stroked his head.

'Sorry, Bobbi,' she said, as she fastened a lead to his collar. 'Let's go home. We have to prepare. I still cannot reach Agravain, but Arthur will need us before long.'

The words reminded her and, cursing, she dug her hands into her jacket pockets. Nimuë pulled her house keys from her left pocket and her waterlogged mobile phone from her right.

Muttering, she set off up the beach towards her cottage.

~~~

England
Christmas Day 2020

Arthur sat perched on the edge of an armchair with an ill-fitting, crumpled, orange tissue paper crown on his head. He felt bloated, and he waved away a tray of pineapple chunks and cheddar on cocktail sticks that an elderly lady held out for him.

'Thank you, I couldn't eat another thing,' he intoned, his face aching from all the forced smiling.

This was not his usual Christmas experience, but he had to adjust, he reminded himself as yet another package, wrapped in ridiculous candy cane patterned paper, was thrust into his hands while Slade blared in the background.

He tore open the paper to reveal a book about the First World War. It took all he had not to throw the damned thing across the room, and his heart rate leapt when he saw the photograph on the cover of an English soldier making his way across no-man's land. Images of his own experiences flashed before his eyes, but he widened his smile and nodded, hoping to appear grateful as his hands trembled ever so slightly. He hoped nobody would notice.

'Cat said you were interested in history,' said Caitlyn's mother, setting down her tray and plucking the book from his hands before he could make a comment. She turned it over and started reading out the text on the back of the book and pointed at the pictures.

'Thank you. You're very kind,' said Arthur. He felt Caitlyn curl a sympathetic arm around his shoulder, and she kissed him on the forehead. He was grateful for that, for sure.

'He's *already* got it,' said her father, sitting in an armchair on the other side of the room, arms folded and cheeks red, his moustache stained port red. 'I told you he would. He's ex-military, Veronica.'

'I'm sure he hasn't, Dad,' said Caitlyn.

'It really is very gracious of you,' said Arthur, as he stood. He set the book down and took the old lady in an embrace before crossing the room with the aid of his cane to shake Roger's hand.

The old man grunted and nodded in acknowledgement.

'I haven't read it,' said Arthur. 'Thank you both.'

Veronica blushed and told him it was nothing then reached for a tray of mini pork pies and cocktail sausages with silverskin onions on sticks.

This, reflected Arthur, *was going to be a long day.*

Not so very far away, deep within the woods where both Caitlyn and Arthur made their respective homes, a pool occupied a clearing in the trees, its waters murky and its surface still.

Trees creaked, birds called, but the woods were empty of wandering humans, all of whom were busy elsewhere that Christmas afternoon. The dog walkers had walked their dogs and abandoned the woods in favour of hearth and home.

All save one.

Bobbi the border collie waited, stretched out with his head on his forelegs beside the pool, his eyes fixed on the spot where his mistress had disappeared, except for the odd occasion when a squirrel distracted him. He resisted the temptation to follow.

Bobbi raised his head suddenly, and moments later, the still surface of the pool was broken by the tip of a sword bursting from the depths. Birds took to the skies as the rest of the sword emerged, and a woman's hand appeared, grasping the hilt.

It held Excalibur aloft, seemingly already dry, a faint green light emanating from the blade.

The dog tilted its head and watched as, still holding the sword, Nimuë rose from the pool, naked and beautiful, her pale body slick with water. She walked up onto the grass, shivering, and wrapped Excalibur in a length of cloth before slipping into her clothes and sitting down to pull on her boots.

Later the same evening, Caitlyn drove Arthur back to her home, down the private road through the very same woods as those that surrounded the pond into which Arthur had thrown Excalibur a year ago, after Merlin's death. Once she parked, they walked through the gate to Hunter's Cottage and, arm in arm, up the path to the front door, surrounded by towering trees, centuries old.

Samson, Caitlyn's Rottweiler, met them at the door with a mix of glee at their return and resentment at having been left in the first place.

'Thank you for coming with me today,' she said, closing the door behind them, 'I know you'd rather have been elsewhere.'

Arthur paused, sitting on a chair with one boot off and in the midst of prying off the other. He finished the task and stood to take Caitlyn in his arms.

'It's a privilege to spend the day in your company, wherever we may be. Your parents are . . . ' he frowned, searching for words, ' . . . considerate, and they love you very much, that much is clear.'

'Smoothie,' she scoffed and ducked out of his arms.

Arthur smiled and hung up his coat.

'Get a fire going,' Caitlyn called from the kitchen. 'I'll make hot chocolate and then . . . '

Her head appeared, sideways in the doorway.

'Presents!' she grinned. Arthur laughed as she disappeared again and did as instructed.

Caitlyn joined Arthur where he sat on the rug by the fireplace, and set down the mugs, topped with tiny, chocolate-sprinkled marshmallows, on the stone hearth. They sat almost too close to the flames, and Arthur felt his skin protest, but it was a somehow pleasant sensation.

'Thank you,' he said, sipping at the hot chocolate then wiping his mouth when Caitlyn nearly spat hers out, laughing at how the marshmallow stuck in his moustache.

He leaned in and kissed her on the cheek. When he pulled back, he saw that she was holding out a gift, wrapped in brown paper and tied with two ribbons, one red and one green.

'For you. Happy first Christmas together,' said Caitlyn. She sat cross-legged, leaning back against an armchair, and stroking Samson.

His heart beating a little faster, slightly nervous about finding what was inside and worrying how he would react, Arthur carefully began to remove the ribbon and unfold the paper.

'So delicate! Just rip it open!' teased Caitlyn.

He did so, and found a beautiful, hand-crafted box within, a tiny brass lock in its centre.

Arthur turned it in his hands, looking it over with a growing smile upon his lips.

'Open it,' said Caitlyn, her voice quiet.

Arthur set down the box and opened the lid to reveal several smaller items, wrapped in different shades of tissue paper.

'Caitlyn,' whispered Arthur, moved by the care she had taken in presenting the gifts.

She made no reply, but sidled next to him and leaned her

head against his shoulder to watch as he revealed first a jet-black fountain pen with gold trim, then a silver pocket watch and then, finally, an earthenware mug.

'For your coffee,' she said, adding cautiously, 'Do you like them?'

Arthur set the box down and kissed her on the top of her head.

'I love them, and I love you,' he said.

'You're a wise man, Grimwood,' she said, drawing him into a kiss.

'Now,' she said, pulling back, closing her eyes and holding out her hands, 'Gimme!'

Gifts were exchanged with success, Arthur felt, and then the two of them whiled away the early evening together. Arthur prepared a light supper, all they could manage after the over-indulgent lunch, and Caitlyn dozed off on the sofa. Arthur kept an eye on the time and, eventually, covered her with a blanket and slipped into the hall.

'Are you going?' Her voice floated after him.

He fastened his coat and turned up the collar before stepping back into the living room.

'I'm meeting Tristan and the others,' he nodded. 'Do you want to come with me?'

Caitlyn shook her head.

'Go have fun,' she said. 'I'll kidnap you tomorrow.' And with that, she closed her eyes once more. Samson settled down on the rug beside Caitlyn as Arthur headed out into the dark of evening, snatching up his cane from the stand beside the door as he went.

The woods were dark and silent, but Arthur knew the way. The branches of the trees formed an arched tunnel over him as he walked up the slope away from Hunter's Cottage. He emerged on to the wide public bridleway, lined on one side by great oaks. On the other, a nearly treeless meadow stretched away from the path, and Arthur had a clear view of the night sky. No clouds, and the silver arc of the moon looked down upon the former king of Britain as he made his way past the monument and down to the main road. No cars were on it, which would be unusual on any other day.

He crossed over, pausing in the middle of the road to watch three deer emerge from the trees and dash for cover again. He followed the tarmac as it wound back and forth to the left until he saw the double gates of his estate, set in a high stone wall.

As Arthur drew closer, he heard raised voices. He frowned, reminded of the night the previous year when Branok the Ravenmaster had violated his home with his raven familiars, killing Percival and mutilating Merlin. The old wizard's warlock apprentice had been dead for a year now, but Arthur picked up the pace, ignoring the protests from his injured leg.

The dim moon and starlight showed him Tristan and Kay, also using a cane now, apparently remonstrating with a third person whose back was towards him. A black and white border collie wandered between them, sniffing at the men. Tristan's arms were folded across his chest, his brow lowered, while Kay gesticulated with his free hand.

'Is everything alright?' asked Arthur as he approached.

As the third person turned, Arthur caught a glimpse of a sword in her hand. Of Excalibur.

He hesitated momentarily, caught between springing forward in instinct and holding back, knowing the havoc his sword could cause, the blade that felled both Merlin and Branok.

But the woman turned Excalibur's hilt towards Arthur, holding it out to him, and he recognised her.

'Nimuë,' he said, his voice low, as much to himself as to anyone. He had met the woman, who had sealed Merlin away for centuries before Arthur's return, only once; in 1888. That meeting had lasted less than a minute.

She smiled and offered him the sword.

'You lost this, Arthur,' she said, 'You have lost much this past year, it seems.'

'I gave it up,' he replied, saying no more about his other losses, for he did not know how much the enchantress knew.

Does she know about Merlin?

'You gave it up?' said Nimuë, but she did not sound surprised. 'The fates have not idly bade me return to your company, it seems. We must talk of Agravain. Shall we?'

And with that, as though she had issued an undeniable command, Arthur led her through the gates to the estate and up the path to his home.

'Agravain is in prison, Nimuë, and will be incarcerated

for some time yet.' The thought pained him, despite the rift between them, especially since his company had finally begun to age since Merlin's demise, his former brother's vitality dwindling day by day in a cell.

Nimuë let out a little laugh and when Arthur met her gaze, he saw she was smiling.

'You do not know Agravain as well as you think,' said the enchantress, and she passed under the boughs of the oak in the centre of the courtyard, making for the warm light that spilled through the door to Arthur's mansion.

Chapter Two

The 5th Century
Mordred, the son born of sorcery and incest to Morgana Le Fay, Arthur's half sister, wages war against King Arthur. It is mere weeks until father and son will slay one another during the battle of Camlann.
Morgana Le Fay counsels Mordred and though it is he who vies for the throne, he is but her instrument. While Mordred leads his army, the sorceress wields power through more subtle means, as she has ever done.

Arthur paced back and forth across his great hall, smoke billowing from a central fire, next to which his many hounds were dozing. Tapestries adorned the walls, hanging from beams, and a large, round table made of oak stood upon the dais, behind which was the throne itself. Sir Tristan, Sir Agravain, Sir Bors and Sir Kay were seated around the table, each waiting patiently. Finally the door behind the throne opened, and

Merlin emerged through it, flanked by two attendants. He paused and bowed his head first to King Arthur and then to each of the knights, who rose and bowed to him before taking their seats once more as Merlin moved to stand behind the throne.

'Welcome home, Merlin. Your return has been long anticipated. What news do you bring? Have you had word from Sir Malagant?'

Merlin laid his staff upon the throne and, hands clasped behind his back, he stepped down from the dais to stand before his pupil and king.

'I bring ill tidings, lord,' said Merlin. 'I have ridden far alone and met with Morgana Le Fay.'

Arthur knew better than to chide the wizard for acting on his own initiative.

'What had she to say of our offer?' he said instead. 'Why has Sir Malagant not returned with her answer?'

'Alas, sire, your sister will not be dissuaded. She means to put Mordred on the throne at any cost. As for Sir Malagant,' said Merlin, 'you have been betrayed.'

Arthur tucked his thumbs into his belt, glowering at Merlin.

'Be careful, Merlin. I will not have the name of one of my brothers besmirched without proof,' he said.

The wizard shook his head and muttered something which Arthur could not comprehend.

'Malagant came late to your service, did he not?' said Merlin.

'Aye, it has been less than a year since I knighted him. He felled thirty of Mordred's men, holding open a pass through the hills for one of my defeated companies,' said Arthur.

'I saw it with my own eyes,' said Bors. 'When I arrived to aid Gareth, the remnants of his people had already escaped while Malagant stood alone against all comers.'

'Noble, brave, foolhardy,' nodded Merlin, stepping onto the dais and standing over the knight.

'Indeed,' said Bors, looking up at the wizard, who sighed at his response.

'A contrivance. You are no judge of character, Sir Bors,' said Merlin, rounding on Arthur.

'He was sent by Morgana to listen at your table and return with tidings. He has fulfilled his task and more.'

Arthur dropped to sit on a bench with his back to the fire, stroking one of his hounds when it came to him for affection.

'How many more of those I hold close to my heart will prove faithless before the end, I wonder?' said Arthur.

'I wonder,' said Merlin, casting a look back at

Agravain. The knight frowned.

The wizard retrieved his staff and stood beside the throne.

'Those you sent with Malagant have all been imprisoned or slaughtered, save one man. I found him, a beggar on the road, walking back to you to tell all he has seen and heard on the way,' said Merlin.

'And what is that, pray tell?' asked Arthur.

'That Sir Malagant has taken up the command of Mordred's lands on our southwest border. That Morgana has taken him to her bed. And worse . . . '

The king and knights waited for Merlin to continue.

'That Malagant was never a man at all. Your sister summoned him up from the Otherworld to wreak terror on Mordred's behalf. It is said that he feeds on terror, growing stronger as his enemies run before him.'

'Should you not have sensed such a thing, Merlin?' said Bors. 'You are no judge of character, wizard.' He grinned, and all the more so when Merlin scowled at him.

'That is the talk of the small folk, no more true than their tales of pixies and goblins,' said Arthur.

Merlin sighed, shaking his head.

'I thought it best not to return without seeing

this with my own eyes,' said Merlin. 'And so I rode to the borderlands. The villages within your realm have been burned, the children lie dead in the streets, and from every tree, your people hang by their necks, Arthur. Men and women alike wander as refugees, mutilated or driven mad by torture. Those who have escaped Malagant's reach speak of him as the Dread Knight. They say he rode in the midst of the carnage, arms outstretched, his eyes naught but empty sockets, drawing the life from his victims.'

Arthur said nothing.

'When I met with Morgana,' said Merlin, 'she was not alone. A man rode with her, and I did not recognise him until he spoke as though he knew me well. When I heard his words, I discerned the truth of the rumours which trouble all the lands, Arthur. Malagant is no man, but a spirit who had but possessed the body of the man we knew as Malagant. He had taken a younger, more handsome host, perhaps to better please Morgana. As my trepidation grew, I could feel him drawing on my fears, until I resisted him with all my will and cast him back. He was flung from his saddle, and I saw that his arm was badly broken, though he did not cry out. Malagant rose from the injured man as a red mist and after a moment, he possessed one of Morgana's guards. I saw the abandoned body crumble into dust before my eyes. I could not contest both the sorceress and her Dread Knight alone, and so I withdrew and now stand before you, whole,' finished Merlin.

'And I am glad of it,' said Arthur, 'if not of your tidings for they are ill indeed. It seems that if I ride to meet Mordred, Morgana and Malagant may devour my realm while I do battle.'

'Malagant cannot be allowed to rampage across the borderlands, tormenting the small folk,' said Agravain. 'They are defenceless with all our strength gathering to do battle with Mordred's host.'

Arthur brooded on the words of both Merlin and Agravain.

'I cannot send an army to deal with Morgana and Malagant lest I find I am too weak to withstand Mordred,' said Arthur.

'Morgana knows that full well,' said Merlin, 'but strength of arms may not be enough to fell the Dread Knight. Perhaps given time, I could draw him forth and banish him, were I defended whilst so doing,' mused Merlin, 'but if his body is slain, he would but take a new host. Only my arts or Excalibur can rid us of Malagant, I deem.'

Arthur looked up as Agravain pushed back his chair.

'Those are my homelands he has ravaged, my people he has put to the sword,' said the knight. 'With your permission, sire, I will ride out and aid Merlin in putting an end to the Dread Knight.'

'You could go with but a small company,' said Arthur. 'You are willing to take the risk?'

'Malagant must be brought to justice for his crimes, sire,' said Agravain.

Tristan stood, as Arthur had expected he would, so close were the two knights.

'I will go with him, if the king desires it,' said Tristan, 'though I am reluctant to leave your side when war is brewing.'

'It may be that the three of us can achieve by stealth what could not be wrought with strength,' said Merlin. 'These two are your boldest knights, Arthur. Together, we may prevail.'

Arthur caught Bors scowling at the wizard.

'So be it,' said Arthur. 'Go forth. Bring Morgana and Malagant to justice.'

One week later

'This may have been a mistake,' said Tristan, just audible above the shrieking of the gulls that made their nests on the sheer faces of the nearby cliffs, spending their days wheeling high above the crashing waves. Tristan shrank down to squat behind the boulder beside Agravain, both men clad in leather armour and soft boots, hoods covering their heads. Agravain supported himself on a wooden quarterstaff.

'What did you see?' he asked. 'Any sign of Merlin?'

'At least twenty of Malagant's soldiers crossed the road while I was watching. Who knows how many more guard the gate?' said Tristan.

Agravain grunted and turned back the way they had come.

'Where are you going?' hissed Tristan, but Agravain made no reply. Tristan hurried to keep up, staying low as they ducked into the cover of the trees beside the coast.

'We have to at least try. Morgana and Malagant could be up there,' he whispered.

'I know,' said Agravain, 'but you said attacking the gate was a mistake. Don't say I don't listen to you, brother.'

Agravain pressed on through the trees as the land began to slope downwards, confident that Tristan would follow on behind.

Finally the trees gave way to scrubland, and Agravain could see a sandy beach strewn with rocks between him and the ocean. Before Tristan stepped out to block his view, Agravain saw that the beach stretched away north at the base of the cliffs, the woods they had just crept through atop them. The land curled out into the sea and there, perched at the very end, was a broken-down stone fort, the seat of Malagant's power for miles around.

Agravain nodded towards the distant stone fort then started off in that direction, tucking himself in at the base of the cliffs as he moved.

'This way,' he said, leaving Tristan staring up.

'You're mad,' the knight whispered, but seeing few other choices, he set off after Agravain, watching for signs of scouts as he did so.

Once they had rounded the bay, Agravain stepped back onto the beach and looked up, contemplating the task ahead of him. He stood over six feet tall, muscled and lean, his black beard and hair streaked with grey. The height overcame him, and he staggered slightly, then heard Tristan laugh.

'You really want to do this? You've nearly fallen before leaving the ground,' said his friend and brother knight.

Agravain grunted.

'We'll see if you are still as amused once your face is in a gull's nest and your feet are slipping out from under you,' he said, and without waiting for a reply, he set off towards the cliff.

Agravain lay both hands on the cliff face, hung his head and closed his eyes while he said a silent prayer. He heard Tristan move up beside him.

'Good luck, brother,' said Agravain, and Tristan slapped him on the back of the shoulder.

'To us both,' said Tristan.

Arthur's knights searched for somewhere they could get purchase and began to climb.

⁕

Less than head-height off the ground, Agravain lost his footing. He cried out as first his left foot went out from under him and his right followed. He held on with his fingertips momentarily then dropped and rolled on the sand below.

He lay on his back and looked up at Tristan far above, looking back down at him, a panic-stricken expression on his face, but unable to call out. The knight started to step back down, but Agravain held up his hand as soon as he realised he was intact. His heart was beating fast, but he took several deep breaths, steadied his nerve and began the attempt again.

He moved slowly and steadily, ensuring he was grabbing and standing on solid rock, wiping sweat from his eyes on the sleeve of his shirt whenever it threatened to spill into his eyes. His whole body shook with fear and the exertion as he crept up and up.

The higher the knights climbed, the more the wind buffeted them.

At one point the calling of gulls intensified and a spray of shingle hit Agravain in the face. He blinked as grit got into his eye, and he froze where he was, blinking furiously, terrified that he would lose concentration and fall. The moisture in his eye did the job, his vision cleared and he looked up to see Tristan fending off a gull with one hand, having drawn too close to its nest.

Tristan, strong but also nimble like Agravain never would be, moved swiftly away from the ledge and continued his climb. Breathing hard, Agravain adjusted his route and climbed on.

By the time Agravain had reached the top, he had drawn level with Tristan, and he could see the younger knight's body shaking. Agravain, who was the stronger, moved in beside him and supported him as they climbed up onto the top of the cliff into the narrow space between the base of the castle wall and the drop below.

'Are you aware, oh knights, that there is a path up to the gate down yonder?' said a quiet voice. Agravain looked up, still gathering his breath, to see Merlin leaning back against the wall, a knowing smile upon his face.

'You . . . old . . . goat,' said Agravain. He clambered on to his knees and, once standing, he hauled Tristan to his feet.

'Goats climb. Wizards arrive,' said Merlin. 'Take a moment to recover, and we'll see what we shall see inside.'

⁂

The three men kept close to the wall of the fort, which bowed out towards the bottom and was bolstered by rotting timbers. It was largely intact at ground level though they had to clamber over stones which had tumbled down where the walls had crumbled during the years the fort had stood empty. Tristan took the lead and the others halted when he approached a section where a crack ran down from the top of the wall. He came back and whispered to Agravain.

'We could shin up there and climb over.'

Agravain looked back at the drop behind him, and, reluctantly, nodded.

Both knights were on their way up when they noticed Merlin had settled down to sit upon a rock and was looking out across the churning grey ocean, far below.

'Merlin,' whispered Agravain. 'Are you with us?'

'Goats climb,' Merlin repeated without looking up at the knight. 'I will join you when I am needed.'

Agravain muttered a curse under his breath and continued to climb, already regretting having looked down.

They struggled over a gap in the wall on the seaward side of the fort and dropped into the rear of the camp. Tents, huts and rudimentary stone buildings were crowded all about.

Agravain led Tristan forward, both men crouching with short swords drawn, moving stealthily towards the sound of voices. Oh so carefully, Agravain listened at every tent, peered through every gap while Tristan watched out.

Finally, the knights took cover behind a wagon at the edge of a clearing in the centre of the tents.

Various men in simple armour were standing around a fire, warming their hands, playing dice games and talking.

'We'll surprise them,' said Tristan, and, seeing that his companion was readying himself to spring into the circle, Agravain took his arm. When Tristan looked back at him, he shook his head then nodded towards a particular tent, outside which hung Mordred's banner, a green dragon on a black background.

They circled back behind the last row of tents and began to work their way towards Mordred's tent, but before they were halfway there, the sky lit up above the gate, and the ground began to shake. Just out of sight, stones tumbled from the fort and crashed down to the beach below. Agravain readied his sword and both he and Tristan looked all about them as raised voices travelled away from them towards the gate.

'Merlin,' whispered Tristan.

'Now's the time,' said Agravain. He burst into a run towards Mordred's tent, still using the tents to shield himself from view until the last second. He burst into the clearing, Tristan close behind him, to find the campfire deserted and just glimpsed the last of the soldiers disappearing between the tents.

'The Dread Knight!'

Agravain wheeled as he heard Tristan's cry, turning towards Mordred's banner. He saw a man with his eyes closed, arm outstretched, fingers clawing at the sky in the direction that the soldiers had run, and it seemed as though tendrils of black clouds were drawn in through his fingertips, forming from the air a few metres ahead of him. The man was tall and pale with long brown hair flying out behind him in the wind, his beard reaching down to his waist. He wore a fur-trimmed cloak over mail, a mace hung from his belt, and the man was smiling, his eyes closed, as though savouring a sensation. Black veins crept all over his white skin.

Malagant, thought Agravain, *but is Morgana here as well?*

Malagant, the Dread Knight, opened his eyes, hearing Tristan's call. For a moment it appeared as though the sockets were empty, a glowing, swirling green mist within, and then the Dread Knight blinked. His eyes returned to normal and he started at Agravain.

Agravain and Tristan raised their swords and charged.

Malagant raised both hands, reaching out as though to seize the knights by the throat though they were still some distance away. Agravain felt his windpipe constrict and was suddenly struggling to breathe. He slowed and heard Tristan spluttering beside him. They strove forward, but Agravain saw a plume of red smoke emanating from Malagant as vapour rises from a warm body on a cold day. It swirled around Malagant, who grasped at it with his fingers, taking a deep breath. Agravain felt Malagant strumming his fears like the strings of a lute. He shivered, his steps faltered and a terror welled up in him so that he felt for a moment that he must escape, must do anything he could to get away.

'Enough of that,' said Merlin, striding into the firelight from the direction of the gate, and

Agravain noticed for the first time that the voices in that direction had fallen silent.

Merlin held up his staff as Malagant's head snapped around, and the Dread Knight's mouth fell open as though he had been shot between the eyes with a crossbow bolt. He staggered and fell back into the canvas of the tent. A woman's cry issued from within.

'Take him,' ordered Merlin, his ancient voice rising to compete with the crashing sea below. Agravain, his courage restored, ran towards Malagant who lay dazed on the floor.

The king's sister stepped out from the tent.

'What is . . . ' she said, but her words turned into a low growl as she laid eyes on Merlin.

'Morgana,' he said, walking towards her. For an instant, her brow lowered, her countenance fearsome, Agravain thought she might dart forward and leap at the wizard, but instead she dashed away between the tents, her cloak billowing behind her.

The wizard stalked after her, not increasing his speed, and as Agravain and Tristan approached the rising Dread Knight, who shook his head free of the spell, Merlin and Morgana were lost from sight.

Malagant held out one hand and raised his mace in the other. Agravain hesitated, cowed by the towering figure, gripped with fear, knowing the rumours of Malagant's creation, how he had been summoned by Morgana from the Otherworld. Stuff of stories, he knew, and yet he could not dismiss his trepidation.

The Dread Knight grinned as the knights crept forward and once more that icy terror swept through Agravain. Malagant drew the wisps of red smoke from him.

'There is nothing more potent,' said Malagant, 'than the terror of a powerful man.'

He took a step forward, hissing, and Agravain flinched. The Dread Knight laughed, and his fingers toyed with the smoke. He gathered it up into his fist and released it into his eyes.

Once more the sockets were empty, that swirling green mist billowing out and into the wind.

'Do not stand between me and my mistress,' said Malagant. He strode forward and swung the mace at Tristan, then arched his back when the knight parried, and Agravain's sword sliced the air where his throat had been less than a second before.

White light flashed from the seaward side of the fort, and a woman's scream rent the air.

Malagant's eyes appeared once more and, a pained expression on his face, he turned and ran back into the tents behind him. Agravain saw Tristan give chase and, rather than follow, he darted left in the direction that Merlin had walked, thinking to cut the Dread Knight off as he went to assist Morgana.

He could hear Malagant and Tristan's footsteps nearby, and ran around the tents towards the screaming, which intensified as they drew near to the perimeter wall. He broke the line of tents just as Malagant stepped into view.

Both men stood aghast upon seeing Merlin down on one knee, his staff raised and white light emanating from him as though he were a star. Morgana drifted above him, thirty feet in the air, suspended. She flailed her limbs, roaring in anger, and, Agravain could see, she was pointing a finger towards Merlin. The wizard seemed to dwindle even as he kept the sorceress imprisoned, his hair turning from grey to white, his shoulders hunching.

Malagant stepped forward, but Tristan hit him from behind, throwing his arms around the Dread Knight's waist and carrying him off his feet so that both men landed hard in the dirt.

Agravain moved up to Merlin, calling his name and laid a hand on the wizard's shoulder. He felt a jolt run up his arm and tried to pull back, but it was as though his hand was stuck fast. He felt the energy drain from his body and when he looked down, he saw that the fingers of Merlin's hand were thrust into the soil and pearlescent vapour twisted up the wizard's arm.

The wizard forced himself to his feet as the vapour wreathed his staff. Agravain, still holding Merlin's shoulder, became light-headed, but then the wizard let out a bestial cry and thrust his staff towards the sky.

Morgana was flung high over the wall, struck by an invisible force that sent her wheeling high, still shrieking until she dropped, falling down to the sea, her screams echoing all around. Merlin sank to his knees.

'Morgana!' cried Malagant.

Agravain turned to aid Tristan, but saw that the Dread Knight was on all fours, his head hanging, his mace lying some distance away at the base of the stone wall. Agravain realised Malagant was weeping. Tristan clambered to one knee and grappled the fallen Dread Knight around the throat, hauling him over so that he lay face up, chest exposed to the approaching Agravain.

'Do you yield?' asked Agravain.

Malagant reached out his fingers, but all fear had departed Agravain, who now fully understood the source of the Dread Knight's power, of how terror nourished him.

Malagant's body began to shake, but Merlin

clambered to his feet, panting and stood over him. Tristan's arm pressed harder against the struggling Dread Knight's throat.

'Yield,' he uttered and stopped struggling. 'I yield.'

Agravain stood over him.

'You will answer for your crimes, Malagant. The law will judge you when we return to Arthur's hall,' said the knight, hauling the sobbing Dread Knight to his feet.

'So ends Morgana Le Fay,' said Merlin as the two knights led Malagant towards the gate and their horses, hidden in the woodland nearby.

'For now,' said Malagant. 'Death is not the end.'

Agravain felt his skin turn to gooseflesh as the Dread Knight spoke, the words like clammy fingers running over his body. He and Tristan secured the Dread Knight on a spare horse then made for home.

⁂

Sir Malagant, the Dread Knight, spoke no more on the long ride back to Arthur's hall. Agravain sometimes heard him weeping or muttering when he thought the others could not hear. The knights took the Dread Knight before Arthur, who charged him with treason and a list of atrocities which had been compiled. Malagant gave no account of himself during his trial and stood silent as witnesses were called. When Arthur sentenced him to death, Malagant smiled and offered no resistance as he was led away to his cell, there to pass his last night on Earth.

When morning came and Arthur sent Agravain to fetch the condemned Dread Knight, the reason for the prisoner's nonchalance became apparent.

One of the two guards lay slain in the corridor outside the cell, his body punctured in many places. Agravain raised the alarm and ran to the cell, seeing it was still barred from the outside. He looked through the small barred window at head-height and saw Malagant's clothes in a heap in the middle of the cell. Of the second guard, there was no sign.

'Malagant must have possessed the guard and escaped,' said Merlin, shaking his head.

'I was foolish to have so few watch over him,' said Arthur.

'Let me ride out once more,' said Agravain. 'He has been condemned, and I *will* carry out his sentence on your behalf, sire.'

But Arthur shook his head and held up his hand.

'There is no time now. Mordred's host is nearly upon us, and I must have you with me,

Sir Agravain,' said Arthur. 'Like as not, the Dread Knight will join his master, and if he has fled elsewhere, there will be time enough to hunt him down when battle is done.'

───※───

Arthur, Merlin, Agravain and the rest of the knights rode to meet Mordred at the head of their host. Little did Arthur know that the coming battle at Camlann would be his last.

He defeated Mordred's army, and killed his son in single combat, but was mortally wounded himself. Merlin cast a deep enchantment, binding his soul to his body. Merlin lay Agravain and the other knights to rest and to wait in their tomb beneath Stonehenge, where they would sleep until the 17th century, when the wizard and the Ravenmaster would summon them to England's aid.

While the Dread Knight roamed free.

Chapter Three

England
Christmas Day 2020

Arthur followed Nimuë up the steps and into his home. She swept into the hall and stood, hands balled on her hips, looking left and right, up and back down the stairs, then turned to face him, eyebrows raised expectantly.

'Where shall we talk?' she asked, waving one hand about at the various routes.

'Follow me,' said Arthur and led her towards the drawing-room. Tristan and Kay began to follow, but as Arthur turned the door handle, he nodded towards the kitchen.

'Perhaps the lady would like some refreshment?' he suggested. Nimuë smiled.

'Tea would be lovely,' she said, then added, 'peppermint tea if you have it.'

Arthur could have sworn she relished his reaction.

There would be peppermint tea in the kitchen, which nobody had ever drank but Percival. Arthur saw the box every time he opened the cupboard, and it never failed to wound him, but he could not bring himself to throw it away. He had never asked, but he assumed his companions felt the same. How they had ribbed poor Percival over his choice of drink and so many other things, relishing how ready he was to blush.

'Would you mind?' he asked Tristan, who made no reply, but set out down the corridor towards the kitchen. Arthur showed her into his drawing-room and closed the door behind him, noting that Kay had taken up position just outside.

Arthur watched as Nimuë circled the room, fondling every ornament, lifting and flicking through every book, caressing the frame of every picture. The way she whirled around the furniture, dashing from here to there, reminded Arthur of a dance. He laid Excalibur across his desk then settled into an armchair by the fire and waited for Nimuë.

Tristan brought coffee for Arthur and peppermint tea for Nimuë, the scent of the latter inflicting yet another wound as it drifted up under Arthur's nose.

'Thank you,' Nimuë said, smiling, and she took the mug from him, seemingly not bothered by the heat, and sat in the chair, Merlin's chair, by the fire.

Arthur scrutinised her as she made herself comfortable, remembering the first time Merlin had come to this house, when a scenario much like this had unfolded. Nimuë cut quite a different figure as she tucked her legs up beneath her on the wingback chair, but she also had an unmistakable aura about her, of confidence, of power and of . . . knowing, Arthur decided.

He waited for Nimuë to speak, spending several minutes watching her stare, smiling, into the fire. He could stand the silence no longer.

'Merry Christmas,' he said. Nimuë gave a little laugh, but did not turn to look at him.

'And to you, Arthur,' she said, then added, 'I wonder, do you think Agravain is very merry, stuck in his cell, quite forgotten?'

Arthur made no reply. Nimuë finally looked at him over her mug as she sipped, holding the mug with both hands.

'You have heard much about me,' she said, 'and I will not waste my time trying to persuade you that you have had a false account. You love Merlin too ardently. I can feel the grief rising and brimming in you, ready to spill over. I am sorry for your loss, truly I am. I am not without pain myself. He was, after all, my teacher.'

'And you betrayed him,' said Arthur.

Nimuë smiled.

'As I said, I will not waste my time. Very well, I betrayed him, but ultimately no harm has come of it. I am not the villain of the piece. *He* has only lately reasserted himself,' said Nimuë. 'I did seal Merlin away to sleep, but he awoke in time, once the enchantment faded, and he went straight back to being Merlin, but without following Nimuë at her heels,' she said.

Arthur was going to reply, but she held up a finger, wagging it from side to side.

'No, I do not wish to discuss it further. It is not why I have sought you out,' said Nimuë.

'Why did you then?' said Arthur, his voice low.

'I was not unskilled when fate thrust Merlin and I together, but he taught me much of the role our kind has in guiding others who would make changes in the world and protect it. I played my part in the years while Merlin slumbered, but I never had the desire to meddle with the royal line, involving myself in the politics, as he did. Once Merlin was free once more, I kept away from him and from you out of respect for the old man and out of fear that you would consider me an enemy.'

Nimuë caught Arthur's frown and laughed.

'I was justified in that, I see,' she said, smiling so that crow's feet formed at the corners of her eyes.

Wary as he was, Arthur could not bring himself to dislike the woman curled up in Merlin's chair. She had a wistful, dreamlike quality and a smile ever on her lips, he noted, a nature so worldly and yet benign that he found himself warming to her, and, he realised, trusting her.

'But Merlin has been gone for a year now, and it's my role to guide you now, as he taught me. I was biding my time, assessing the need, but it seems an old adversary has resurfaced. The land whispers and tenses,' she said. 'Agravain will ride out again for his task is not yet done.'

Arthur saw Nimuë's smile fade as she mentioned his knight's name. Agravain, who had rivalled Tristan as Arthur's truest, boldest knight, was midway through a prison sentence.

'His task? Agravain has decided his own tasks for a long, long time, Nimuë. Of whom do you speak? If you refer to

Branok, that threat has ended,' said Arthur.

'You are his king, Arthur. You always have been, and you always will be. He never broke faith with you, just parted from you for a time, as all your knights once did, to quest. He felt a calling and answered it. He has done much good these last centuries, even if he did not concern himself with the greater issues. He has prevented many crimes, saved many lives and watched over the small folk who would otherwise have faced injustice and been forgotten. Do not speak ill of Agravain, not in my company,' she said, her voice growing louder and her frown deepening as she spoke. Arthur held up a hand to placate her, and Nimuë gradually relaxed back into her chair. Arthur saw that her hands were shaking as she picked up her mug once more.

'I did not intend offence, lady,' said Arthur. 'Perhaps I am bitter about the manner of our parting, but there is no enmity between us.'

'No enmity but little kinship. Little concern for his doings too,' said Nimuë. 'Before he was arrested, how long had it been since you had seen him? What do you know of his life since he left you?'

'Too little,' Arthur admitted. Since Merlin's death, the days had begun to take their toll on his previously immortal body, new grey hairs appearing in his hair and beard as they had not since the English Civil War. Arthur had more often thought of Agravain running down the clock in a bare cell, his body gradually failing. The guilt rose up in him.

'Yes, too little,' said Nimuë. 'It is time that you summoned him back to court, Arthur. I have heard nothing of Malagant since last we met in 1888, and I assume he stayed away while Merlin was still with us, but he knows that your wizard is dead, and he will not fear me as he did our mentor. I had hoped him dead, but seldom is the world so lucky, and I felt it was not true in my heart. I am going to visit Agravain in the coming days, though he will not be happy to see me, for we too were sundered, but I am not only honour-bound to give him the news, I need his help.'

'What can he do from prison?' asked Arthur. *One who has shamed us all*, he thought, but did not say aloud, wary of Nimuë's wrath.

She laughed then stood to circle the room once more.

'You have either forgotten his nature, or you never truly knew him!' she exclaimed. She turned on the spot, arms outstretched to point out Arthur's furniture, books and other possessions.

'Such fine things, Arthur, such a beautiful house you have acquired. The years have been good to you. If you could see where Agravain was living when I first met him, the hovels he has lived in down the years!' she said.

'I have always sent him funds. He has been well taken care of,' said Arthur. He felt under attack and wondered if he deserved the criticism. He was wealthy, it was true and perhaps his lifestyle could be considered lavish, but was it his fault that Agravain had gone his own way and chosen to live in a different manner? What had he done with the fortune Arthur had sent him?

'Agravain does not care for such things. Lord, I berated him for it often enough, as one who appreciates a comfortable life, just like you, but I have come to respect his Spartan tendencies, his tenacity and his dedication. He serves at Her Majesty's pleasure because he honours the rule of law, not because he has no choice in the matter. He would be content to serve his time, but when he hears what I have to tell, no bars will hold him. Agravain will escape, Arthur, and you must make a decision. Will you aid him in the days to come, will you thwart him or abandon him?'

Before Arthur could answer, Nimuë crossed the room to stand over him. She leaned down.

'This concerns you too, Arthur,' she said in a low growl. 'You passed sentence on the Dread Knight, but it was never carried out. Only Agravain has pursued your justice down the centuries.'

Arthur leapt up, forcing Nimuë to step away. He paced across to the other chair and turned back towards her, gripping its back with one hand, unable to process the information.

'If this is true, where has he been for the past century? Why has he come back now? It makes no sense.'

Nimuë smiled pityingly.

'You are all aging now that Merlin is dead, are you not? If Malagant has unfinished business, it can no longer wait. He may not be a threat to the United Kingdom's stability like the Ravenmaster, but his hatred for you and yours, particularly Agravain, is unabated. Agravain put a stop to the worst of his activities while Queen Victoria still lived, but with Merlin dead and Agravain imprisoned, fear will stalk the streets and terror reign if Malagant is not stopped.'

'Do you think he means to resurrect Morgana?' said Arthur, thinking of his final confrontation with the Ravenmaster, during which the warlock had summoned Mordred's spirit and bound it to a new body for a short time.

'Malagant has no knowledge of the arts, though he may well have petitioned Branok for just that before Agravain disrupted his plot. He may have found a way, but I think not. Malagant has been content to be a parasite for millenia, but I deem he has not forgiven you or your company, and it is that which prompts him to act now,' said Nimuë.

Arthur closed his eyes and pinched the bridge of his nose between thumb and forefinger, wondering how many more spectres from the past would rise up before his time was done.

Could Malagant have found a way to bring his mistress and lover back to life?

Finally, he regained his composure and saw Nimuë sitting in his chair, watching him. He perched on the edge of hers, thinking of his new life with Caitlyn, wondering if he would ever be at peace.

'What would you have me do?' said Arthur, and Nimuë smiled. She reached into a pocket and pulled out a folded piece of paper and several photographs.

Chapter Four

Stonehenge, England
The 5th Century

Merlin ended his chant, the words in an ancient tongue fading to whispers in the breeze. He leaned against one of the great standing stones while he recovered his strength.

He thought of Arthur and his knights, now sealed far below in the secret crypt, and his eyes brimmed with tears.

'Hope slumbers,' he said aloud, though there was nobody there to hear it.

After a few minutes, Merlin had recovered enough to walk, and left his friends behind him to seek a place to rest and recuperate.

※

As he walked the world in the coming days with no home and no place to be, Merlin took stock of a time without his boy, in which all his machinations had come to nothing. Arthur had died, like Uther before him, and the Britons were without a king. Next would come the age of the Anglo-Saxons, Merlin deemed.

The wizard was lost, a traveller and a beggar on the road, sleeping under the stars and, for a time, without purpose. His only source of comfort was also his only regret.

Arthur would live again when the time came, as would Tristan and Agravain, Gareth and Percival, along with all of their brotherhood. And yet, he had dabbled in a forbidden magic in casting such an enchantment, and he admonished himself for his weakness.

Yet he determined in the end that he would do the same again, for the land and for his boy.

On he wandered, as the weeks and months passed, healing the hurts of the land as best he could, listening to her breath and drawing power from her.

The world continued though Arthur slept, Merlin realised, and he turned his thoughts towards how he would spend the coming years, however long they may be.

He would wait for whoever was to succeed Arthur to assert him or herself and then do as he had done before, move in close behind the throne and work his arts to gain influence. He would find the good amongst the powerful and perhaps, in time, find someone with the same potential as Arthur.

The thought heartened him, but there was a knot in his stomach at the prospect of the difficult task ahead of him.

Merlin need not have worried, for his fate had been written already in a book that he could not read, nor can any among the living save those who dabble in the forbidden arts, as Branok, Merlin's apprentice, would later do in the 16th century. His apprentice, yes, but not for hundreds of years, and not his first.

Petroc's Stowe, Cornwall
The 5th Century

Merlin travelled south and west until, one sunset, approaching the west beach of the Camel River estuary just north of Petroc's Stowe, the wizard heard a woman singing.

He stood still to listen and a welling, warming sensation overcame him, signalling, to Merlin at least, a moment of significance. He set down his pack and moved carefully towards the water.

The singing grew louder.

His booted feet touched the sand, and Merlin saw the enchantress, Nimuë, for the first time in the failing light. His shadow stretched out before him, seeming to mark a path towards her, and it did not go unnoticed by the wizard.

Nimuë bathed a short distance out, the water splashing around the skin of her waist. Her naked body glistened, and long red hair tumbled over her shoulders, its ends floating on the river. Merlin moved down across the sand, not thinking to preserve the woman's modesty or to avert his eyes. He stopped and watched as Nimuë sank below the surface of the water, and it took him a few moments to realise that her singing continued unhampered. The merry song sounded as loud as it had before the woman ducked below.

Seconds turned to minutes as the wizard waited for the singing woman to surface, and he began to frown, unable to decide what manner of creature could possess such attributes. Perhaps a creature from the Otherworld?

'We shall see,' said Merlin, and he set about searching the beach. It did not take long for him to spot the heap of what he presumed were the woman's belongings, a little further north up the beach, and beside them he saw a large black dog lying in the sand. It raised its head when first it heard Merlin's approach then sprang to its feet as the wizard drew in close.

The black dog lowered its head and began to growl, stalking forward.

'Oh enough of that, now,' blustered Merlin, fluttering the fingers of his left hand as though trying to shake a cobweb free.

The dog tilted its head and stopped growling.

'That's better, my friend,' said Merlin, scratching behind the animal's ear. 'Now, let's see if we cannot unravel this mystery.'

His knees clicked as he squatted down and began rifling through Nimuë's belongings. He lifted her clothes one by one, hoping to uncover a clue about their owner's nature.

The dog began to growl, this time mere inches from Merlin's face.

'We had this discussion,' said Merlin, once more fluttering his fingers at the dog, but it snapped out for them with his teeth. The wizard fell onto his side and held up his hands to protect his face.

'Stay,' said Nimuë, and the dog, never taking its gaze from Merlin, ceased growling.

The wizard shuffled sideways and rolled so he was sitting.

The woman stood before him, fully naked, her nipples protruding through the mass of her long red hair, now sodden and wine dark. She stood with her legs apart, her hands planted on her hips, and she looked at him with fury in her eyes, yet Merlin saw a slight upward curl of her lips.

Was she taking pleasure in his discomfort? Merlin felt the blood rush to his cheeks, and he stammered, for once in his life, unable to find words. He tried to give an account of himself, to draw his eyes away from the lines and curves of her magnificent body to look her in the eyes, but ever they drifted south.

Nimuë circled around him, and Merlin pushed himself away on his backside to give her some space. He watched as she retrieved her simple gown and turned the material over in her hands until she had it orientated correctly to don the garment. She paused, seeing the flustered wizard taking her in.

'Make the most of it,' she warned him, 'for you will not see me unclothed again, old man.'

She stretched up her arms, taking Merlin's breath away. The gown fell, and she wriggled into it until she was covered once more, and Merlin marvelled that her words had struck him like a blow. To be forbidden such a sight? Unthinkable. Who was this marvellous creature?

He felt a sudden, overwhelming desire to know her better and in many ways.

But for the moment he contented himself with clambering to his feet and fetching up his staff until he looked a little more himself.

Nimuë fastened a girdle over her hips, and Merlin spied many small cloth wraps fastened to it with twine. Nimuë crouched and stroked the black dog, and the animal seemed to relax.

The wizard gathered his wits, and, cheeks still burning, he straightened up as best as his aging back allowed.

'I had no intention to intrude, I assure you,' he said, attempting to sound put out, but the woman was not fooled.

'And while you were turning your back to retreat and leave me in peace, you tripped and rolled down to my things. I caught you flailing amongst my vestments, thrashing as you tried to stand? Is that correct?' said Nimuë.

Merlin's cheeks seemed to replace the sun, they burned with such intensity. He muttered an inadequate response, and the hint of a smile on her lips blossomed full. She laughed.

'I suppose I might forgive an old man for forgetting himself, as he has done me no harm, and I deem he does not intend any?' Her words turned up, making a question of the statement.

'No harm,' Merlin admitted, abashed and relieved all at once. 'I apologise, and if it is of any comfort to you, it was not your flesh that drew me down the beach, but your singing, and it was not your form that made me stay, but your disappearance below the waters while your song remained above.'

'You have the tongue of a poet, but you

exaggerate,' said the woman, tying back her hair. 'I but dipped below, and my song perhaps echoed from the rocks.'

Merlin reached out with his mind, and he saw the woman gasp as he swirled around her being.

The dog began to growl again, and Merlin felt the woman placate the animal with a thought.

He knew her better now, and began to understand.

'Nimuë,' he said, drawing himself up to his full height. 'I am Merlin.'

He had some expectation that she would have heard of him, but her reaction took him by surprise.

'I am honoured, my lord,' she said as she rushed towards him. 'I have followed your journey, and hoped our paths might cross. There is much that I might learn of you, if you are willing to teach me, I . . . ' she released the old man's rough hand. 'You know my name?'

'I am Merlin,' said the wizard, rejoicing in having the upper hand once more.

⁓⧫⁓

Nimuë led Merlin back to her cottage, and there they dwelled for many a month, the old wizard and his apprentice, already so skilled an enchantress with her natural affinity for nature.

They spent their days wandering the coast, discussing their arts and practising them, picking plants and fungi then returning home to settle in by the fire while the night lasted. Merlin schooled Nimuë, whose wont was to concern herself with the small doings of nature, teaching her of the great responsibility their kind had to watch over the lands and to counsel the leaders.

'I do not teach you for its own sake, girl. There may come a time when I am gone, and it will fall to you to offer Arthur guidance in my stead,' said Merlin, and he was happy that the enchantress warmed to the idea as the weeks passed.

He told her of Arthur's many foes and of Malagant, and, to his surprise, Nimuë shuddered.

'You know of the Dread Knight?' asked Merlin, but Nimuë shook her head.

'I have only heard the legends of his deeds, but when you speak of him . . . I don't know, I have an ill feeling. A sense of foreboding.'

The enchantress closed her eyes and her power thrummed around Merlin.

'He is distant, but the world cries out from afar nonetheless.'

※

Nimuë would ask questions about his time with Arthur, and Merlin never tired of regaling her with stories of the deeds of those whose names were carved into the round table, now lost. When Merlin asked Nimuë about her past, however, of her family and where she was from, the enchantress would say nothing.

Just before sunset, Nimuë would slip from the house down to the very same beach where Merlin had first spied her. At first, the wizard made no attempt to witness this ritual, but the more time he spent with the young woman, the more his heart yearned for her, and his loins as well.

When first he asked, she frowned and replied,

'Never again unclothed, Merlin. Nobody bears witness to my communion with the waters.'

He said nothing the first time, respecting her wishes, but it would not always be so.

Merlin sulked and brooded while he brewed potions and teas from the plants they had collected together, pondering his desire to possess Nimuë. His thoughts began to darken, and he thought back to how he had disguised Arthur's father, King Uther, so that Igraine would take him for her husband, but he banished the thought from his mind. He must win her heart without the use of his arts, he knew.

Nimuë would return once the sun was down, her hair dripping on to the reed-strewn floor of her cottage. He would fetch her a towel to dry her hair while she sat by the fire, stretching out her long legs and wiggling her bare toes.

Coming to know Nimuë's mind and abilities was less of a frustration to Merlin. Through both conversation and her demonstrations, he came to understand that while they both drew their power from nature, his abilities were strongest when seeing into the hearts and minds of humans, while Nimuë had an aptitude for understanding animals and the elements themselves. He envied her that, loving the world as he did, feeling diminished by her affinity with the land they walked and the river, which accepted her as a friend, not something to drown and consume. What was he in comparison? He felt the rhythms of the land and tapped into them, he was learned and wise, perhaps a master of nature. And yet Nimuë seemed to be of it, part of it. When they contested each other's will in this regard, such as when competing to commune with an animal, Merlin was brushed aside by the lady. But should he wish to, and he attempted it only once, he was able to circumvent her efforts by ignoring the animal and manipulating her thoughts. In that, Nimuë was defenceless against him. She would cease her efforts, and Merlin could concentrate anew on the animal and achieve his desires.

I am a master manipulator, he thought to himself, and the thought gave him no pleasure.

Astute and dedicated, Nimuë learnt fast, almost fanatical about both what Merlin had to say as a mentor and about his status within their ever-dwindling community. She was not, however, blind to his growing obsession with her, Merlin deemed, and when he started slipping out of the cottage to follow her to the beach, he felt a change come over her.

Nimuë never broached the subject with Merlin, never admitted to knowing that he followed her nightly, hunkering down in the rocks to watch her slip out of her clothes and disappear, singing, into the river, but there was a cold determination in her face and her questioning during their lessons grew more intense, as though she were trying to bring them to a conclusion. She chose to concentrate her studies on seeing into the minds of humans and manipulating them, something only Merlin could teach her.

The wizard became more desperate as it became apparent Nimuë would not succumb to his advances, and on many occasions his hand would linger on Nimuë's shoulder too long or she would withdraw her hand from beneath his when he placed it atop hers. He reached out to her mind before making these attempts in the latter days and was shocked by the disgust she felt, so well disguised by her smiles and their civil everyday interactions.

Merlin asked Nimuë to become his lover, and she at first told him no, but when he disappeared for several days, he found she had softened towards him upon his return. He asked her once more and her answer was a little more vague. Heartened, the wizard continued teaching the enchantress, and when they walked the coast together, sometimes travelling far afield on excursions that lasted many weeks, he taught her the last of what he knew. Nimuë could not contest him in the arena where he was strongest, but she was learning, and he was confident that, in time, she could become the power behind the throne should it become necessary. She had, he noticed, a hint of prescience about her. She could not tell exactly what would happen in the future, but it was as though she sometimes discerned the foreshadowing of fate's plan.

All Merlin's hopes came to fruition on a distant beach at the base of the cliffs.

Merlin reached for Nimuë's hand as they sat upon the sand and she did not pull it back. His heart leapt into his throat, and she turned to look at him, smiling. He detected something in her expression, but could not quite fathom its meaning, so he reached out for her mind and found barriers up, barriers which he had taught her how to raise.

Merlin frowned, but was distracted as Nimuë stood, still holding his hand, and helped the wizard to his feet.

'Go into the cave yonder and find us a place to lay, my lord,' said Nimuë. 'I would bathe alone before I break my promise to myself and undress before you.'

Merlin hesitated, to his credit, but his blood was up and he did as she bade, taking with him his staff. He approached the base of the cliffs and, looking back once more at Nimuë, he slipped into the dark cavern. It delved deep, sloping downwards, and the ground was covered with pebbles. Merlin moved carefully over them and rounded a bend. There, out of sight of the beach, he removed his cloak and spread it out upon the floor, his heart beating fast in his chest.

A weariness came over him, and he steadied himself against the wall of the cave, shaking off the feeling. This was no time to give in to fatigue.

He sat upon his cloak, muttering as he felt the stones protruding through from beneath.

Merlin yawned a long, exhausting yawn that left him more weary than before. He laid back on the cloak to test the surface and, without warning, he closed his eyes and fell asleep.

Nimuë, still fully dressed, crept into the cave and stood over Merlin's sleeping form.

'You have taught me much, Merlin, but you need to rest to cool your ardour. I hope in time you will forgive me, for if I had not acted, you would have pursued me until the ends of the Earth, dishonouring yourself. I would not have it so.'

The enchantress retreated to the beach and stood with her back to the sea. She raised her hand, fingers outstretched, closed her eyes and exerted her will.

With a great groaning and heaving, the face of the cliff began to shift and grow, sending little rockfalls down upon the beach. The stones impacted before Nimuë's feet, but she never opened her eyes, muttering words in an ancient tongue under her breath, the same words that had sealed Arthur and his knights into their crypt and disguised the entrance. The same words that would seal Branok into the Tower of London many centuries later, charming anyone who approached so that they forgot that there had ever been a door.

The entrance to the cave closed.

Merlin, immortal and asleep, was sealed inside, and Nimuë was once again free.

'We will see each other again, no doubt, Merlin,' she said to the cliff face. 'In a thousand years or so.'

Nimuë began to sing and, slipping out of her clothes, she made her way down to the sea.

Chapter Five

Her Majesty's Prison Stonegate
January 2021

The situation went from nought to sixty in the space of time it took Agravain, or John Marlow, as he was known to the court system, to bust out two reps. He saw the commotion out of the corner of his eye, more a blur of movement than anything distinct, but he'd heard the preceding conversation and noted the tone. It sounded like trouble, and Agravain did not like trouble. He'd never liked trouble.

He rested the barbell on the cradle while both voices grew louder. He heard a heavy metal door opening a little distance away. Back-up, no doubt, but close enough?

'You can fuck off,' said Carter, a small, lean inmate pacing back and forwards, barring entry to the prison gym. 'Fuck . . . right . . . off,' he said to one of the prison officers.

Agravain spun into a sitting position, immediately recognising the rising tension. He wiped down the bench with his towel and slung it around his neck. Holding the ends of it in each hand, he silently crossed the gym towards where the officer, now joined by another, was edging closer to Carter, who was clearly revving himself up for a fight.

'You've had your warning. Back to your cell,' said the officer. Carter threw a punch at his face. Agravain, over 6ft tall, muscular, salt-and-pepper stubble covering his face, loomed behind the shorter man. The officer would take the blow right on the nose, unless . . .

Agravain wrapped an arm around Carter's throat and yanked him back, so that his fist missed the officer's face by inches. Agravain threw the prisoner to the ground in the same motion.

Carter spluttered and immediately sprang up, just as the two prison officers recovered from the shock of Agravain intervening. They started forward.

'Wait . . . ' Agravain's tone was firm and his voice even, in stark contrast to the effing and blinding coming from Carter. The inmate coughed and took a few steps towards Agravain, puffing out his chest, chin tilted up and arms out straight. 'I'm not afraid of you, come and get some' could have been tattooed between his bare nipples.

Agravain folded his arms across his chest, unimpressed.

'I'll fucking do you,' Carter shouted, then, hawking up phlegm from his throat, he gobbed it at Agravain.

That was when the two officers launched themselves at Carter and within seconds, still kicking and shouting obscenities, the inmate was pinned to the floor.

The phlegm ran down the centre of Agravain's face. Smiling, he wiped his hand up the side of his nose and scooped the matter into his palm.

'You're a goddamned amateur, Carter,' said Agravain, as

he squatted down. The two prison officers were kneeling on Carter's back, all of their hands employed in controlling the man's arms.

'Get back, John,' wheezed one of the guards, tiring from the exertion.

Agravain rubbed the phlegm in Carter's hair. The prisoner gnashed his teeth and howled.

'John! Get back!' shouted one of the officers, the one who had almost had a face full of knuckles.

'Any time you think you're ready, boy,' whispered Agravain to Carter before adding, 'Yes, sir.'

He stood and backed off, hands outstretched as if to say, *I'm no threat*. Agravain turned to walk back to the weights bench, and as he did so, he added,

'You're welcome, officer.' before resuming his set.

There's no justice in the world, thought Agravain, as he was escorted back to his cell, gym time cut short for helping one of the officers. He'd caught the man's look of gratitude as he passed him on the way out though, and that was reward enough. After all, there was no shortage of days in this place, plenty of time to kill.

They locked Agravain in his cell, one of the oldest in HMP Stonegate, its walls decorated with his own drawings of people he had known and lost. Agravain lay back on his bunk then stretched to pick up his reading glasses and book, Great Expectations by Charles Dickens. He had just disappeared into 19th-century life when the door to his cell swung open.

'You've got a visitor, John,' said the prison officer. 'Coming up?'

Agravain looked at the officer over his reading glasses.

'Who is it?' he asked, still holding the book open on his chest.

The officer yawned.

'Solicitor,' he said.

Agravain folded up his reading glasses and set them down on the closed book.

'Alright, I'm coming.'

⁂

The officer led him up to the visiting area, through a series of corridors leading to small rooms containing a table with chairs on either side and surrounded by walls of glass. He was shown into the first room and locked in while the officer went off to the visitors' waiting area.

What could the solicitor want? There was nothing in the works.

But it was not his solicitor. Agravain spied the officer returning up the corridor, followed by a woman with long red hair, red hair that reminded him of . . .

'It can't be,' Agravain said aloud. He felt the blood drain from his face and his head began to swim. His knuckles turned white as he gripped the arms of the chair. He looked around for a bin, foolishly, because the room was devoid of oddments, as he fought the impulse to throw up.

By the time he had realised there was nowhere to vomit but a carpeted corner or across the table, the officer had unlocked the door.

Agravain looked up as Nimuë stepped into the room, dressed in a suit and carrying a briefcase.

'I'll keep an eye out, but hit the panic alarm if you feel the need. You'll be alright though, won't she, John?' said the officer.

Agravain nodded.

'John's a good old boy. One of our most long-standing guests,' said the officer, as he fiddled with his key. 'Alright, I'll be in the corridor.' The man retreated, and Nimuë eased herself into the space between the table and chair without bothering to pull it out.

'John,' she said, smiling, but her expression was strained.

'So you're a solicitor now? What are you going by these days?' asked Agravain.

'Just Nimuë,' she said. 'I thought a little white lie was in order. I needed to see you.'

Agravain nodded, unsure what to say next, wondering why the hell she had come to bother him after so long. He rubbed his Adam's apple between his thumb and fingers, the stubble rough to the touch.

'You look strange. I always hated your moustache, but now that it's gone . . . ' she stuck out her lower lip and raised her eyebrows. 'Well, we don't appreciate what we have at the time, I suppose.'

'I always did,' said Agravain. 'Why have you come?'

She made a show of opening up her briefcase and pulling out some papers, then slid one sheet over to him, spinning it around at the last second so that he could read.

'They're back,' she said quietly.

Agravain squinted at the piece of paper, lamenting the lack of his glasses. He wondered what Nimuë would make of those, and then scolded himself for wasting time on such fripperies when clearly there were greater matters at hand. There had to be, if Nimuë was back. It had been, what, near enough 130 years since they had spent any significant time with each other. Queen Victoria had still been alive, and he had still lived in London.

Why did I ever leave? Why would I? He could not find an answer. It was as though he had shut the memories away.

Agravain held the paper up to the light, judging the thickness as he did so; 140 GSM cream wove writing paper, good quality. It took him a moment to put a name to the watermark, but recognised it immediately; Cookson of Oxford Street. He turned his attention to the letterhead, which was embossed with the shape of an eye, surrounded by emanating light beams. He set the paper down and ran his finger over the ridges of the symbol, nodding. His heart rate picked up as memories flooded back to him, and he licked his suddenly dry lips.

'Malagant and the Order have been quiet for so long,' said Agravain.

Why did I ever stop hunting them?

'Read on,' said Nimuë.

'Do you have the envelope?' he replied.

'I think so,' she said, rummaging in the briefcase, 'Yes, here.'

The envelope matched the paper. The first-class postage stamp aligned with the top and right edge perfectly, allowing a 3mm margin. Agravain took in the name, written in emerald ink, in a sloping hand. John Marlow Esquire % Sunset House and an address that he did not recognise.

'Your address?' he asked, stowing it away in the back of his mind.

'Until lately,' she said quietly.

He returned his attention to the envelope.

'Postmarked November 18th, in Cambridgeshire,' he said. 'That doesn't ring any bells with me. You?'

Nimuë said nothing.

'Either Malagant or one of his people is based there or they went to pains to send the letter from a place where they have no connections,' said Agravain.

He set down the envelope beside the letter.

'What's this all about? You abandoned me when I needed you most, only showing your face for brief moments for years afterwards. We don't speak for decades, but now you come parading in here like you own the place and slap down a letter that is only ever going to signal bad news that I can do nothing about. Why, woman?'

'I have tried to reach out to you many times since we last met, but your mind has been closed to me. You shut me out, John. Then when I saw your photograph in the newspapers . . . well, I thought not to torment you by coming to visit.'

Agravain said nothing.

'Merlin has been dead for a year now,' said Nimuë. 'Arthur will need guidance, and this,' she tapped the long red nail of her forefinger on the letter, 'concerns you and I in particular. I am not the only one to hear of the wizard's demise. All manner of evils are creeping out from their hiding places, up from the sewers and out of the dark places.'

'Evil never went away,' said Agravain. 'I've been hunting it all of my days since you left.'

'Not this brand of evil. Malagant and the Order fell silent long ago, thanks to you, but they are back and they have you where they want you. And they want you to know it.'

Agravain looked down at the paper, upon which was written, in that same sloping hand, emerald on cream:

From hell

Mister Marlow,
Sir,
I may make use of the bloody knife that took it out if you only wate a while longer
signed
Catch me when you can Mister Marlow.

The content had been tweaked, but the style was all too familiar, even if the handwriting was different.

Nimuë retrieved a sheaf of papers from her briefcase and pushed them across the table.

A list of names and addresses with accompanying photos, taken with a long-range lens.

'You're bleeding,' said Nimuë.

Agravain drew in air, releasing his teeth from his bitten lower lip to do so. He wiped the blood away with the back of his hand.

'Why now?' he asked.

'To taunt you,' said Nimuë. 'He knows you are trapped in here, and he is free to eliminate them. To taunt you, and to lure you,' said Nimuë. 'He knows that no prison can hold Agravain if he wills it. This is an invitation for a final confrontation.'

His hands still shaking, Agravain ran his thumb over the symbol once more.

'The Order of Phobos and Deimos,' he whispered.

'Don't give them what they want, John,' she reached across the desk and took his rough hands in hers. 'You are safe here. Leave it to Arthur. Leave it to me.'

'I cannot spend my days lifting weights, snacking on cereal bars and reading Dickens while the Order runs rampage,' Agravain hissed. 'This list,' he pointed at the names and addresses, 'they are but a few of the many he will target. I have a duty to protect them. We have a duty, though you have long shirked it.'

Agravain regretted his choice of words as Nimuë looked down at the table, knowing he had spoken unfairly.

'I told Arthur it would be so,' she shook her head, a wan smile on her face, crow's feet wrinkling the corners of her eyes.

She retrieved the papers and photographs from him and looked straight into his eyes, but when she spoke again, he heard the words inside his mind and her lips never moved.

'We must speak of Agravain's escape.'

Chapter Six

1666 - The Great Fire of London
Merlin, Arthur and the knights of the Round Table are awake again, and Branok, the Ravenmaster, desiring revenge for the death of King Charles I, has used his dark arts to cause suffering and fear, first by stirring up the Great Plague and then fanning the fires that have devoured London. Merlin, aided by Arthur and his knights, has just sealed Branok into a chamber high within the White Tower of the Tower of London, at the cost of Sir Geraint, felled in the battle with the warlock's six raven familiars. Branok sleeps, as Merlin once slept.
No longer stoked by Branok's magic, the Great Fire of London dies down, leaving England's devastated capital to recover, and the knights to bury their fallen brother.
The threat from Branok the Ravenmaster has abated, for now. His raven familiars stalk the grounds of the Tower of London, watching and waiting for their master's return.

Agravain brought up the rear as eight of Arthur's knights carried Geraint through the Tower of London and down to the water at Traitors' Gate, where their boat was still tied.

He stood and watched as his brothers laid their comrade in the craft and set about readying for departure. Arthur and Merlin stood beside Tristan and Agravain on the stone steps.

'I can scarcely wait to leave this damnable city behind us,' said Arthur, and when Agravain looked towards him, he saw that the king was unable to take his eyes from Geraint's corpse, and that his face was drawn.

Merlin patted Arthur's shoulder, shaking his head slowly.

'How long are we to linger here, sire?' asked Tristan, helping Gawain down into the boat.

'We have achieved our ends and paid dearly for it,' said Arthur. 'We will fetch our possessions as quick as we can, then set out downriver to escape the city. We will build Geraint's funeral pyre on the bank of the Thames before dawn.'

Tristan nodded in acknowledgement and stepped down into the boat. Agravain watched as his friend extended both hands and aided a grumbling Merlin to step down into the craft.

Agravain did not move as Arthur stepped forward, his head lowered, seemingly under great burden.

'Sire,' he said, the word sounding harsh and urgent, as though it has escaped him rather than been said. Arthur turned, frowning.

'Agravain?'

'A moment, sire?' he said, making as though to walk back up the steps, continuing only when he saw his king meant to follow.

The two men wandered through the Tower side by side, Agravain's hands clasped behind his back and his head bowed, saying nothing.

'What troubles you?' said Arthur, and he took hold of Agravain's shoulder, bringing him to a halt by the Bell Tower in the shadow of the inner bailey by the King's House.

Agravain tried to raise his head, to meet his king's gaze, but instead his head remained bowed, and he closed his eyes as Arthur gripped both of his shoulders.

'I ask your leave to remain behind in London, sire. I did not anticipate so swift a departure,' said Agravain, his voice low.

'I do not understand,' said Arthur, releasing his grip on the knight and stepping back.

Agravain looked up and raised his head, but his eyes fixed on the wall behind Arthur. He said nothing, unable to articulate that he felt a traitor for asking, a betrayer and yet was compelled to do so.

'You are the boldest amongst my company

and my oldest friend, Agravain, and yet you cannot meet my gaze?' said Arthur in a kindly voice, but Agravain heard strain, too, and hurt.

He stood straight and stalwart once more, looking straight into Arthur's piercing blue eyes.

'I am ashamed, sire. Ashamed to ask and bereft at the thought of leaving the brotherhood,' said Agravain.

'And yet you seek to leave our company and abandon that brotherhood. Why?' said Arthur.

Agravain stepped forward, anger flashing across his face, and Arthur's mouth fell open, but his knight made no move against him.

'Say not that I abandon the brotherhood, Arthur. I seek to leave your company, but not your service!'

He recovered himself, though he could feel his heart pumping, the blood rushing through his veins, still angered by the perceived slight. His arms twitched as though he was readying to strike out, but he instead folded them across his chest, standing taller than Arthur and looking down at him.

Arthur, too, recovered and he draped his left hand over the pommel of his sword. Agravain saw Arthur was searching for the right words, and he dropped to one knee before him.

'Forgive my insolence, sire,' he said, eyes

fixed on the ground between Arthur's boots. He had a strong desire to reach out and lay hands on them, to be close to Arthur and seek clemency of his lord like a beggar sprawled at his feet, but instead he felt Arthur's hand beneath his chin, lifting it so that Agravain raised his head. He saw a sad smile upon Arthur's face, broken only when he asked Agravain to rise, telling him there was no need for apologies, just explanation.

'I . . . ' he began, at first unable to find the words. 'I feel something here, Arthur, in this place. A sense of belonging that I have only ever experienced in your company.'

'Apparently superior to it,' said Arthur.

'No, sire,' said Agravain, 'but there is something I must achieve here. A bond is forming between the city and I, strengthening with every new pain she feels. We have spent these last days pulling down her houses, helping her people escape the fires that burn outside these walls even now.' He looked westward where the sky glowed brilliantly above the Tower's outer wall.

'Much of the city has been destroyed and will need to be rebuilt. Her people, sire, they are in great need of aid, of someone to watch over them. We owe them that, the people of London. They have suffered great losses thanks to the plague and the fire, both,' Agravain concluded.

Arthur sighed.

'This city is not what I envisioned when I dreamt of uniting the land and building a great capital at her heart, a beacon for those in need, a place of inspiration,' said Arthur. 'London is overcrowded, cramped, filthy and disease-ridden. There is a depredation of spirit here, her people are denizens of hell on Earth, wrought by man and his notion of progress. I cannot stay in the city, Agravain, cannot commit to that. Branok encouraged the plague and stoked the fires, and perhaps we do owe them a debt as he was once one of Merlin's brood, as are we all, but I owe my allegiance to all the people of this land, not just those who live in her capital,' said Arthur.

'Let me be your representative here, sire, and I shall seek my purpose. I feel a calling that I do not yet understand,' said Agravain. 'I will serve you still. Sometimes a man's lot might be as simple as to look after those less able to protect themselves.'

He saw Arthur drop his eyes and begin to wring his hands before him as he contemplated Agravain's words. He knew his king was as torn as was he, between keeping the company together and letting his knight follow his own road.

Finally, Arthur looked up, and Agravain stood to attention, ready to receive his king's judgement.

'Very well,' said Arthur. 'I grant your request. You shall be my representative here for a while. May you find the purpose you seek and ever be a protector for London and her people, until the time is right for you to return or I call upon you, whichever comes sooner.'

Tears welled in Agravain's eyes, finally spilling down his cheeks.

'Thank you, sire,' he said, his voice trembling, but Arthur stepped forward and took Agravain in an embrace.

'I will miss you, brother,' said Arthur.

'And I, you, my king,' said Agravain in a whisper.

The two men drew apart.

'I will slip away. I cannot face them,' said Agravain with a final bow of his head. He turned and walked towards the gate of Middle Tower, knowing Arthur was watching him go, the man whom he had served since his youth, so many centuries behind them.

Before leaving, a thought struck Agravain and he made his way back towards the White Tower. Keeping out of sight, he peered around a wall and watched the six ravens strutting on the lawn, sitting on walls or perching in the branches of trees.

They would keep watch, and so would he, thought Agravain as he left the Tower and returned to work creating fire breaks, this time alongside the Trained Bands, London's part-time militia.

※

Agravain left the Tower of London and made his way north, skirting the fire-ravaged areas to the west as he progressed up Tower Hill, fighting his way through crowds of Londoners trying to make their escape.

Two pairs of eyes watched him stop to assist a family, shouldering furniture and walking ahead of them, forging a path north. Once Agravain was out of sight, they stepped out from the shadows together, a man and a woman.

'He went in with the others, my lady,' said the man, 'but leaves alone.' The man wore a powdered wig and a grey coat, which came down to his knees, over a grey waistcoat and brown breeches. He adjusted a pair of spectacles that perched on his nose.

'Do we know him?' said the woman. 'We ought to know him.'

A long cloak covered her dress entirely, but a pendant in the shape of a red eye hung around her neck and was displayed high, nestled in her clavicle.

'That was Agravain,' said the man. 'Malagant will want to hear of this.'

'I wonder where he is going,' said the lady. 'Come, we should check on Branok.'

She offered her hand, and the man took it. Together, they walked towards Middle Gate.

The soldiers guarding the Tower, now free of Merlin's influence, challenged the couple, but the woman showed her pendant, and the man, after a moment of rifling through his clothing, withdrew a pocket watch, a green eye on the lid.

The soldiers let the man and woman pass inside.

As they moved through a narrow passage they heard a caw and a raven fluttered down to land before them.

The couple stopped.

'Is it you?' asked the lady, her voice high and nasal, but quiet.

Faster than they could perceive, the raven transformed, one moment a bird and the next, a black-haired girl, clad in simple dark clothing. She stood before them, hands on her hips, challenging.

'Good evening, Daisy,' said the man.

'Where were you?' said Daisy, moving her head to and fro in a movement that spoke more of bird than human.

'Watching,' said the man. 'We are not soldiers.'

'Quiet, Sir Henry,' said the woman. 'What of Branok? Is he unharmed? Can he keep the fires lit?'

Daisy bared her teeth in a soundless snarl.

'No, Lady Fitzroy, he cannot. Arthur and the wizard managed to reach him. He lies within, but we cannot discern where he lies sleeping or how to wake him. Branok cannot assist your Order now,' said Daisy.

'That is most unfortunate,' said Sir Henry. Daisy took a step forward, a furious expression on her face, and Sir Henry held up a hand to pacify her. 'I am sorry for your loss, of course, but we had rather pinned our hopes on raising Morgana for the Dread Knight.'

Daisy looked Sir Henry up and down then looked as though she was about to spring into flight.

'You will have to be patient. Perhaps when Branok wakes again. Until then, you'll have to find new ways to feed your master, since ours can no longer torture the people who cast the House of Stuart aside. We will watch over the Tower until the Ravenmaster returns. Our business is concluded,' said Daisy, crouching, ready to leap.

'Perhaps not,' said Lady Fitzroy. 'Perhaps you could help us in his stead.'

Daisy's head snapped round and as she

opened her mouth her lips stretched into a beak. She let out a shrieking caw, which caused both Sir Henry and Lady Fitzroy to jump. Daisy grinned. The idea had a certain appeal.

'I am too angry to speak of your scheming and dealings tonight. Come again, but not soon,' she rasped. Then, without waiting for a reply, she leapt into the air, turning back into a raven as she did so.

Agravain travelled with the displaced Londoners until he reached the city wall in the north. There he passed out through Moor Gate and into Moorfields, where a camp had sprung up, a clutter of tents, shacks and hastily built ramshackle shelters. Over 400 acres of London had been destroyed, including more than 13,000 houses. Hundreds of thousands of people were wandering out of the city, and as Agravain travelled with them, he felt for them, looking about for some means of aiding them. Not one of them asked him for anything, but he gave all he had, and helped where he could, purchasing bread and supplies from the safe markets around the perimeter once they were established at King Charles II's command.

He laboured with the people of London, returning to his lodgings only when he was so exhausted that he thought he might collapse. There he found Arthur had left him ample coin to sustain him for some time. He locked his room, pulled off his boots and dropped down asleep on his bed, still wearing his clothes, the reek of smoke and sweat about him.

Chapter Seven

January 2021

'You do not owe him anything, Arthur,' said Tristan as they walked in the garden together.

Arthur laughed.

'You do not readily forget a slight, do you, Tristan? How many years has it been? Eighty years, and still you bear him ill will?' said Arthur.

'He walked away from his responsibilities. Abandoned you. Turned his back on the rest of us,' said Tristan. 'He has dishonoured both himself and our brotherhood by association. He is in prison, for God's sake, sir! And worse, he struck you after you went to his aid.'

'I have forgiven it,' said Arthur, all too aware he had not forgotten, 'and you should as well. He came back to us after that and made amends for many years before he went his own way again. He is still one of our own, and it is unfair to say he walked away from his responsibilities; rather say that he views the world differently to us, and he has acquired new responsibilities. He did other work in our name. As for his conviction, I now suspect there is more to it, especially now

Malagant has expressed an interest.'

Tristan said nothing, clasping his hands behind his back at Arthur's side, eyes everywhere, looking for hidden threats, even within the haven of their home.

They passed under the bare branches of a rowan tree, and Arthur looked up as a robin alighted on a twig, which swayed just overhead. The bird looked at him, and Arthur thought it looked curious.

'How will he get out?' asked Tristan, but Arthur shook his head, returning his attention to his knight once more.

'I doubt even he knows at this point, but we must be ready to assist him once he escapes,' said Arthur.

'Won't that put the rest of us in jeopardy, those of us who have never fallen foul of the law?' said Tristan, with not a little bitterness in his voice.

'Perhaps, but we will be careful,' said Arthur, thinking of Caitlyn, her cosy house nestled in the woods, and her dopey dog. He had hoped he would be allowed to settle down to enjoy a retirement, now that Merlin was dead, and Arthur had begun to age alongside the rest of the world.

'And in the meantime?' asked Tristan.

Arthur withdrew the folded list of names and addresses along with the photographs from his trouser pocket and handed it to his knight.

'These people are at risk, if Nimuë can be trusted,' said Arthur.

'Which she can't,' said Tristan without looking up from examining the names.

'Who are these people? What is their significance?' he

said, when he had read it several times. 'I don't recognise any of the names.'

Tristan smacked the paper with the back of his hand.

'Why are we troubling ourselves with this?' he snapped. 'What are Nimuë and Agravain playing at?'

'I have no answers on that score. Nimuë is as mysterious as Merlin. He evidently taught her well,' said Arthur. Tristan grunted and tried to hand the list back, but Arthur waved it away.

'That's your copy. I need you to take this in hand,' he said, leaning on his cane as he stopped, turning to face Tristan. 'We have limited resources, but we are going to watch over these people. Maybe we can outsource it through one of the security companies. Can I leave it with you?'

Tristan nodded. 'I'll start right away. Kay can lend a hand, work from here. I'll call the others.'

'Thank you, brother,' said Arthur, patting Tristan's upper arm before the knight walked back in the direction of the house. Arthur sighed and looked for the robin, but it was nowhere to be seen.

He wandered the gardens for a while before taking his dogs for a walk, stopping to check on his horse, Hunter, who was being fussed over by a groom.

Restless, Arthur put the dogs away, and pushed his way through the kitchen door. There was no noise except the ticking of a clock and the occasional drip of the kitchen sink tap. Arthur tightened the tap and leant on the counter, looking out through the window and thinking of Agravain. He remembered first laying eyes on the tall, broad teenage son of a blacksmith when Merlin brought him to his father's court, of how they had trained at arms together. Agravain had always been taller, stronger - a brawler, but, and the thought made Arthur sigh, he had always had a fierce sense of justice and a desire to protect the weak. It was always Agravain who had spent time helping villagers rebuild after Mordred's forces razed their homes, their barns and their fields. He was a staunch ally in the field, but rarely at court between battles, choosing instead to see to the needy. Arthur supposed, then, that his decision to remain in London in the aftermath of the Great Fire in 1666 was not so surprising. He had never fully understood Agravain's desire to lend a hand on the ground when there were far larger scale problems to face, but a pang of guilt told him that perhaps, just maybe, he was not being entirely candid with himself.

The desire for coffee came over him, as it did many times a day, but it was the box of peppermint teabags that he opened on the counter. He set the tea to steep, the mint aroma making him think of Percival. It was a day for nostalgia.

Arthur replaced the box of teabags and walked the passageways and stairs of the house, peering into rooms where the doors were open, stopping occasionally to consider a painting or ornament. His home was all too quiet these days since he had given the knights leave to set about their own lives. Arthur had not seen Gawain, Ector and Lucan in months, but Dagonet, Gareth, Bedivere and Bors had homes locally. Only Tristan and Kay still lived with Arthur.

Despite the ticking of the clock and the murmur of Tristan and Kay talking in a nearby study, Arthur felt as though he was walking through a building which had seen its life, like a young couple's first home, which has seen them grow old, their children grow up and leave, until only memories and waiting remain.

Arthur stopped by Percival's door, laid a hand upon the wood and sipped the tea.

He still could not stomach it, but he finished the cup all the same.

Eventually, he found his way to his own bedroom, and there he laid upon the bed, listening to the wind rattling the windows.

'You alright?' asked Bors, appearing in the doorway. He was still wearing his coat and was taking off a pair of fingerless gloves, tucking them away into pockets.

Arthur turned his head and nodded, offering a smile he did not feel.

'Tristan called. Told me about Agravain,' he said, leaning against the door jamb. 'Bit of a turn up,' he concluded.

'We may be seeing him again sooner than anticipated,' said Arthur as he shifted to sit on the edge of the bed.

Bors nodded, looking thoughtful.

'How is it going with Caitlyn?' he asked, provoking a smile from Arthur.

'Well,' he said. 'Very well. She's an old soul, wiser than I.'

'Good to have the companionship, no doubt,' said Bors in his gruff voice. He cracked his knuckles. 'Worried this business with Agravain will disrupt things?'

Arthur considered this for a moment.

'I don't yet have a sense of what is coming, but I would be loath to change the status quo, I admit,' said Arthur. 'I don't like lying to her, and I may have to do so.'

'More than you are already? Have you told her you're a resurrected legendary figure? She tells you about what she was wearing in the eighties, you tell her about how you can't get used to how straight the roads are since the Romans arrived?' Bors grinned, and Arthur laughed.

'Not quite. I want to tell her, but come on . . . ' said Arthur.

'No, I know. You'd be a fool to even try,' said Bors. 'She'd think you the biggest kidder going, or mad as a March hare.'

Arthur said nothing, leaning on his cane as he got to his feet.

'I've given what I can. We're veterans, I'm from old money, I'm largely retired from my involvement in the family corporation. No doubt she thinks it strange I am holed up in a mansion with friends,' said Arthur.

'Fewer friends than before,' said Bors, who had bought himself a flat in the nearby town.

'True. As far as Caitlyn is concerned, I helped Tristan and Kay out when they came out of the Army, set them up with jobs on the estate,' said Arthur.

Bors grunted.

'All very well until the two of you want to set up home,' he said. Arthur said nothing, instead easing past Bors, out on to the landing.

'What brings you here?' said Arthur, thinking that he already felt that the mansion had been home, but no longer; that now he yearned to relax with Caitlyn in her tiny cottage, surrounded by oak trees.

'You'll want help with Agravain, of course,' said Bors. 'Figured I'd preempt the call to arms. Gawain, Ector and Lucan won't be able to get back quickly, so here I am.'

'You don't have your own commitments?' asked Arthur.

'Of course, terribly important business, but it can wait. There's only so much fishing and watching rugby one man can do, after all,' laughed Bors. 'What do you need, Arthur?'

Arthur patted Bors on the shoulder.

'We have to make plans for a prison break,' said Arthur.

Chapter Eight

Just north of London
1724

A waning crescent moon cast scant light on the highway as David Bowlby rode along it. He reached a particular, familiar tree and, looking up and down the road before doing so, he urged his horse to leave the road. Soon both the view of horse and rider were obscured by trees and hedgerows from the view of anyone on the road.

The highwayman dismounted, tying the horse's reins to a low branch.

Bowlby searched around for his stone marker and having found it, he paced out the distance. One, two, three, four, five, six, seven paces.

Agravain watched from the shadows in the copse as Bowlby dropped to his knees and brushed the dirt aside to reveal a wooden plank. He pried it up with his fingertips and, his hiding hole exposed, Bowlby wiped his hands on his breeches then retrieved a purse from his coat pocket. He emptied the coins back into his left coat pocket and withdrew two rings and an emerald necklace from the right. He had dropped the rings into the purse and was just slipping the necklace inside when Agravain made his move.

'Don't move, Bowlby,' said Agravain, stepping out from behind a tree, a pistol aimed at Bowlby's back. Agravain wore a long brown leather coat and a tricorn, pulled down low so that he peered out from under its peak. He advanced on the startled Bowlby as the highwayman let out a cry and fell on to his side. He scrambled to get up then froze when he saw the weapon.

'Do not move, sir,' said Agravain, 'or by God above, I'll sully the grass with your heart's blood. Do not move.'

'Who the devil?' said Bowlby, caught on one knee, his hands in the very dirt he had so recently displaced.

Agravain planted a boot on the man's back and forced him to lie face down on the ground.

'You are arrested, sir,' said Agravain, pressing the muzzle against Bowlby's skull.

'Who the fuck are you?' asked Bowlby, and Agravain thought the man was practically in tears.

'A thief-taker, that's all you need to know,' said Agravain.

'A goddamned thief-taker!' Bowlby hawked up phlegm and spat.

'Hands together behind your back,' said Agravain. 'Quickly now.'

'Take what I've got,' said Bowlby. 'There's more hidden hereabouts. Just let me go.'

'Hands together behind your back, and once you're secure, we'll talk about a price,' said Agravain. 'Do as you're told.' He pressed down with the pistol. Bowlby cried out and clasped his hands together behind his back.

Agravain knelt on Bowlby's shoulder blade and set the pistol by his own right foot. He quickly set to work securing the highwayman's hands with crude manacles. He felt Bowlby shifting under him and so applied more of his weight to the man's neck through his knee.

'Stop moving,' Agravain ordered. Satisfied the manacles were secure, he fetched up his pistol and moved to tie the highwayman's legs at the ankles.

'What's the price then?' asked Bowlby, lying with his hands and feet fastened together.

'£40 for your conviction,' said Agravain and dragged the highwayman to his feet. 'Move.'

x

Having successfully delivered the wanted man into the hands of the authorities later that morning, Agravain left empty-handed, as he would not be paid until the man was convicted. He dutifully entered the debt in the journal he kept tucked in his inner coat pocket.

Agravain paid a call to the house of his employer, hoping to collect the private commission on the arrest, provided by the family of Bowlby's victim, but a servant informed him that the master of the house would not be at home until that afternoon.

As such, Agravain found himself uncommitted.

Carts rattled by him, men driving cattle through London's streets as Agravain walked, a heavy stick in his right hand, not to provide support while walking, but gripped halfway down the shaft, like a weapon.

He tipped his tricorn to all he passed, searching faces and looking all about him, taking in the tiniest details of his environment.

Before long he reached home, but stopped short. A woman stood by the door to his home. By the look of her, she was waiting. For him?

'Good morning, madam,' said Agravain, and he removed his hat out of courtesy as he approached her.

The woman flinched as though a fly had hit

her nose, and Agravain thought he had broken her daydream.

'I'm sorry, I did not mean to startle you, ma'am,' he said.

'You didn't, sir,' said the woman, smiling a broad, unconcerned smile at him.

No hint of deference in her demeanour, but no condescension either, he noted.

'I am glad of it, ma'am. Can I be of assistance?' asked Agravain.

The woman raised an eyebrow.

'That, I judge, is ever the question on your lips,' she said, stepping forward and looking him straight in the eye. Agravain shuddered, feeling as though he had fallen into icy waters.

Yet he was not so distracted that he failed to notice her accent. Not from London, maybe the West Country - Devon, perhaps, or Cornwall.

The woman laughed and held a hand up to her mouth in a gesture of apology.

'I'm getting ahead of myself. I apologise,' said the woman.

Agravain tucked his tricorn under his arm and leant on his stick, curious and perhaps a little titillated by the encounter. Who was this woman, who waited at his door and spoke of his nature to him without so much as an introduction?

'Should I know you, ma'am?' he asked.

'Perhaps, but only by name. We have never met and yet I came in search of you when I sensed you were nearby and alone. The city sings your name, Agravain,' she said. Agravain sighed and stepped towards his door.

'You'd better come in,' he grunted, then stopped and leant in close. 'Unless you're planning to murder me under my own roof, oh strange creature who knows too much and speaks in riddles?'

A sweet scent rose from her, and he felt the hairs on the back of his neck stand up. A scent of the forest and the rivers all at once somehow, comforting, familiar and alluring. She was smiling at him.

'Not at the moment, no, sir,' she laughed, 'I but seek the company of one who is like myself . . . ' she made a show of looking about to see if anyone was listening, then stood on her tiptoes to stretch up and whisper in Agravain's ear. He turned it towards her.

'One who is immortal, like myself. One who has seen ancient days and marched down the centuries unfettered by age,' she whispered.

Agravain drew himself up to his full height and scoffed.

'Do you not see the grey in my hair and beard, ma'am?' he asked, stalling while he absorbed the meaning and implication of her words.

She smiled that damnable smile of hers once again, and he was not blind to how it distracted him.

'Ah, yes, but I'd wager it grows no greyer year on year,' she said, then reached out her hand to him.

'My name is Nimuë. I knew Merlin,' she said, quietly and, he decided, wary of how he would react.

As it was, Agravain let out a laugh and Nimuë took a step back, seemingly alarmed, her eyes wide.

'Nimuë? That is a name I have heard before, God love you!' he exclaimed. 'The girl that got the better of Merlin? This I must hear!'

Nimuë had dropped her hand, but Agravain snatched it back up again and graced it with a kiss.

'Do come inside, ma'am,' he said, his voice breaking up with the remnants of the laugh. He pushed open the door and she followed him inside.

'I will come in,' said Nimuë, 'but be warned, I will not stay forever . . . '

Agravain watched her as she walked into his room while he puzzled over what she meant.

'I belong to a place far from here, and to that place I will return, though fate, it seems, will delay me here,' she said, and, to Agravain, she seemed inexplicably sad.

'May I sit down?' she asked as she sat down and untied her bonnet with gloved hands.

Agravain lived in a single-storey brick building that faced on to a narrow road, overlooked by far taller buildings. He had a bedroom, which had no window, and a day room in which was a table with two chairs, another chair by the fire, a chest and nothing more. Agravain swept and dusted his quarters daily, and though the furnishing was sparse, his home was presentable and clean. He hung his tricorn and his coat on the hook secured to the back of his door, revealing his buttoned waistcoat and pistols hanging under his armpits, secured by buckled leather straps, then straightaway set about building a fire, crouching by the grate while Nimuë settled in her chair and removed her gloves.

Nimuë watched him at work, sighing so sorrowfully at one point, that Agravain turned and asked her what was the matter.

'I predict I will want to stay, but I shall not be able to bear it.'

She would say no more on it, and, puzzled, the thief-taker turned back to his task.

Once the fire was alight, Agravain hung an iron kettle over the flames then plumped down in the chair he had dragged over from his table so he could sit across from Nimuë.

'We'll have tea in a minute, if you like,' said Agravain.

'Such a gentleman,' said Nimuë in a singsong voice, almost absentmindedly as she examined his room.

Agravain shifted in his chair, feeling that he was under scrutiny. He leant forward, elbows on his knees, clasping and unclasping his fingers. He felt as though he were naked on a stone slab while Nimuë ran her fingers across his skin and pinched at his flesh, evaluating every inch of him. His skin turned to gooseflesh.

'You do not spend much time here, do you, Agravain?' said Nimuë, moving to the table, the top of which was covered in scattered papers, yet not in a state of disorder. Everything had its place and was quite where it should be. A stack of journals, all identical in size, perfectly aligned and devoid of dust, occupied the far right corner of the table, butted up against the cracked plaster wall.

'I do not go by Agravain,' he said, leaping up as Nimuë picked up the top journal and started turning the pages. He plucked it from her grasp and set it back upon the stack. When he looked back at Nimuë's face, a single arched eyebrow and the faintest of smiles spoke of mischief and feigned contrition.

'What do you go by, if not your true name?'

she asked, and he adjusted his quills and bottles of ink, turning away from her.

'John Marlow,' he said, 'of the Marlow Foundation.'

'John? How imaginative,' said Nimuë. 'Well, John, shall we talk and drink our tea and talk some more?'

She returned to her seat. Agravain joined her and stretched out his hands to warm them over the fire, his pink fingertips contrasting with the dark material of his fingerless gloves, splattered with mud.

'What can I do for you, Nimuë?' he asked. Agravain lit his pipe after igniting a spill in the fire and sat back in his chair.

'I'm yet to fully decide *that*, John,' said Nimuë. 'I am far from home and my wanderings have brought me to your door, perhaps that is enough.'

'And so if I turn you out after you've drained your cup, our business will be done?' said Agravain.

'Don't be so impatient,' Nimuë scolded.

'Speak plainly then, woman. I have little time for dancing,' said Agravain.

'Shelter would be appreciated. Hospitality,' she said, raising an eyebrow and nodding towards the cast-iron kettle beside the fire. Agravain sighed and made the tea.

'You do not spend much time here,' she said again.

'You have a keen eye,' said Agravain.

'When you've lived as long as I, it is important to have a purpose and not shrivel away by the fire of your own home. I sleep here, I keep my books, I warm myself sufficiently then return to London's streets and walk them,' he said.

'You haunt the streets,' she said, and it was not a question. 'They whisper your name, you know.'

'Who does?' asked Agravain.

'The streets, the birds, the river, the air, the rain,' said Nimuë, leaning in confidentially.

The thief-taker, still crouching by the fire, looked up at her, enthralled by her nonsensical words, for a moment feeling as he had first done when Merlin came to his village when he was a boy, child Arthur in tow, and the wizard spoke to him with truth, of things greater than himself.

'You remind me of Merlin,' he said quietly.

Nimuë cradled her cup between her hands, looking deep into the tea within as though scrying, or looking down through rushing water to a river bed, a mysterious smile creeping onto her lips.

She smiles so readily, thought Agravain,

pitying himself, who lived behind a frown, for whom the world was a serious, dangerous place full of people in need of either protection or arresting, or he mused to himself, perhaps both.

'I remind you of Merlin? Is it the beard, perhaps?' Nimuë laughed, then changed the subject, seeming to pick up on his thoughts. 'It is quite the burden you have assigned yourself, John. The immortal lawkeeper, London's watchman.'

'Hardly that,' said Agravain, gruffly, then added: 'You are not content to rifle only my belongings, but must also plunder my thoughts, ma'am.'

She is beautiful, he thought, and Nimuë blushed. Agravain's cheeks grew hot as coals. He coughed and sipped at his tea.

'You are kind, sir,' said Nimuë. She reached out and took his hand as she returned to the previous topic.

'Nobody is quite like Merlin, but there are similarities for certain,' she said, sitting back once more and releasing Agravain's hand. He unfurled and furled the fingers of the hand Nimuë had grasped. He rubbed his thumb and fingers together.

'Tell me,' he said, scarcely louder than a whisper, the fire crackling and the room growing warm.

'How does Merlin tell it?' Nimuë asked, sipping at her tea and watching him over the cup.

Agravain hesitated, gauging how honest he should be and whether he would be betraying a confidence, but forthright as ever, he spoke true.

'Merlin does not tell it, lady. All I have heard of you is through literature written by outsiders and rumour amongst Arthur's company. The literature speaks of you as the Lady of the Lake and, sometimes, as though you were a different person entirely, who dwelt with Merlin in the latter years before he was... before he slumbered. The rumour amongst us, spoken only when the wizard cannot hear, is that you are a powerful enchantress, a pupil and lover of Merlin who sought to usurp him and sealed him away for centuries. That he allowed you to trap him because his love for you was his weakness,' Agravain finished, his eyes lowered, barely able to look at her while he revealed the unkind account, even if they were not his own words.

Nimuë did not seem in the least put out.

'These things I too have heard,' she said, smiling. 'A kernel of truth here and there, but it seems even myth cannot decide about Nimuë. I was a pupil of Merlin, true enough, but we were not acquainted until after Arthur's death.'

'So you did not gift him Excalibur?' said Agravain.

'No, I have watched your king since his return, but never met him,' she said. 'Merlin would not abide it.'

'Indeed, no,' said Agravain, shaking his head. 'He does not speak kindly of you. Forgive my candour.'

'I did imprison Merlin, but not to usurp him, but for our own mutual good. For the same reason I do not approach Arthur and his company even now.'

Agravain pressed her on the point of Merlin's slumber, but she insisted it was best she did not say more. The knight felt uneasy, frowning as she refused, wondering who she was protecting, Merlin or herself?

Had the wizard been misrepresenting events between them all these years since Arthur's rebirth? If he had misrepresented what occurred between him and Nimuë, what else had he twisted?

It seemed he would not find out that day, however, and so Agravain let the matter rest, attending fully to Nimuë once more.

'I am closely concerned with this land, as is Merlin, but less so her rule. That is his domain. I am satisfied to live on, coming to know the waters and the woods, listening to all creatures that will speak to me. I have a deep love for my home and though I wander abroad now to come to know the land, I will return, if I can. But I have not abandoned my role in Arthur's story or forgotten Merlin's teachings. There may come a day when I replace the wizard as Arthur's counsel, but until then, perhaps I can offer guidance to his wayward knight?'

'You would offer me counsel,' Agravain realised.

'Quite so,' said Nimuë.

'I see,' he replied, 'and what would that counsel be?'

'Malagant is in London,' Nimuë said, and the words were almost lost under the sudden cracking of a log in the fire, 'as are those who follow him.'

Agravain frowned.

'The Dread Knight? He is still alive? It's been centuries,' he said.

'Malagant was always a fell creature, perhaps from the Otherworld. Time's teeth can find no purchase in a malignant spirit such as he. He has gathered a following since he escaped Arthur's hall in the 5th century. The lands never stopped whispering his name, but those whispers became shouts as I travelled towards the capital. His power is growing. I know not his intentions, only that no good can come of them,' Nimuë finished and drained her cup.

'Tell me what you know,' said Agravain, remembering the face of Morgana, the king's sister, her white eyes, devoid of pupil, her long silver hair, darkening to black at its ends.

Morgana and Malagant, thought Agravain, *a pair indeed.*

'Very well,' said Nimuë, 'but I will not stay forever.'

Chapter Nine

London
1724

Agravain gave Nimuë the bed and slept clothed in the chair by the dying fire. He awoke in the early hours of the morning with a crick in his neck to find that she was still sleeping. He shivered and set about building the fire as quietly as he was able. She stirred, but did not wake. Once the wood was ablaze, and he was content that Nimuë would be warm enough, Agravain strapped on his pistols, pulled on his coat and tricorn then snatched up his cudgel from behind the door, heading out into the dark and locking the door behind him.

He took a deep breath of the cold air and began his daily patrol of the streets alone, considering all Nimuë had told him. Alone, though the city was a dangerous place, some 74 years before the first organised police force would come into being. Yes, there were constables, but one only had to look around to see the signs of violence and depredation. Yet Agravain knew the streets and those who walked them knew him by the sound of the heavy footfalls and his steady gait, unflinching and unyielding, no matter what he came across as he walked lonesome in the dark. London was a living breathing thing, Agravain felt. The buildings were its organs, the streets were veins, and the populace the blood that ran through them. What was he then? Something . . . *other*. A tonic administered of its own accord without consultation or prescription, something to restore the balance and keep ill health at bay. There was only so much he could do, he knew that, but as he often thought and sometimes said aloud, 'One can only do what one can do.'

Agravain spied a bundle of rags in a side street and on closer inspection he found a shivering man in tattered clothing slumped up against the wall, filthy and reeking of alcohol. He would be dead by morning, left to freeze.

Agravain tipped his hat to the man, who shrank back and raised a hand protectively.

'Have no fear, brother,' said Agravain. He dug into his coat pocket and pulled out a shilling.

'Let's get you somewhere warm and some food for your belly.'

Agravain was true to his word, and once he had found the man somewhere warm to sleep, he continued to walk south and east through the city, making his way into east of Aldgate Pump, into the deprived East End of London. Here folk lived in cramped quarters, poor people moved in from the country, refugee French Protestant Huguenots, Irish immigrants, Ashkenazi Jews and many more besides. A dangerous place to walk at the best of times, where desperation, hunger and crime were such daily realities that even cries of murder did not bring people to their windows and doors. Luckily for them, they had Agravain, though they knew it not.

Men roamed the streets, some drunk, some looking for drunks to rob, and prostitutes plied their trade on most streets as Agravain reached Whitechapel. He sought out the people and the places that the sensible kind avoided. And he began asking questions.

※

In the coming weeks, Agravain would spend many a night doing just that. He seldom slept for more than four hours at a time, and rarely when the sun was down. He did not abandon his usual business, of course, taking on private commissions to hunt down thieves and robbers, collecting his dues on conviction and his fees besides.

When he saw crimes, he put a stop to them. Where he saw poverty, he did his best to intervene. He looked for potential in the poorest of places and paid well for information from loyal boys, girls, men and women whom he took under his wing. He read the newspapers, spoke to the constables and the magistrates, he looked for patterns and listened to the chatter in the ale houses.

Throughout that time, despite her constant warnings that she would not stay forever, on occasions when Agravain returned home, he would find Nimuë there or signs that she had yet to depart. Homelier touches. Not enough to occupy more than a few minutes of her time, but enough to suggest she had been present. Sweet smelling herbs hung on the walls and occasional bottles of something interesting.

One afternoon, Agravain had dozed off on his bed when the sound of a knock at the door woke him. He groaned and wiped saliva from his beard on his way to opening the door.

Nimuë stepped inside and planted a kiss on his cheek then stepped back, frowning.

'You look haggard,' she said. 'Walk with me? I will treat you to a meal and, even better, my company, sir!'

Nimuë did not wait for an answer, fetching Agravain's hat and coat.

'You will not need that,' she said, as he picked up his cudgel, but he ignored her advice and took it anyway.

'Will you tell me what you have discovered?' she asked after they had been walking for much of the afternoon, finally out of the city and northwards along the bank of the River Lea.

'There is not a great deal to tell,' he said. 'Nothing conclusive.'

'But?' asked Nimuë. She walked to the edge of the bank and, removing her shoes, she sat and dangled her feet in the water, reaching down to rub and clean them. Agravain stood towering over her for a moment then threw down his cudgel and he too removed his boots. He took a sharp intake of breath as his toes hit the cold water, and he recoiled, but when Nimuë laughed at him, he plunged both feet fully under, in defiance, regretting it immediately, but hiding his reaction. She grinned, and he knew that she had discerned much from the twitches of his face and nuances of his expression. She knew too much about everything, he decided, and yet he liked having her as a companion.

He knew he must cut a ridiculous figure, swathed in a long coat and tricorn like a highwayman, weapons tucked here and there, but dangling his feet in the water like an idle child. But there was nobody to see them sitting in the shade of a willow tree, with fields stretching away on all sides. He took a deep breath, exhaled slowly and let loose some of the tension in his shoulders.

'That's better,' said Nimuë. 'Now, tell me what you have found.'

'There are whisperings, but not much more, rumours of organisation. There have always been murders, random killings, but I have my suspicions.'

He reached into a pocket and withdrew a bundle of chains and pendants, some green, some red, but all in the shape of eyes.

'What are they?' asked Nimuë, taking one and letting the pendant dangle so that the eye span slowly one way, then another, sometimes catching her in its gaze.

'I am beginning to think they signify membership,' said Agravain. 'I have seen them many times before over the years, but more and more often of late. The green eye and the red eye. I have found them on the persons of criminals and, only once or twice, they have been found near the scenes of violent crimes, perhaps pulled from around the wearers' necks amidst the struggle, left to fall as they made their escape.

'Membership of what?' asked Nimuë.

'I don't know,' said Agravain, 'but if Malagant is in London as you say, and a movement is underway, this,' he took back the pendant, 'is the only clue that I have so far. And I mean to follow the trail.'

Without speaking, Nimuë pushed off the bank with both hands, sinking knee-deep into the cold water. She turned to look at him and pulled her dress up over her head until she stood naked in the water.

Agravain felt his cheeks flush, and he looked away, but not before he caught her smiling. He heard her wading out into the water and looked when he heard a splash. Nimuë had dived beneath the surface and hung there, lying facing the sky, fully submerged, but seemingly ignored by the rushing current.

When nearly a minute had passed, Agravain began to fear that she would be drowned. He shrugged off his coat and leapt in after her. He lost his footing and went under himself, only to find himself manhandled back into a standing position.

Nimuë rose from the water ahead of him, laughing. She drew in close until her body pressed against his, and she began to undress him.

'Where does the trail lead?' she whispered.

'I've been given an address in the city,' he said, unable to fully comprehend what she was doing until she had thrown his shirt up onto the bank and reached out a hand to gently take hold of the back of his neck. She pulled him towards her, and he relented, taking her in his arms. They kissed there, standing in the waters that flowed down to the East End of London.

※

When they had returned home that evening, after several hours in bed together, he arose, leaving her swaddled in the blankets, sleeping, Agravain prepared to visit the address he had been given by a fence he knew on Whitechapel High Street.

He locked the door behind him and swept westward and south through the streets, preparing himself to meet an old adversary, one Agravain knew he was ill-equipped to destroy alone, possessing neither a knowledge of magic nor the sword of the land. He would have to content himself with a scouting mission.

It took nigh on an hour to reach the address, a townhouse nestled in a quiet road. Agravain peered around the corner from the next street.

There was one man on the door. *A big fellow*, thought Agravain, *so big that he would likely be overconfident*, or so the knight told himself to maintain his courage.

Agravain stepped around the corner, whistling, cudgel in hand. He strolled down the street, feeling the man's eyes on him. He looked up when he was still a way off then shot the man a nervous smile and tipped his tricorn towards him. The man nodded back just before Agravain drew level.

Three. Two. One.

Agravain took a two-handed hold of his cudgel and whirled to his left, smashing the man in the gut. The big fellow cried out as he doubled over and let out an 'oof', which was what Agravain had been counting on. He drew back the cudgel, took aim and brought it up to connect with the underside of the big man's chin. His mouth hanging open after the blow to the stomach, the man's teeth smashed together, his head snapped back and he collapsed unconscious against the door with a thump.

Agravain checked all around, but nobody had seen, as far as he could tell. He hitched up the fallen man's legs by the knees so he was fully concealed in the doorway, and patted him down. He left the man his few coins, but withdrew two keys.

Agravain found what he was looking for almost immediately. A pendant in the shape of a red eye on a chain around the big man's neck.

So, thought Agravain, *he would have to pay heed when the Whitechapel fence gave him information in future.* It only remained to see whether the red and green eyes were connected to Malagant, who may well be beyond the single door. Agravain took a moment to consider his approach. Perhaps he should send word to Arthur or enlist Nimuë's help?

You're here now, thought Agravain. He tried the first key, but it did not fit. The lock clicked when he tried the second.

Agravain slipped inside and closed the door behind him.

An intense, cloying heat hit him as he entered the candlelit hall, dark wood and grim portraits looming over him.

He gathered his courage and stepped forward.

'Are you afraid?' said a voice, and it echoed all around him.

Chapter Ten

London
1724

'Are you afraid?' the voice repeated. Agravain was, to his core, standing alone in the dark, in what could only be Malagant's lair, he knew now. In that moment, he wished for nothing more than to have Tristan by his side, but he had forsaken the company of his brothers.

He regretted it.

Agravain recognised the lilt in the man's accent, and looking up, an icy hand gripped his heart as a shadowy figure stepped into view at the top of the broad staircase.

'Why should you fear me, Agravain? I was no match for you and for yours when last we met. You have made a habit of sneaking and skulking, haven't you? Hardly characteristics associated with the noble knights of King Arthur.'

All of the candles spontaneously leapt into

flame in their sconces, suddenly illuminating the hall and the staircase.

Malagant, Morgana's Dread Knight, walked slowly down the stairs towards him. He had taken a new host, thin and graceful. Gone was the long brown hair and beard, replaced with a powdered wig, moustache and goatee. He wore a long, green velvet robe and jewelled rings on his fingers. Agravain saw wisps of green smoke drifting up towards Malagant, and when he looked down at his hands and body, he could see it seemingly escaping his body, as though his soul was casually drifting away.

Malagant stopped walking and tilted his head to one side with a bemused expression on his face.

'You look bewildered, Agravain,' he said, caressing the drifting smoke with his fingers.

'You are not as I was expecting, Malagant,' said Agravain. He could feel his hands beginning to tremble.

'No, quite,' said the Dread Knight, 'and I barely recognised you. The years have not been kind to you. I had heard you roam the city like a stray dog.' Malagant smiled.

Agravain drew his pistol and took aim at Malagant's chest in what he knew was a futile gesture, but the Dread Knight held his hands out at his sides.

'Would you trespass in a man's home and shoot him though he be unarmed, meaning you no harm?' asked Malagant. He slowly lowered his hands and clasped them behind his back.

Agravain kept his aim steady, checking his peripheral vision for movement at the doors leading off the hall.

He tucked his cudgel under his arm in one swift motion then withdrew the handful of pendants from his pocket, holding them up for Malagant to see.

'I understand,' said the Dread Knight, stepping closer. 'You have followed a trail to my door.'

'Are you responsible, then?' said Agravain. 'For the violence, the murders, the disease?'

'Responsible? Hardly, but when one is offered a tasty morsel, why should one not devour it?'

Agravain licked his dry lips.

'For example . . . ' he closed his eyes, took a deep breath and sucked in the twisting smoke. Agravain took a step backwards, fear rising in him, and his shoulder blades banged against the door. Malagant's eyelids flew open, revealing the green mist that swirled inside the empty sockets.

'Will you shoot me, sir knight?' he asked, his tone mocking and yet, Agravain thought, genuinely curious.

Agravain lowered the pistol, after all, what good would it do?

'You ask if I am responsible for the murder, the violence and the disease? How long has it been since you charged Branok the Ravenmaster with these crimes? I was here as the masses fell to the plague, tasted the sweet terror in the air as Merlin's apprentice stoked the Great Fire and the city burned, but was I responsible? I did not lift a finger, I simply observed. Did I take glee in panic and the chaos, the desperation? Of course, but I laid not a hand on a soul. I will not tell a lie, I know of others who did, but not by my command.'

'What of the pendants, the red and green eyes? Your followers?' asked Agravain.

'Ah, they signify allegiance to my little organisation,' said Malagant. 'I do find people flock to secret societies. Ridiculous, but it serves my purpose.'

'What purpose?' asked Agravain, finding he was losing all sense of what he was doing in this place and what he had been hoping to achieve.

'To feed. To sustain oneself, as we all must,' said Malagant.

Agravain raised the pistol once more, levelling it at the Dread Knight's face.

'You feed on fear,' said Agravain, his voice low.

'Fear is stale bread and hard cheese. Terror is milk and honey,' Malagant grinned. 'And right now, Agravain, you are quite the delicacy.' He waved his hand, and Agravain saw the smoke, no longer green, but red swirled about the room as if to illustrate the Dread Knight's point.

'I have a duty to put a stop to this,' said Agravain. 'Arthur passed judgement and sentenced you to die. You are under arrest.'

'Killing me won't stop anything, human nature being what it is. The city is merely a hub, where all that I need is intensified and, somehow, the right kind of perpetrator is drawn to me. They go about their business, and I breathe in the taint in the air. I am not responsible, sir. I hear their tales, I listen to their supplications, I offer due reward where it is in my power to do so,' said Malagant. 'And they repay me in loyalty.' He called out that final word, and doors swung open down the length of the hall. Men and women stepped into the candlelight, all manner of folk, high-born and low. They crowded into the hall, slowly walking towards him.

'You might find that arresting me is a little more problematic than you anticipated,' said Malagant, as the vapour poured from Agravain's body until the Dread Knight's hollow eyes were filled with a red mist. 'The Order of Phobos and Deimos, the twin gods of fear and terror. Of the green eye and the red.'

His terror overtook him then, and he turned his back to the cultists, tucking away his pistol and fumbling to open the door.

'We will see more of one another, Agravain, I have no doubt,' Malagant's voice reached him just before the door slammed. Agravain stepped over the fallen form of the watchman and ran in a blind panic down the street, only stopping once he had rounded the corner and tucked himself into a doorway, breathing hard and sweating profusely.

'Get ahold of yourself,' he said aloud. 'This will not do.'

He considered going back, cutting them all down before him to get to Malagant. He could have done it in his youth and perhaps now, but to what end? He knew not what crimes they had perpetrated, could not conceive of exactly what he was laying at Malagant's door. And to execute the Dread Knight, he knew he would need more than a pistol and cudgel.

Nimuë, he thought, *I must speak with Nimuë.* The thought had barely taken root before he was striding back towards his home, a prickling sensation across his back, as though ghostly fingers stroked his spine. He could not bring himself to look back and see if it was so.

<hr />

Two weeks later

Nimuë stooped and kissed him on the forehead, her lips warm against his skin. She sat on the edge of their bed, and he could feel her eyes on him as he sat wringing his hands.

'I have heard from Arthur,' said Agravain. He took a swig of brandy and offered Nimuë the bottle, but she frowned and waved it away.

'Is Merlin coming?' she asked.

'Arthur has not seen Merlin in some time and does not know where he dwells at present. He does not feel it is necessary to come to London immediately, when Malagant has roamed free for so long. Arthur tells me that the Jacobites seek to dethrone King George, and countering their efforts takes up much of his time. He tasks me to watch over the Dread Knight,' said Agravain, frowning, 'and to send word should matters escalate. He will bring Merlin when the time is right.'

Nimuë said nothing for a moment, but sighed.

'Well, I suppose you have already taken on a duty to this city,' she said quietly. 'To watch over it. To keep the peace?'

AGRAVAIN'S ESCAPE

Agravain thought for a second then nodded slowly.

'I suppose I have,' he said. 'Still, I thought Arthur would come. It is his judgement that Malagant has escaped. He must choose between his past judgements and present strife, I suppose.' Even Agravain heard the doubt in his voice.

'There is no choice in the matter, not for you,' said Nimuë, interlocking her fingers and looking down at the floor. 'You are the city watchman. So go about your business. Bring people to justice. Keep the streets as safe as you are able, and take comfort that you know of Malagant and his people now. You are better informed than you were. You know where they meet. You know where to keep an eye, do you not?' she concluded.

Agravain sighed and made no reply.

'You are troubled beyond what you have told me,' said Nimuë.

'I am a coward,' he said. 'I turned from Malagant, and I ran. It heartened me to think my brothers would come to my aid.'

She reached out for his hand and took it in hers.

'All men feel fear. If that was the first occasion you gave into it, then you are bolder than most,' she said.

'Will you stay awhile?' he asked, looking up, longing for companionship and respite.

'I will,' said Nimuë, and she stood to fetch them hot tea, 'but not forever.'

Agravain nodded.

That is something, he thought. A shiver ran through him as an image of Malagant's eyeless face appeared in his mind, red mist spilling from the sockets and a widening demonic grin stretching the Dread Knight's pale skin, distorting the face.

Agravain stood and curled an arm around Nimuë's waist.

Perhaps it was better that Merlin had not come, as Nimuë would surely have left to avoid the wizard. He could not stand that, he realised.

London is my city, Agravain decided, *Arthur has no love for it, and Merlin cannot see beyond his own machinations. This is my duty, mine alone.*

So many ways to disguise the words, 'I will not risk her.'

───※───

Agravain received word from one of his informers that evening, by way of a note pushed under his door.

The house where he had confronted Malagant had been abandoned, and there was nothing to suggest where he had relocated. Agravain sighed and screwed up the note.

He would go on to make his patrols, to develop his charitable foundation as the years passed, and he saw no more of Malagant for a long time, though the red eye and the green were ever present in London. He continued his long reign as city watchman.

Chapter Eleven

January 2021

Cooking the weekly Sunday roast with Caitlyn had become something of a ritual. Arthur's instincts as a chef reflected the excitement of a man who, first, had never had to cook for himself during his first lifetime and, secondly, that of a man who dwelled now in a new epoch, where spices and seasonings were available from parts of the world that he had not even known existed as a young man. It had been fascination with far-off places that stirred his imagination when it came to coffee beans, and he marvelled at roasted potatoes, which could never have graced the tables in King Uther's halls when Arthur was a boy, still hundreds of years before the Spanish would bring them across the Atlantic for the first time. Cinnamon had been a medicine when he was king, cloves fascinated him and even sugar still felt like a novelty. He was over-fond of the latter, he knew, and as his frequently loosened belt attested.

Caitlyn was a more practised hand in the kitchen, and she liked things as she liked them. Her potatoes were sliced thin and scored with crosses, dusted with flour, just as her grandmother had made them. She preferred to steam green vegetables and roast the roots, but liked a dollop of mashed potatoes mixed with salt, pepper, butter and a little cheese.

Arthur leant towards game, boar, venison and even hare, while Caitlyn preferred chicken and sometimes lamb. They danced around each other's tastes, negotiated and quarrelled until they had established a new tradition between them.

Midway through preparing the gravy, Arthur's mobile phone began to ring. He excused himself and stepped into the hallway, still wearing the apron that amused Caitlyn so.

'Go ahead,' said Arthur upon answering.

'Mr Grimwood?' said a female voice on the line.

'Speaking,' said Arthur.

'Ah, sorry to bother you, sir, it's Priti Acharya from Asherman Law,' said the woman.

'Good afternoon, Miss Acharya,' said Arthur, his mouth drying out immediately. He licked his lips.

'I've just had a call from John Marlow,' she whispered, as though that would help if someone was listening in on the call. 'He asked me to pass a message.'

'Go ahead,' said Arthur, picking up a pen. He made notes as the solicitor recounted the tale, knowing it would need to be decoded.

'Who was that?' asked Caitlyn, when Arthur walked back in, and then she added, 'Are you alright?'

'Hmm?' said Arthur, looking up, then immediately smiling. 'Yes, sorry, just a call from my solicitor.'

'On a Sunday? Is the world ending?' she said.

Arthur cursed inwardly as he returned to stirring the gravy.

It's the little slip-ups that betray you, he thought.

He could not think of a reply.

'Arthur?' she said again.

'Give me a minute?' he snapped, turning to look at her, and, for the first time, she scowled at him.

'Fine,' said Caitlyn, and she returned to serving up.

Arthur sighed. He set down the fork and slipped an arm around her waist. She shrugged him off.

―――

They ate in silence, but then Arthur could take it no longer. He took a big swig of red wine, set down his glass, cleared his throat and made his attempt.

'I'm sorry I snapped in there. The news was not good.'

'So . . . bad then,' said Caitlyn, not looking up. 'It was bad news.'

I'm in trouble, thought Arthur, as he heard her mock him under her breath, repeating 'the news was not good' in a gruff imitation of his voice.

'Caitlyn,' said Arthur, softly but still scolding, 'there's no need for that.'

She looked up at him, scowling, but he saw her expression soften as her temper settled.

'Sorry,' she said. 'What's wrong?'

Arthur refilled their glasses and then drained his.

'It was bad news about a friend,' he said, not really sure

where his story was going and realising how reluctant he sounded. Caitlyn set down her cutlery, and she crouched down beside Arthur, taking his hand.

'What's happened?' she said, and all trace of the previous animosity was gone. Arthur loved her all the more for how quick she was to forgive and forget. Tristan could learn a few things from this woman.

'It's not easy for me to talk about,' said Arthur. 'John meant a great deal to me, but he did something in anger for which he is still paying the price.'

Caitlyn was frowning at him, and Arthur considered how much he should say, especially given that Agravain meant to escape imminently. It would be in the news, it would implicate him, surely? Perhaps he could cover up his involvement. Maybe this was the beginning of the bigger lies. Perhaps his time here was about to come to an end, forced to move on and go into hiding.

'John Marlow served under me, years ago. We . . . drifted as time passed, but I heard a few years ago there had been an incident. John's always had a strong sense of right and wrong, got in all kinds of trouble intervening where perhaps the police would have been better suited. He killed some people,' Arthur paused, unable to stop himself imagining what Agravain's face looked like whenever he fought, when the red mist descended.

'Jesus,' said Caitlyn. 'What happened?'

'John never gave an account to the police or in court. He's been a brawler all his life, but usually because he could never stand by and let anyone get hurt. He's a very strong, very experienced fighter, and I entirely believe he acted in good conscience. Nevertheless, he was convicted of murder.'

Caitlyn returned to her chair, took a sip of her own wine.

'Why didn't he explain what happened if he was trying to help? I mean, it's terrible that people died, but if your friend was trying to help? It hardly seems fair,' said Caitlyn.

Arthur shrugged.

'Perhaps, but it's the law,' said Arthur. He picked up his fork, but realised his appetite had diminished.

'So what's happened now? Why is your lawyer calling?' asked Caitlyn.

'I paid for his defence,' said Arthur. 'He passed her a message for me.'

'Why doesn't he tell you himself? What message?' asked Caitlyn.

'We are not on speaking terms,' Arthur admitted, dropping his gaze. 'He walked away years ago.' He pushed back his chair, caught his cane as it slid along the table edge and took his plate to the kitchen.

He paused by Caitlyn's chair on the way.

'He's not been well, and he's just been diagnosed,' Arthur lied. 'The prognosis is uncertain.'

Perhaps, he thought as he left her to digest the information, *given what would come next, the lie had been a good one.*

AGRAVAIN'S ESCAPE

Monday 11th of January 2021
08:00

A pool of blood spread on the cell floor like the blossoming of a crimson flower, its smooth, wet petals unfurling around Agravain's body as he contorted on the floor, his hand clamped over the wound to his left wrist.

A prison officer opened the cell door. He started to offer a 'good morning', but then saw Agravain and spluttered something unintelligible. He froze momentarily, his eyes wide and mouth hanging open before getting on his radio and shouting to his nearest colleague.

✧

Monday 11th of January 2021
08:30

A stolen van on cloned plates, carefully chosen to ensure they were for the correct make and model of vehicle, stood with its engine idling in a supermarket car park, positioned so that the driver, Gareth, had a clear view of the main road. Tristan sat in the passenger seat. Both men were dressed in branded tracksuits, both wore baseball caps with the peaks pulled down low in an attempt to shade their faces from overhead cameras.

✧

Monday 11th of January 2021
08:35

Bors, his arm in a sling, walked into the A&E department of Stonegate Hospital. He queued, semi-patiently, then took a seat in the overcrowded waiting room. Babies screamed, men clutched bloodied limbs, people rested heads on shoulders, nurses looked harried and doctors were conspicuously absent. Coughing, an unpleasant smell and waiting. Bors closed his eyes and rested the back of his head against the wall.

———

Monday 11th of January 2021
08:40

A little of Arthur's coffee slopped on to the dining room table as Caitlyn set his mug down beside him.

'What *is* wrong with you this morning? You can't sit still! Look! You're bouncing in your seat and staring through the wall. What's up?' she tousled his hair. 'Thinking about your friend?'

Arthur nodded.

'Sorry,' he said. 'I'm not good company at the moment.'

Caitlyn kissed his brow.

'We all have *those* weeks, and you've better reasons than most. Have you got much on?' she said.

'How do you mean?' said Arthur.

'Well, can you take some time for yourself? Do something to take your mind off it?'

'I'll try, but I doubt anything will,' said Arthur, staring up at the clock.

―⁂―

Monday 11th of January 2021
08:45

An ambulance pulled out of the airlock gates leading through the towering walls of Her Majesty's Prison Stonegate and began the short journey to Stonegate Hospital.

It passed by a trading estate on the main road into town.

'There it is,' said Tristan. 'We're on, lads.'

Gareth put the van into first gear and then Arthur's knights were on the move.

Chapter Twelve

London
1734
Ten years after Agravain confronted Malagant

Agravain pushed open the door to his small home and looked around at the fireplace, table, chest, bed and two chairs as though it was the last time.

Nimuë sat by the fire in one of the chairs, unmoving. Agravain was able to creep up on her while she cradled their swaddled daughter, so transfixed was she by Ariadne's tiny features, seemingly fascinated by what she had made from her own flesh.

As Agravain came to stand beside her, he noticed the baby frown momentarily then purse her lips and relax.

'She's dreaming,' he said, resting a hand on Nimuë's shoulder and stooping to kiss her head, relishing the sweet scent of her hair.

She looked up at him, and he caught a glimpse of a contented smile on her lips before it faded, her eyes briefly shining with a new magic before the light went out. The dark circles appeared all the darker against her pale skin as she looked up at him. He sensed her sudden sadness at his presence and was about to crouch and ask her what was the matter when she spoke.

'Do not delude yourself,' she said softly. 'This will not last. I will not stay forever, and neither will she.'

He took a step back as though pushed, and anguish must have been clear on his face as she reached towards him, and her expression changed to one of kindness. He took her hand, cold against his warm skin, and she drew him to her, resting her head against him.

He recovered somewhat, and caressed the nape of her neck with his rough fingers. She responded with a little shiver, and he smiled, his fears put aside.

'I come from our new home,' he said. 'A place fit for a family. It's about time I spent a little of my stipend from Arthur on myself.'

Nimuë laughed.

'On yourself? You would not have purchased such a house if you were alone, John Marlow. You have done this for your daughter and I,' she said, and Agravain blushed.

London
1737
Three years later

The woman staggered through the back streets of Holborn, often falling against the buildings and, once, tripping so that she fell on her front in the mud. She cursed angrily, but before long, she was back on her feet and singing despite her grazed hands and ripped dress.

Agravain trailed her at some distance, a looming figure, apparent for all to see, the lurkers in the shadowy alleys and those who hunted the byways of London.

Agravain walked unnoticed behind the woman until, finally, she reached her door. He waited until she was inside then walked back the way he had come.

Will Nimuë still be there?

Every night the same thought as he climbed the stone steps to his three-storey townhouse. So often he found a note left in Nimuë's place, sometimes just to explain that she had gone down to the river, but occasionally it informed him that the enchantress had business elsewhere and that she would return to her wandering for a time, leaving the care of the children to him and their servants.

He unlocked the door and moved into the darkness within.

Silence.

Agravain lit an oil lamp and set it down while he removed his boots. He hung up his coat and tricorn then climbed the stairs, keeping to the edges to minimise creaking, casting his gaze all about him for signs of intruders.

He reached the top floor and carefully opened the door to the nursery. Agravain crept across the room to the cot and leaned in to listen for his baby son's breathing. He licked the back of his index finger and held the moistened skin above Henry's nose until he felt breath upon it.

Thus reassured, he moved down the hall and checked on Ariadne. She was tucked up safely in bed, sleeping soundly.

He approached his own bedroom, and once more the thought intruded.

Will she still be there?

He turned the round handle and, holding his breath, opened the door a crack, peering through.

His eyes adjusted, and he could just make out Nimuë's shape beneath the blankets. He breathed out and slipped into the room.

London
March 1744
Seven years later

'Lay them on the grave,' said Agravain, holding baby Caroline in his left arm as she burbled, eyes looking all around, following the sway of the thin branches overhead.

'You don't have to be afraid, Arthur,' said Ariadne, stooping down beside her younger brother. The infant clutched a posy of spring blooms in both hands and stepped back so that his back bumped into Agravain's leg.

'It's alright,' said Agravain, squatting down so that he was at the same level as his son and daughter. 'Ariadne can do it instead, if you like, but there is nothing to be afraid of. Henry was your brother.'

Ariadne attempted to pluck the posy from little Arthur's hands, but he held on tight and stepped forward. The boy bent down and dropped it on the grave. Agravain did not notice how the flowers suddenly freshened and flourished as he did so.

'Good lad,' said Agravain, tousling the boy's hair. He winked at Ariadne, and she smiled back at him.

'We should go home, Cook will have dinner ready very soon,' he said.

He reached out and laid a hand upon the headstone, his heart all but breaking as he spared a thought for his son, buried in the dirt beneath his feet, felled by scarlet fever.

'Will Mother be back tonight?' asked Ariadne as she walked along the path out of the graveyard.

Agravain did not reply immediately, fearful of telling a lie. He answered out of hope and belief when he did speak.

'Not tonight, but soon. Your Mother travels, but she always comes back, doesn't she?'

Ariadne nodded.

Though she may not always stay, he thought.

'Come along, let's see what Cook has in store,' said Agravain and cast one eye back to where his infant son rested beneath the earth.

―⁂―

London
Christmas Day - 1762
Eighteen years later

The Marlow family sat around the table in their dining room, Agravain at one end and Nimuë at the other. Ariadne sat next to her husband on one side with her baby on her lap, and Arthur's wife sat between him and Caroline, opposite them.

Once the servants had laid the Christmas feast upon the table, Agravain led his family in prayer, and once they had given thanks for the meal and for each other, he went round the table and filled all of their glasses with wine.

He returned to his seat and, smiling wistfully, nodded once to Nimuë. They both stood at their respective ends of the table, and Nimuë spoke.

'To absent friends and family. To Henry, to Jemima, to Alice, whose lives were no less brighter for being much shorter.' Her voice broke as she spoke, and more than one cheek was graced by a tear around the table. Agravain felt as though his eyes might burst as he thought of his lost children, victims of the age.

When dinner was done and the meal cleared away, they sat for a while together and shared a drink, catching up with one another's lives.

After a while, Agravain stood and begged leave to head out for a while.

'I must attend to my Foundation obligations,' he said. 'We have many folk distributing food and blankets around the city, and if my people are spending their day thus, it would be remiss of me not to join them.'

He embraced each of his children and Arthur's wife in turn, shaking hands with Ariadne's rather serious husband, Frederick, before sharing a passionate kiss with Nimuë.

'Stay safe,' she said, then wrapped a new scarf around his neck, 'and come back to us for supper and games before it gets too late?' She framed it as a question, but Agravain knew an instruction from his wife when he heard one.

༺◦༻

London
February 1793
Thirty-One Years Later
France has executed King Louis XVI. Great Britain has expelled the French ambassador.

Agravain folded The Times and placed it carefully on the table beside his chair in the drawing-room. He heard the door open and Nimuë stepped through.

'We are at war. The French have . . . ' said Agravain as he looked up, but stopped short when he saw her wild eyes and tear-streaked face.

'What's the matter?' asked Agravain, rushing to her and taking her by the shoulders. He thought she would break down in tears for a moment or two, but she straightened up and a calmness that was even more alarming fell over her.

'Ariadne has passed away,' she said in a

quiet voice, pulling him in close, her head against his chest. Agravain's vision blurred and his knees gave beneath him. He crumpled to the floor, and Nimuë fell with him. He could not hold back the tears and they dropped from his cheeks, soaking into Nimuë's hair. Neither of them spoke as they mourned the death of their eldest child, who had lived to 59, even then outliving their son, Arthur, who had succumbed to pneumonia in his forties. Only Caroline remained alive.

And yet Agravain and Nimuë crept through the years unchanged.

London
1815

Twenty-two years of nearly constant war with France are coming to a close. The Revolutionary Wars gave way to the Napoleonic Wars, and now Arthur and his knights fight at the Battle of Waterloo, where Napoleon will be defeated.

In England, the grandchildren of Ariadne, Arthur and Caroline are growing fast, and some of them have had children themselves.

Agravain and Nimuë have stepped back from the family as questions begin to be asked about their youthful looks and longevity, distancing themselves from their grandchildren, while acting as benefactors from afar. Now Caroline, the last of the children, is on her deathbed, surrounded by her own sons and daughters. Agravain and Nimuë have been to her home and said their goodbyes.

The couple remained silent on the carriage ride back to their home, and when Agravain reached for Nimuë's hand, as much for his own comfort as for hers, she folded her arms and turned to watch through the window. Agravain sighed and, resting his head back, he closed his eyes and remembered his lost children, feeling hollow and all the more lonely for being unable to reach out to his wife on that day of all days.

──◈──

Nimuë walked into the house ahead of him. The door was barely closed and their outer clothes taken away by their servants before Nimuë turned on Agravain, her eyes red and streaming tears, but her jaw set. She sounded determined when she spoke, firmly, and without emotion.

'Our children are all gone,' she said. 'The time has come.'

Agravain folded his arms over his chest, then let them hang by his side, then folded them again. As he replied he unfolded his arms once again, gripping the lapel of his jacket with his left and scratched his sideburn with the fingers of his right hand.

'The time?' he said, knowing full well.

She tilted her chin up, and he thought she was barely holding herself together, fighting to maintain her resolve.

'Our children are all gone. Their families and our neighbours begin to ask questions. I always told you that I would not stay forever,' she said, the words sounding harsh and uncaring to his ears, though he knew that her heart must be breaking.

He objected, he cajoled, he railed and he pleaded with her as she bustled from room to room, gathering a few of her possessions and some clothing together, but she would not relent except that when she reached the front door, she turned and kissed him, long and slow, and Agravain felt the love that passed between them.

'Goodbye,' she said, and with that, Nimuë departed and swept out of his life.

Alone once more, Agravain's life reeled back nearly a century. He stepped back from his Foundation to become a silent donor, he sold the family home, unable to dwell in the empty shell with only the ghosts of his children to keep him company.

He returned to the streets, and took rooms in the East End, not far from Whitechapel High Street.

And he turned his full attention to London once more, haunted by the memory of a life now lost, watching over his grandchildren, and their children, and their children's children as the years went by, aiding them where he could, but never a word spoken to any of them, unless it was as a stranger, benefactor or employer.

Chapter Thirteen

Monday 11th of January 2021
09:00

Monday morning traffic being what it was at the tail end of the rush hour, it was not long before the van containing the knights fell behind, and they lost the ambulance from view.

'Lost it,' said Gareth.

'It doesn't matter, we've confirmed it's heading towards Stonegate A&E,' said Tristan. He pulled a cheap pay-as-you-go phone from his pocket and sent a text to two other similar phones, recently bought and unregistered.

'Keep on towards the hospital,' he said. 'Keep it steady. We'll get there when we get there,' said Tristan.

∽⚭∽

Monday 11th of January 2021
09:00

Sitting in A&E, Bors felt his phone vibrate. He hooked it out of his pocket and read the message.

Confirmed

He put the phone away and, casting a look around as he did so, getting a sense of whether earlier recces had represented the situation on the actual day, he made a note of how many security staff were around. First, he found the toilets; next he went in search of a vending machine, eyes everywhere, searching for the information he needed, ensuring that nothing had changed.

There were two security guards in A&E, just as they had expected.

Monday 11th of January 2021
09:00

Confirmed

Nimuë stared at the word on her phone screen.

'Not long,' she said to nobody, her heart beating fast. She opened the driver's door and stepped out into the chill, fresh air, leaning on the second-hand car, bought for cash the previous day and not yet registered with a new keeper. She looked out across the grass beside the quiet road, over the treetops to the upper floors of Stonegate Hospital beyond.

She moved around to the passenger side of the car, opened the door and put the keys in the glove compartment.

Nimuë walked up the street, thrusting her gloved hands into the pockets of her long coat, and she disappeared around a corner.

Monday 11th of January 2021
09:15

Bors stood outside the main doors of A&E and watched as the ambulance pulled into the circular area by the ambulance bay outside Stonegate Hospital. He saw the paramedic who had been driving jump out and run to the rear doors. She opened them and after a few moments, the second paramedic stepped out, along with a prison officer in black shoes, black trousers, a white shirt with a black jacket over the top, hitched up over a radio on his belt.

A second officer stepped down, and Bors saw a stretcher come into view with a man lying on it, a man he had not seen in decades, a man handcuffed via a long chain to the second prison officer.

The first paramedic began pushing the wheeled stretcher towards the entrance to A&E, flanked on each side by the burly prison officers. The second paramedic closed up the ambulance and ran to catch up as they passed inside the dedicated entrance, disappearing up an empty passageway. Bors headed back inside, texting as he did so.

In

Monday 11th of January 2021
09:25

'They'll be booking him in now,' said Tristan, turning back over his shoulder to address the knights as Gareth parked the van in a side street near the hospital, making sure he was not on yellow lines or causing any obstruction. He and Gareth unclipped their seatbelts and slipped out of the van.

'Make yourselves comfortable,' said Gareth, before closing the doors and walking away together towards the main road. They did not worry about cameras, but kept their heads down as they walked and talked until they were a few streets away.

Monday 11th of January 2021
12:00

Once Agravain had been triaged, his wounds were seen to and bandaged, and he was moved to a private room for some further tests and a mental health assessment.

The prison officers went with him. One sat by the bed, handcuffed to Agravain's left hand, between Agravain and the window, and one moved a chair to block the route to the door.

Agravain said nothing, lying back on the bed with his eyes closed.

'You alright, John?' asked the prison officer by the door, and the concern was genuine. Agravain made it his business to get on with all of the prison staff, passing the time of day with them, enquiring after their own interests. John Marlow was a people person. Not today it seemed, and the officers with him were as perturbed as anyone that John made a suicide attempt, however half-hearted.

Agravain did not reply, but nodded his head ever so slightly. The two officers exchanged a look.

Monday 11th of January 2021
12:05

Bors left A&E and took the short walk to where the van was parked. He got into the driving seat, checked if anyone was looking then shrugged off the sling.

'Dag, Bed, you're up,' said Bors, after checking all around through the windows and in his mirrors.

The rear door to the van opened. Dagonet and Bedivere stepped down, both wearing blue trousers and bomber jackets, zipped up at the front, baseball caps shading their faces. Once they were walking towards the hospital, Bors started the van and drove away.

Monday 11th of January 2021
12:10

Dagonet and Bedivere, both dressed in nurses' scrubs with jackets and caps in hand, made their way through a door to the podiatry department at the side of the hospital and headed through the corridors that would, eventually, lead them into the main hospital without having to pass through main reception or any kind of security.

AGRAVAIN'S ESCAPE

※

Monday 11th of January 2021
12:15

Not being able to call anybody at the hospital was infuriating. After Caitlyn had left for work at *her* hospital, alibi witness secured, Arthur walked back home in search of Kay. He, too, was not fit for action if things went wrong because, unlike Arthur, whose lingering injury was caused by machine-gun rounds at the Somme, Branok's familiar, Joseph, had hacked off Kay's left leg at the thigh during their final showdown at the Tower of London. His prosthetic enabled him to get around, but he had less mobility than Arthur.

Arthur called out as he pushed through the front door, and Kay's greeting in reply came from upstairs.

He found his knight in the study, monitoring the news sites, careful not to search for anything incriminating.

'Anything?' asked Arthur.

'Nothing yet,' said Kay. 'This is killing me. I should be out there with them. This is like waiting in the trenches, poised to run, whistles set to blow at any time.'

Arthur's heart rate sped up at the mention of the trenches, and when Kay met his gaze, he saw recognition in his knight's face. Kay changed the subject.

'Are you sure about letting Nimuë help?'

'She has more of a vested interest than anyone, and she will be needed. The world has moved on, but if one of our brothers makes the approach, well, they have a distinct . . . look . . . about them.'

―⁂―

Monday 11th of January 2021
13:00

Nimuë backed into Agravain's room with a jug of water and a cup. The officers sat up, attending carefully, but relaxed as they saw a woman in scrubs.

'Sorry,' she mouthed, smiling, scrunching up her eyes a little and hunching her shoulders a little as though to say 'silly me'.

She set the jug and cup on the overbed table.

'Something to drink for you, lovely,' she said, affecting a change in accent. Agravain opened his eyes and looked at her. She panicked in that instant, wondering how he would react, but he looked at her with a blank expression, said 'thank you' quietly, then closed his eyes once more.

She made for the door, but before stepping through she turned back.

'Can I get you gents a tea or coffee?'

'Could murder a coffee,' said the man in the chair by the door.

'Tea would be lovely,' said the handcuffed officer, sitting on the far side of the bed.

'How d'you have it?' said Nimuë, eyebrows raised, looking from one man to the other.

'Milk and two sugars, please,' said the handcuffed officer.

'Julie Andrews,' said the man by the door.

'What, my love?' said Nimuë, flummoxed.

'White nun,' said the handcuffed officer. 'Sorry about him.'

Nimuë laughed, although she did not get it, never having watched The Sound of Music.

'One tea, milk, two sugars, one coffee, just with milk?' she checked.

'That's it,' said the man in the chair.

'Be right back,' said Nimuë, setting off to find the tea station, avoiding doctors and nurses as best she could.

Monday 11th of January 2021
13:30

Dagonet and Bedivere paused at the correct corridor intersection. A few nurses moved between rooms, but there wasn't a constant flow. They found a suitable spot by a window and struck up a conversation about a fictional affair one was having with a fictional doctor's fictional girlfriend, hushing whenever someone walked by, but not quite enough that they couldn't be heard.

Dagonet looked up at the sound of more footfalls, and he saw Nimuë walking towards them.

She greeted them as though they were close colleagues, passed on the location of the room and made her way out of the hospital.

Dagonet and Bedivere knew they had to be quick. They

checked signs as they passed, although both had pored over plans of the hospital in the past days, pulling on latex gloves before reaching their destination.

Finally they stood before the correct room, and Bedivere pushed inside. Dagonet followed him in.

The two officers were slumped in their chairs, not quite unconscious, but fading in and out, heads lolling. Dagonet and Bedivere lifted the chair holding one of the officers and moved it against the door then as fast as they could, set to work.

'Agravain,' hissed Dagonet as he crossed to draw the curtains, but Agravain made no reply. He didn't even open his eyes. Bedivere stepped up and shook him gently and was rewarded by Agravain opening his eyes.

'I knew you would come,' he said flatly. 'Get me out of here.'

Monday 11th of January 2021
13:40

The door to Agravain's room pushed open and a prison officer stepped out into the hall carrying a cap and a jacket.

A minute later, two male nurses also emerged and split up, moving off into the hospital. The alarm may have already been raised if the unconscious prison officers had not checked in at some unknown allotted time. The police could already be on the way.

AGRAVAIN'S ESCAPE

Monday 11th of January 2021
13:50

A genuine nurse backed into John Marlow's room, ready to take observations and wheeling his monitor with him. He turned, ready to speak to the officers, but swore as he saw that the bed was empty and the officers, one still handcuffed, were slumped unconscious in their chairs, wearing nothing but socks and boxer shorts.

One empty cup sat on the overbed table, the other had been left by the skirting-board by the door.

Monday 11th of January 2021
13:50

Agravain, now wearing a jacket and cap, along with unremarkable black trousers, left the hospital by a side door and checked the map he had been passed by Bedivere, before setting out across the car park towards the treeline.

He passed through the trees and saw the car Nimuë had left parked on the kerbside across a stretch of grass.

Agravain set off towards it, grinning as he did so.

Chapter Fourteen

London
October 1837
The first year of Queen Victoria's reign

Mary Stevens, a serving girl, hurried towards Lavender Hill, eager to arrive at her workplace on time and running a little late after visiting her parents in Battersea. Her feet pounded as she crossed Clapham Common, south of the Thames, far from Agravain's stomping grounds to the north of the river.

Mary walked with her head down, trying to master her breathing as anxiety rose in her at the prospect of the day ahead.

Just do your job and try not to be so clumsy, she told herself.

A figure clad all in black leapt in a great arc, inconceivable for a human, or so it seemed to Mary, and landed before her in the street, arms reaching for her and cloak billowing out behind it. She started backwards and let out a guttural groan before properly seeing what now stood before her in the otherwise empty street.

It gripped both of her arms with cold, clammy claw-like hands and held her fast. She screamed again. The creature grinned, showing long yellowing teeth and darted in to plant kisses on her lips and cheeks and forehead even as Mary struggled. The creature began to tear at her clothes, and Mary recovered enough to scream. Her attacker released her, still grinning, and ran off with a leaping stride.

Mary continued screaming even as local residents were drawn to her cries. She told them of the attack, and they began a search of the common as Mary was taken to safety.

The creature was never found, but tales began to spread of a creature that leapt great distances, a devil perhaps, with horns and glowing red eyes.

The following evening, a coachman was driving a carriage down a street not so very far from Mary Stevens' home when that same figure clad all in black, his cloak billowing, leapt from a side street, landing before the coachman's horse, causing it to rear. The coachman caught a glimpse of a creature, its arms outstretched, a grin on its face, and he hauled on the reins.

The carriage swerved, but, try as he might, the coachman could not regain control of the vehicle. It smashed into a building, throwing him to the street. The creature made off, seen by many witnesses, some of whom would later claim that they saw it leap straight over a fence which stood no less than nine feet tall, babbling and cackling as it did so.

The legend of Spring-Heeled Jack began to spread.

London
10th of January 1838

Agravain walked the streets alone, gas-lights visible behind the windows, and a cacophony of laughter, fighting and chatter from the public houses filled the air. He kept out of the way of the carts and carriages that splashed through puddles.

He wore a greatcoat over a frock coat, and his tricorn had been replaced many years before by a tall top hat. Instead of a cudgel, he now carried a cane which concealed a long blade, and his flintlock pistols had been replaced by a pair of state-of-the-art Colt Paterson revolving guns, each loaded with five rounds, requiring partial disassembly to reload. He wore his sideburns long. They were black, turning to grey halfway down, and his handlebar moustache was also flecked grey and white. He had not shaved the rest of his face in two days, and stubble lined his jaw. His riding boots were scuffed and muddy, and he made no trouble to avoid the worst of the mire as he walked.

He stopped beneath a lamp, and retrieved a small journal from inside his greatcoat. At the top of each page was written a name, and at the bottom were a single circled page number in the corner and an index of other numbers along the bottom, referring to other pages in the book. Addresses were scrawled under the names. Some of the names had been struck through, and the writing on those pages had faded. On others where the names were still intact, all but the most recent addresses had been scrawled through.

Each name was written in either red, blue or green ink, indicating which of his children the person was descended from, although in truth he no longer thought of his descendants as grandchildren, great-grandchildren or even great-great-grandchildren. They were the living blood of his Ariadne, Arthur and Caroline, and he cherished them, though they did not know him, except as an agent of a distant Foundation, which offered financial aid when it was needed, and as a stranger who, when he happened to be in the right place at the right time or had investigated and intervened, might intercede on their behalf. An abusive husband would be set right. A job lost might result in an introduction. A robbery might be thwarted.

Agravain could not be everywhere or save them all, but he did not take fatherhood lightly, and he did what he could.

And I can only do what I can, he reminded himself, thinking of his many failures.

⁂

Another family lived in Agravain and Nimuë's townhouse now, and he had taken a small set of rooms in the East End. They were not as meagre as his lodgings in Moorfields, which were long gone, and Moorfields itself had been developed as the city expanded, the area now replaced by Finsbury Circus. His rooms were not large, but they were secure, warm and comfortable. He did not have much furniture, but he ran his businesses from the premises, his living room doubling as a study.

The only decorations hung about the walls were his own art, the product of many an evening's work, drawings of Nimuë, his children and his grandchildren in coloured inks, each carefully framed.

Agravain slumped in his chair, almost ready to fall asleep, but decided to read through that day's papers to push him over the edge. There seemed to be more and more newspapers springing up of late, he thought as he began to cast his eye across the text.

All of them were filled with reports of a figure becoming known as Spring-Heeled Jack. It seemed the Lord Mayor had convened a public session and revealed an anonymous letter of complaint about someone taking a wager to adopt disguises in order to spread mischief. It complained that seven ladies had been 'deprived of their senses' and one woman in particular who had opened her door to find a spectre standing before her had yet to recover from her swoon. The tone of the stories was almost hysterical at times, and Agravain read on, ever sceptical. The next day, he attended another session called by the Lord Mayor and listened with interest to the news that letters reporting such attacks, pranks and incidents were piling up.

Over the coming weeks, tales of Spring-Heeled Jack, dressed variously as a demon, a bear, a ghost and other such creatures, became widespread in London.

The newly burgeoning media helped to spread the tales, terrifying illustrations accompanying exaggerated accounts. And yet Agravain could not help but wonder if Malagant was involved. The fear of Spring-Heeled Jack was becoming tangible. He was the talk of taverns and dining rooms alike. The Dread Knight was surely feeding well, and was it impossible to believe that if not him directly, one of his cultists had taken this wager? Had Malagant laid it himself?

Agravain decided that he would find out.

London
21st of February 1838

'I appreciate you taking the time to see me, Miss Alsop,' said Agravain as he seated himself in the Alsops' parlour and prepared to take notes.

'I have already recounted the event to the police,' said Jane Alsop.

'I appreciate that, but sometimes details are missed. Also,' said Agravain confidentially, 'there is a certain amount of professional competition amongst my colleagues when it comes to catching the rascal masquerading as Spring-Heeled Jack.'

Since the formation of the River Police in 1798 and the Metropolitan Police in 1829, Agravain had found many of his patrol duties were eased by constables walking the streets of

London. Pretending to be a police officer himself was useful at times, eliciting co-operation and answers where otherwise he would have found closed doors and silence. He was sure the novelty of an organised police force would wear off.

Jane Alsop exchanged a look with her father and then recounted the tale once more.

'There was a knock at the door. I answered, and there was a fellow standing on the doorstep. He claimed to be a police officer and asked for a light, saying Spring-Heeled Jack had been caught out in the lane,' she said.

'Imagine pretending to be a police officer,' said Mr Alsop.

'Scandalous indeed, sir. Please go on, Miss Alsop,' said Agravain.

'I . . . I fetched him a candle. It seemed the thing to do, and as I came down the steps towards the lane, I saw he was wearing a long black cloak. I went to hand him the light when suddenly he threw off the cloak. Sir, he was of the most hideous and frightful appearance.'

Jane Alsop lowered her eyes momentarily as she continued.

'Other officers have laughed at the rest, but I swear I tell it true, constable,' she said, only then looking up to meet Agravain's gaze one more.

'Go on, miss,' said Agravain. 'I'll have heard worse, I assure you.'

Once more she looked to her father, who bade her go on.

'Well sir, no sooner had I gone to hand him the light, he threw off the cloak as I've said, and . . . well, he belched blue and white flame from his mouth! His eyes, sir, glowing red they were. He took hold of me and scratched at me with some sort of claws. Like metal they were, and he tore up my dress. I shrieked and ran for the house, but the fiend caught me on the steps.'

Here Jane began to shake and sob. Her father intervened.

'See her neck there, constable? The cuts? Her arms are no better. If her sister had not come out, scaring the devil off, I dread to think what harm could have befallen my daughter,' said the father.

'Blue and white flame?' asked Agravain, writing in his notebook.

'I swear it,' said Jane Alsop. 'Though many have cause to doubt it. I remember distinctly.'

'Interesting,' said Agravain. 'Well, let us delve a little deeper, and see if we can't get some fine-grain detail to go on.'

He leant in close, making a show of looking as though he were checking if anyone was listening.

'We can't have my colleagues getting the chap before us, can we?' said Agravain with a wink.

Chapter Fifteen

London
27th of February 1838
8 days after the attack on Jane Alsop

'How sure are you?' asked Agravain, sliding a golden guinea across the table to the prostitute sitting opposite him.

"Ow sure?' she slurred. 'Sure enough for me own reckoning. Telling the truth as I knows it, ain't I? Truth as I knows and truth as does is different a time or two, ain't it?' she concluded. She tried and failed to pluck up the coin with her fingertips, but gave up when her dexterity failed her. She scooped it towards her and caught it in her hand then rubbed it between thumb and forefinger, eyes gleaming like a dragon inspecting its hoard.

'Limehouse?' he asked, but the woman was too busy trying to pocket the coin.

'Hannah,' Agravain snapped his fingers. 'Limehouse?'

'Aye. Lime'ouse. Girls hear fings, don't they?'

'They do,' Agravain conceded. 'And they get paid for what they hear all the better if what they hear turns out to be true and not just an attempt at picking my pocket.'

'Ain't touched your pocket!' Hannah screeched.

Agravain took a swig of his drink.

'Have you somewhere to stop tonight?' he asked her, voice softening.

'Rent's past due,' she muttered, reaching for her cup then draining it.

'You'll find a golden guinea in your pocket, my love,' said Agravain.

Hannah laughed.

'True enough! That'll keep the landlord happy for a time if I don't drink it on the way home. Place to stop tonight? You've a bed to share if I should find myself stricken, I'd wager,' she said, doing her best to look seductive and failing on two counts, the first being that she was all but unconscious under the weight of gin and the second being that she was talking to her great-great-grandfather.

'No bed to share,' said Agravain, fighting to maintain his patience. Not all of his descendants could be pillars of society and sometimes no amount of aid would solve self-inflicted problems or thwart adopted vices. He stood and dusted off his top hat.

'I'll stop by your place in the week, Hannah,' said Agravain. 'If I find you've been evicted, there will be no more coin from me.'

He patted her on the shoulder and pushed through the crowded public house and onto the street.

Limehouse, London
28th of February 1830
9 days after the attack on Jane Alsop

Agravain set off for Limehouse before the sun was up in search of his quarry. He spent the day walking the streets, stopping in for a drink now and then, listening to the talk in public and coffee houses alike, all the time looking for one man in particular.

It took the better part of the day to locate one William Guthrie, a well-known bookie thereabouts, with whom Agravain felt a certain line of enquiry could be progressed.

'Now then, Guthrie,' said Agravain, coming up on the man from behind as he was settling a wager in a side alley. The bookie winced as though shot, and he seemed ready to take to his toes for a moment until he recognised the interloper.

'For the love of . . . pay no heed to him,' he

said to the other party, as he handed over the last few coins. 'He's not law.'

Agravain raised his sword cane and rested it across his shoulder, waiting until the payee had disappeared from earshot.

'Shouldn't surprise a man like that. Get yourself shot,' said Guthrie, adjusting his cravat.

Agravain raised an eyebrow.

'You can discharge a firearm back over your shoulder while you're running and shitting yourself at the same time?' he asked.

Guthrie swore, and Agravain gave a grunt of satisfaction.

'What do you want, Marlow?' asked Guthrie, looking back over Agravain's shoulder.

'I want to hear what you can tell about the Mad Marquess. I have heard tell,' Agravain lowered his voice as he leaned in, 'that he is in town and, as luck would have it, crossing your path from time to time, being a gambling man.'

There had been occasions when Guthrie had held out under questioning, but as Agravain spoke, the bookie massaged his jaw, remembering how, once, it'd been broken shortly before he'd decided it was easier to just pass on what he knew.

It must have been nearing half eight when Agravain approached Green Dragon Alley in a respectable part of Limehouse. He had not quite entered the road when he heard two women scream up ahead. He burst into a run, tearing down the street in time to see a young man stooped over a fallen, fitting woman, who he would later discover was one Lucy Scales, with another woman tending to her.

'What happened?' asked the man as Agravain checked his pace and came to a stop beside them, listening intently as others spilled into the street.

He took in the facts; a tall thin man with a cloak had watched them approach, pulled back the cloak to reveal a lantern and belched blue flame in their faces before walking off at a steady pace.

'Which way?' said Agravain, and he was pointed in the right direction by the woman before she assisted in carrying her sister to safety.

Agravain broke into a run, even as the call went up for the police. He barrelled around a corner into an alley, sending a rat scurrying for cover. He regulated his breathing as he picked up the pace, eyes all about him, looking for any sign of the attacker having passed that way.

Surely he could not be so very far behind if

the man had not run? Agravain powered on, and his efforts paid off. He caught a glimpse of a cloaked man in a tall hat disappearing left down yet another alley.

Agravain drew his Colt and ran even faster, struggling to breathe, not even attempting to be stealthy.

He careered into the alley only to find that the cloaked man had started back towards him and was apparently peering out to see if he had been followed. The man gave a yelp as Agravain, acting on instinct, extended his left arm and wrapped it around the man's throat. His momentum carried him forward and both of them crashed to the ground, Agravain maintaining the hold.

'Henry,' said Agravain, hissing, and speaking without fully thinking it out. 'Malagant sent me.'

The squirming Marquess of Waterford stopped struggling momentarily, fingers wrapped around Agravain's forearm.

He said nothing.

'You've been identified. Come with me. I have a disguise nearby,' he said, releasing his grip. Waterford leapt to his feet, coughing and massaging his throat. He looked back over his shoulder, taking a step that way, but hearing voices, he looked back towards Agravain.

'Henry, come on,' said Agravain, having no

idea whether his guess was correct or not, having only ever seen illustrations of the Mad Marquess, famed for his brawling and bad behaviour, in particular his inability to turn down any wager.

'Lord Waterford,' the man snapped. 'I will have my title from you, whoever you are!'

Agravain nodded.

'Light along there, man, or you're done for,' he said and walked off down the alley at a brisk pace without looking back, hoping his deceit would pay off.

Sure enough, he heard footsteps close behind him.

A few more streets away, taking a zigzagging path where possible, Agravain found a spot he was happy with and rounded on the man behind him. He gripped Lord Waterford by the throat and slammed him up against a wall, pressing the muzzle of his Colt into the man's open mouth as the Marquess gasped for air.

A nearby lamp gave off just enough light to see that Waterford wore a sort of helmet and some kind of contraption which, he guessed, would have hung close to his mouth, had Agravain not broken it in his assault.

'Blue flame, Waterford?'

The Marquess said nothing. Agravain thrust the gun forward and Waterford gagged.

Agravain pulled back ever so slightly.

'Co . . . copper sulphate. Hydrochloric acid. Ethanol,' came Waterford's stilted reply.

Agravain grunted.

'Show me the sign,' he growled, squeezing Waterford's throat. 'Slowly.'

Waterford coughed as his hand began to move. Agravain readied himself for trickery, expectant of some counter-strike, but he had overestimated the man's ability on account of his reputation as a brawler.

Waterford reached into his waistcoat pocket and withdrew a pocket watch emblazoned with the red eye of Deimos, just visible in the lamplight.

'Tell Malagant I'm on to him,' hissed Agravain, his saliva spattering Waterford's face.

'And you . . . ' he said. 'I'm watching you. This is the last I'll hear of Spring-Heeled Jack hereabouts, understand? Else I'll come a-calling while you're sleeping and end his reign of terror for good. The messy way. The bloody way.'

He crushed Waterford's windpipe and forced the muzzle of the gun to the back of his throat.

'Understand?'

The Marquess could not reply, could not breathe, Agravain realised. He released his grip and stepped back quickly, but Waterford crumpled in a heap on the floor.

'Tell Malagant that Agravain sends his regards,' said the knight, and he left the Marquess choking in the backstreets of Limehouse.

Spring-Heeled Jack never really went away, kept alive by public hysteria, penny dreadfuls, stories in the Press and, no doubt, many imitators. Agravain kept watch over Waterford's activities and was satisfied that the Marquess's involvement had ended, especially when he married in 1842 and settled down in Ireland, doubly so after sightings of Spring-Heeled Jack continued after Waterford's death in 1859.

Little true harm came from the many pranks over that short period in the late 1830s, other than a fear of what stalked the streets, but it signalled to Agravain that Malagant was more than a bystander in the proceedings, and it was time to renew their acquaintance.

Chapter Sixteen

London
1838

The house where Agravain had first encountered Malagant in London had long ago been demolished to make way for other buildings. During the time when the knight had been raising his family and watching over his descendants, he had given passing thought to Malagant, but it seemed that little had changed on the streets. Yes, perhaps the Dread Knight was feeding on the fear conjured in the city, but the Spring-Heeled Jack incident was different, the rumours spreading across the country, exaggerated and believed, instilling terror in the populace.

Agravain had heard, but was not sure he believed, that the Duke of Wellington had even ridden out in search of the beast that tormented London.

This was more than the usual fear. This was

a deliberate provocation, an incitement to terror. That suggested to Agravain that Malagant was involved, and the Mad Marquess had all but confirmed it.

Now, after many years of detente between the knight of King Arthur's court and Morgana Le Fay's Dread Knight, their paths were drawing closer together once more.

Lord Waterford was not a subtle man, and Agravain was able to follow him easily enough, paying informers to keep watch when he was forced to retire. He waited for the Mad Marquess to lead him to Malagant's new lair.

Everywhere he went, police constables walked the streets, the Metropolitan Police having been in existence for some nine years by that time. He watched them as he passed by, taking in their uniforms and the authority they had been granted, pondering, as he did every day, whether he should join their ranks, just as he had considered becoming a Bow Street Runner or an officer of the River Police before Robert Peel had instituted the Met.

Perhaps he would have relented and joined, just as Arthur and the rest of the knights had served in the British Army, but he had his own business on the streets of London, other pressing demands on his time these days. His network of informers needed paying, his

Foundation required constant attention and his descendants were many and multiplying by the day, in high places and low.

He was free to pursue whatever lines of enquiry seemed fit, able to blend in or trade off his reputation, but the drawback, he knew, was that he was just one man, always the last man standing, just one well-aimed shot away from oblivion.

When he saw the police constables calling for aid and saw their colleagues come running, it pained him, and he remembered the brotherhood he had abandoned, wondering how Arthur and the others fared now.

Maybe it was time to call for aid? After all, Nimuë was gone, and he had nothing left to lose.

Agravain yawned and bought a newspaper, The Daily Account, from a boy selling them on a street corner.

The front page carried yet another histrionic account of the doings of Spring-Heeled Jack, and Agravain scoffed at the inaccuracies in the report of the attack on Lucy Scales and her sister.

And then something strange caught his eye.

꧁꧂

A little after midday, having made some enquiries, Agravain stood before a narrow building, its facade dirty and its windows opaque with grime. He crossed the street, carefully avoiding a horse and carriage, and made his approach. A brass plaque bearing the words 'The Daily Account' was set on the wall adjacent to a weather-beaten wooden door.

He turned the handle and stepped inside. A bell set above the door rang out. Agravain stepped into a small room divided by an L-shaped wooden counter, a small man in a shabby suit stepped out of a side room, pipe in hand, freshly plucked from his lips, to judge by the coughing fit the man descended into before he could finally ask Agravain his business.

'I come on urgent business, and I need to see the editor. It concerns the true identity of Spring-Heeled Jack,' said Agravain, standing straight and tall as he could manage.

'I see,' said the little man. 'You'll forgive me, but I have had four gentlemen and two ladies come through that very door this morning, all claiming to be able to name the perpetrator. All have proved, well, somewhat unreliable. I would not like to make assumptions, sir, but . . . '

Agravain leant on his sword cane and removed his top hat, making a show of inspecting it.

'I have noticed a detail in the text, and I am sure Malagant will be interested to hear what

John Marlow has to say,' said Agravain.

No reaction from the little man, save for a shallow sigh.

'Malagant? Are you referring to the Arthurian legends, sir?'

Agravain felt his cheeks flush, but he did his best to play his role.

'Do you mock me, little man? Fetch the editor, at once, do you hear?' said Agravain.

'I think not,' said the little man. 'Perhaps you can pass me the aforementioned detail and any name you might have, and I will, kindly, relay the message?'

The door to the street opened behind Agravain, the bell chimed.

'John!' said Malagant, his voice recognisable before Agravain set eyes on him.

Malagant slapped him on the back.

'How long has it been, John?' asked the Dread Knight.

Agravain made no reply. He felt his muscles beginning to tense, his hair beginning to stand up.

'Mr Merryweather, sir, this gentleman has been asking for the editor concerning a detail he has noticed in one of our articles concerning Spring-Heeled Jack,' said the little man.

Malagant grinned.

'And you held your ground and kept the

bounder on this side of the counter, Perkins? Good man. I shall have to promote you. Not in actuality, of course, but metaphorically, certainly.'

Perkins slunk away into the room from which he had first emerged.

Agravain pulled back his coat, revealing one of his revolvers in its holster.

'You set Waterford about his business, use your newspaper to create hysteria and not only do you feed on terror, you have the gall to profit from it too,' said Agravain.

'You have found me out, but in truth, I am doing no more than the other editors in town, John. There is money to be made where sensational stories capture the public's imagination. Are we to have another discussion of the relative merits of our respective lifestyles, John?' asked Malagant, still grinning. Agravain noticed the first wisps of green smoke drifting up from the hand which held his sword cane.

'Those conversations are ever so dull,' sighed Malagant. 'Perhaps, instead, we can accelerate things somewhat and take you off the streets for a while?'

He stepped forward and his face contorted, elongating and his eyes melting away, revealing the green glowing mist within. He shrieked, and Agravain held his hands up to shield his eyes.

As he did so, two things happened. First, Perkins stepped back into the room, drawn out by the noise, and second, Malagant snatched one of Agravain's Colt revolving guns from its holster with his gloved hands. Before Agravain could recover himself, Malagant wheeled, took aim and shot Perkins in the chest. Agravain saw the clerk fall backwards, eyes staring, and his body crash to the floor. Malagant turned the gun's butt towards Agravain, and the knight took it back.

'Murder!' cried Malagant, 'Murder!' He dashed for the door and tore it open, calling out into the street.

Agravain recovered his senses and was taking aim at Malagant when the Dread Knight disappeared outside, shouting for aid.

No time to think, Agravain tucked away his gun and followed. Men were already running towards the building as he stepped into the street. Challenges rang out, 'hey, you there, stop where you are!' and such, but Agravain strode down the street, paying them no heed. One man caught up with him and grabbed his shoulder, but Agravain smashed his nose with his elbow and broke into a run, leaping sideways to avoid yet another man.

'It's Jack!' screamed a woman. 'Spring-Heeled Jack!'

Agravain darted across the street, spooking a carthorse as he did so, and ducked into a side street. He could hear shouts and footsteps behind him, but he out ran them and disappeared into the busy London foot traffic before making many turns, discarding his top hat as soon as he thought he was out of sight. He threw his cane aside as well, shedding anything he felt was recognisable.

He slowed to a walk in a side alley, discarded his coat and his Colts, along with their holsters.

Agravain made his escape.

───※───

He did not return to the offices of The Daily Account, but paid well for word of the newspaper. He was rewarded almost immediately with the news that the owner and editor of the Account had disappeared following the murder of a clerk on the premises at the hands of Spring-Heeled Jack.

Agravain ceased his patrols for a time, staying in his rooms, lest he be recognised and identified as the murderer.

───※───

The Tower of London
1838

Under cover of night, the Dread Knight, Malagant, strode across the lawn south of the White Tower and waited, knowing she would appear when the moment was opportune.

Sure enough, a raven fluttered down to land by his feet. The bird morphed, stretched and distended, growing rapidly before him and even he, wielder of fear, took a step backwards as Daisy took form beneath him.

'You have come in person,' cawed Branok's familiar, her master still sealed in the White Tower behind her, sleeping under Merlin's spell.

'Well, you have declined every invitation my people ever brought you,' said Malagant.

'Why do you think your attendance would make any difference? I have a duty to my master. I cannot abandon him,' said Daisy, tilting her head in a bird-like fashion, staring at him with beady black eyes, long jet hair swaying around her hips, her skin milk-white.

'Oh, come now,' said Malagant. 'I would not ask you to abandon your duty! But stalking the Tower must be tedious, tedious work, and Branok is safe within. Venture out and aid me from time to time, and perhaps by my arts, I can weaken Merlin's spell and release him all the sooner? You will have your master once more, and he can assist me by summoning my mistress.'

The woman before him cawed, and a smile crept on to her grey lips when she saw him startle.

'I will think on it,' she said, and dived forward so that he fell back on to his behind, only to see a raven fly over him and away, cawing in such a way that he was sure it was laughing at him.

Chapter Seventeen

Monday 11th of January 2021

Arthur didn't realise he had been holding his breath until he heard the front door open, and he stepped out on the landing to see Tristan and Gareth walk inside.

He hurried down the stairs and embraced both of them.

'Any news from the others?' asked Tristan, who had not taken his own phone and had ditched his burner on the long road home via various forms of public transport, buying and switching clothes on the way.

'Radio silence,' said Arthur, 'but that was agreed.'

'We're going out of our minds,' said Kay, appearing at the top of the stairs.

'I can imagine,' said Tristan.

'I'm starving,' said Gareth. 'What are we doing about dinner?'

Arthur laughed.

'Your priorities! No-one is going to want to cook. Shall we order in?' he asked.

Tristan shook his head.

'I'll make something. It will keep me busy. Maybe stop

me wondering if anyone has been caught. We *are* the first back?' he said.

'Yes,' said Kay, halfway down the stairs. 'No contact all day. All we've had is the news.'

'Oh?' asked Gareth, who stopped on the way to the kitchen where he planned to make a sandwich while he waited for dinner.

'The story is breaking nationally,' said Arthur. 'Not much detail, just that John Marlow, convicted murderer, has escaped from Stonegate Hospital after incapacitating his escort.'

'I can only hope the police come to the same conclusion,' said Tristan, his voice low. He took off his new coat and dropped it by the front door.

'How exposed do you think you are?' asked Kay.

'Gareth and I, not at all,' said Tristan, 'unless they pick up on the van, but it wasn't directly involved. They'd have to trace someone back to it at the shops. Dag, Bed and Nimuë are the weak points, but none have been arrested before, so forensics don't matter. They were seen by staff at various points, no doubt, but how much attention will they have paid to nurses moving through a hospital? Those people are run off their feet these days, barely a chance to breathe, let alone take a meal break. There isn't much CCTV coverage inside the hospital, so really it will all depend on how much they were picked up and whether they draw any more attention than anyone else. Everyone should be making their way back in vehicles that were never at the scene or on trains, buses and the like. Burner phones should all be ditched. Fingers crossed . . . '

'Indeed,' said Arthur.

'Agravain walked out in different clothes, with a cap, in public view for just a few minutes before, if all went well, he got into a car on cloned plates, and drove away. He has the address for the next vehicle,' said Tristan.

'Which was in the middle of nowhere,' said Arthur.

'A few more hoops to jump through, and we can pick him up tonight, if all went well,' said Kay.

'*If* all went well,' said Tristan and Arthur as one.

The three men followed Tristan to the kitchen, where Arthur broke out his 10-year-old Arran Malt.

Bors returned next, then Bedivere, followed by Dagonet a little while later, and, finally, Nimuë knocked on the front door.

They all changed and bagged up their clothes for disposal. Nimuë, Dagonet and Bedivere showered to remove any potential trace of DNA from the prison officers just in case they were arrested later on.

Eventually, a little before midnight, they all assembled in the dining room and sat at the round oak table with food and drinks for everyone, waiting together. Waiting impatiently.

At three, they would go to the pick-up point. Three more hours.

'Well, isn't this uncomfortable,' said Nimuë, breaking the silence.

Bors grunted. Gareth smiled, but not convincingly. Tristan glared. Dagonet and Bedivere shuffled in their seats, and Arthur cleared his throat.

Nimuë grinned.

She pushed back her chair and, fetching the whisky bottle and more glasses, she poured a round.

'It,' she said, refilling Arthur's glass and then returning to her chair, 'has been quite the day.'

'I'll drink to that,' muttered Kay. 'If I have any hair left, it's a miracle.'

'You didn't have much to lose,' said Bors, and Gareth snorted.

'How did he look?' said Arthur to Dagonet and Bedivere.

'Much the same physically, a little more grey in his hair and beard,' said Bedivere.

'But tired, drawn,' said Dagonet. 'He barely reacted when he saw us.'

'Tired as though he carries the weight of the world. He always has, you know?' said Nimuë, as she took a sip of whisky. 'He barely reacted to me as well. A blank expression.'

'It has been a long, long time,' said Arthur. 'We haven't seen him in decades'

'Neither have I. Since the last time we were all together,' she said. 'He may not have forgiven me.'

Tristan huffed.

'What?' said Nimuë.

'He's the one that needs forgiving,' said Tristan.

'Well said,' said Arthur, raising his voice and rounding on Tristan. 'He does need to be forgiven. Perhaps you should hurry that along, given that he'll be here soon?'

Tristan muttered something under his breath.

'What did he do?' asked Nimuë.

'It doesn't matter,' said Arthur.

'What did *you* do?' asked Bors.

'It doesn't matter,' said Nimuë and Arthur together.

⁂

They drank whisky and talked of other things for a time, all save for Gareth, the designated driver. Gradually, the company warmed to one another and the tension faded, if the anticipation of Agravain's return did not. Laughter rippled around the table as the knights shared stories of their exploits with their long-lost friend while Nimuë listened politely, but, Arthur noticed, not contributing any of her own.

During an extended lull in the conversation, Tristan finished his drink, set down his glass with a bang and spoke up.

'He was the best of us,' he said, slurring his words just a little.

Arthur sat back and gauged the reaction around the table. Many of the knights were nodding.

'He was,' said Gareth.

'And my fast friend,' said Tristan. 'I never did understand how he could walk away from his brothers.'

'From you,' said Nimuë, quietly. Tristan shot her an angry look, but when he saw she spoke in earnest, he nodded. 'Aye, perhaps.'

'The truth is,' said Arthur, 'he was always more of a shepherd than were we, watching over his flock. The rest of us were more like sheepdogs, herding men into battle, lording over them, justly, I hope, but lording over them nonetheless. We were trying to unite a country for its people, but Agravain, he wanted to be among them, taking care of them. He was their watch warden and their keeper. That much I have come to understand. I forgive him, and will welcome him back.'

Tristan did not reply, but Arthur saw him nodding to himself before he reached for the whisky bottle again.

'He will not ever be one of you again, living with you and pursuing your goals, you know?' said Nimuë. 'He has his own agenda.'

'Much has changed since Merlin died, Nimuë,' said Arthur. 'We are in a retirement of sorts. Every man is free to live his own life by his own rules, and Agravain is no different. Yes, freeing him exposes us to the wrath of the law, but he is our brother, and we will do what we can to protect him. We have enough funds to start again.' Caitlyn's face flashed before Arthur's eyes. 'If it comes to it.'

Tuesday 12th of January 2021
02:00

'Let me come with you,' slurred Tristan, as Arthur pulled on his coat, and Gareth stepped out into the night air.

Arthur pushed him away, laughing.

'Go and sleep it off, you idiot,' said Arthur, smiling.

He stepped out of the house and just as he was about to close the door, Nimuë darted out.

'Nimuë, I . . . '

'Don't bother,' she said, pulling the door shut.

Gareth opened one of the rear doors and waved a hand for Nimuë to enter.

'Are you sitting in the front then?' she asked Arthur, who stuttered before responding that no, he sat in the back.

She grinned and walked by him, head down, lifting her gaze and poking him in the chest on her way.

'How elitist!' she said, still grinning, eyebrow raised. He was still thinking how to respond when she disappeared into the front passenger seat.

Gareth moved to open the rear door for Arthur, but the word 'elitist' rang in his ears, Arthur opened it for himself and slipped inside, resting his cane against the seat.

❦

The electric car slipped through the gates and on to the road that twisted through the woods, the trees towering over them, lit eerily by the headlights. Arthur looked out of the window as they drove, picking out the movement of deer by the side of the road every now and then.

The murmur of conversation in the front reached his ears, and Arthur looked over at the back of Nimuë's head. She laughed, and he returned to watching out of the window, feeling instantly alone. He wondered if Caitlyn was in bed or had fallen asleep cuddling Samson on the sofa.

Out of the woods they travelled, on to a wider road, which passed through a village and north to an A-road, which eventually became a dual carriageway.

The minutes ticked away, and Arthur considered why Agravain needed to escape now specifically, and what was coming. He determined that he would do whatever he could to assist and to draw Agravain back into the fold, but that tomorrow he would go and see Caitlyn, no matter what was happening at home, in his secret world.

Half an hour passed, 45 minutes and then, around 03:00, Gareth turned the car off the road down a country track, pulling into a layby next to a stone wall that surrounded an abandoned church and graveyard with many toppled gravestones.

They waited. And waited. Arthur and Nimuë stepped out of the car, walking around the church together.

Half an hour passed, 45 minutes and then, around 04:00, they began to get the sense that Agravain was not coming.

They waited until dawn, retreating into the warmth of the car.

Agravain was nowhere to be seen.

Chapter Eighteen

Highgate Cemetery, London
30th of August 1888

Something drew Agravain to the cemetery that day of all days, though he could not have said exactly what. The cemetery gates stood open, and he walked beneath the shade of the trees between the many extravagant stone tombs and individual headstones, crows calling overhead and wind rushing through the trees.

⁜

Agravain had witnessed London grow, its population doubling from five hundred thousand to one million people in the years since he had first made his home in the city at the time of the Great Fire in 1666. The city's longtime dead were piled in mass graves or buried just below the surface in graveyards crammed between other buildings. They threatened to overflow and reclaim the streets and so The London Cemetery Company was established to construct the Magnificent Seven, cemeteries built in the countryside surrounding the city.

Highgate Cemetery stood on the steep slopes north of the city, leading up to Highgate Village. It was beautifully landscaped and with magnificent architecture, its Egyptian Avenue lined with tombs, leading to the Circle of Lebanon, above which towered an ancient cedar tree. Catacombs ran beneath the former site of Ashhurst House's terrace, pulled down to make way for the cemetery.

The landscaping and immaculate grounds, tended by an army of gardeners and groundsmen, were not the only appeal to the rich and wealthy. They could stand in the cemetery, looking out across London, and know their kin, and themselves too one day, would be buried closer to Heaven for when the Rapture came. Jumping the queue, so to speak.

Agravain had purchased a plot at Highgate in late 1839, not long after the cemetery opened, and the construction of his family mausoleum was complete by the winter of the following year. He had not been concerned with the Rapture, but he did have a desire to preserve his legacy somewhat, to make his mark on the city and give his family a permanent home.

Agravain had ordered his children exhumed from their original resting places and had them interred within an elegant stone temple so that they might lie preserved, in peace, for all time there.

He would visit on each of their birthdays, walking the tree-lined paths, watched by the mourning angels on the graves, and making his way to the mausoleum, unlocking the doors and spending time sitting on the cold stone bench in the centre of the room, dusting off the coffins, speaking to his children and, sometimes, even singing to the little ones. Inevitably, his thoughts would turn to Nimuë, and it was only then that he would leave, carefully locking the mausoleum behind him and heading out into the failing afternoon, forcing himself to dwell on other matters. He would pull out his notebook, consult his ever-growing list of descendants, the earlier entries crossed through, and make his rounds.

―⁂―

That afternoon, Agravain left the stone bench, locked the doors to the tomb in his usual way, and, placing his new bowler hat on his head, he took some time to wander the cemetery, troubled by the unexpected urge to visit his family and wondering what it foretold.

He found no answers within, but as he stepped through the gates on to Swains Lane, he saw Nimuë, dressed in the manner of the upper classes, with a fur stole around her neck, and her hands in a matching muff, the hem of her dress barely covering her feet. Agravain thought his heart might fail when he spotted Nimuë waiting for him, the first time he had laid eyes on her in more than 70 years. If anything, she looked younger and more beautiful. Agravain felt suddenly very old, very aware of the grey in his hair though there was no more of it than when he had last seen her, and he staggered, catching the cemetery gates to keep himself upright.

Nimuë did not react, her face unsmiling, and so, for an instant, he wondered if it was truly her, so readily had she smiled when they had been married.

He considered how he must appear to her as he approached, leaning on his cane. He had favoured the bowler hat since the 1850s, and wore a knee-length woollen overcoat over a three-piece suit, and a silver pocket watch in his waistcoat pocket, its chain just visible. He carried a knuckle-duster in his right coat pocket, a small knife in a sheath on his belt, and an Enfield MKI Service Revolver in a shoulder holster beneath his jacket under his left armpit. He wore his greying sideburns long, down to the bottom of his ears, but his face was clean-shaven, apart from a thick, but trimmed moustache. Agravain now thought the twist of the handlebar too whimsical.

He thought he had not changed so very much since he had last seen her, except to adapt a little to the fashions, whereas Nimuë . . ? Well, he thought, she looks as if she has gone up in the world.

'John,' she said, as though that would be enough. Agravain nodded once, slowly, taking her in.

'What brings you back to London?' he asked, struggling to keep back tears, but, he thought, maintaining a fairly convincing pretence at stoicism.

'I flit in and out,' she said, a faint smile brewing. This made Agravain smile, and his heart relented a little as she noticed and cocked her head. He could have swept her up in his arms and carried her away at that very moment without another word between them.

But he just nodded, looked about to see if anyone was watching, then took up her hand to gently kiss it.

'So genteel!' she teased, and he grunted, frowning.

'Well, you are a lady now, it seems,' he said.

'Any fool can buy a set of clothes,' she said.

They were silent for a moment.

'Will you come in and . . . and visit the children?' he asked.

'No,' she said immediately, the smile fading. 'I keep them in my heart.'

Agravain looked down at his shoes.

'Why are you here, Nimuë?' he asked.

'The same as when we first met, John,' she said, and she linked arms with him, leading him down the hill towards the city.

'Something has been simmering. The city has many secrets, and many dark deeds take place every day, a few less than there would be, thanks to you and others like you,' she said.

'None of that is news,' said Agravain. 'There are many evils hereabouts, of many kinds, some supernatural and some, worse, are all too mundane.'

She stopped and turned to him.

'I can feel Malagant like a tensing muscle. His anticipation builds. He is a drawn bow. I cannot explain it better, but the city will find out soon enough. You must be ready. He knows you watch over the streets, he will come for you and for yours.'

'For mine? For ours, surely,' said Agravain.

'As you say,' she said quietly, and started walking again.

'What is coming?' he asked her.

'I don't know, John, I do not have the gift of foresight, but I can feel Malagant draining the air all around. He is exhaling now, preparing for a deep, deep breath,' she said.

'He is in a high position now, he owns several papers, many businesses, he has employees everywhere, policemen and politicians alike in his pocket. Reaching him would not be easy,' said Agravain, who had not been idle.

'Scaling a cliff to assault Mordred's camp with only one man by your side was not easy, but you attempted it,' said Nimuë. 'If indeed the stories are true. Merlin's account of the tale matched your own, so I do not doubt it. I do not doubt my husband,' she said.

He grunted, but after a moment, he turned to look at her, trying to be subtle. Her face was impassive at first, but then he saw her lip curl, and he looked away.

'Will you assist?' he asked.

'I will,' she replied, 'but I will not stay forever.'

They walked on in silence as he mulled over the familiar words and what they might mean for him this time.

'I have missed you,' said Agravain.

'Oh, you will again,' she teased, but to the knight's ear, the words had weight.

That evening, Malagant ceased exhaling and readied to breathe in.

~~~

*London
31st of August 1888*

Mary Ann Nichols had entered the last day of her life. She was in a pub in Brick Lane, Spitalfields, perhaps one of the most dangerous areas of London's East End, a place where thievery and prostitution were commonplace. She had told herself upon entering the pub that she would keep the last fourpence she'd been given by that chap with the bowler hat and moustache, the one from the Foundation, as although she was not above sleeping rough, her body was aching and she longed for a bed, however poor, for the night. No matter what she earned or what she drank, she must keep that fourpence separate, and keep it safe.

Before the first half-hour of the new day was done, Mary's funds ran dry as she fell deeper in her cups, and when she staggered out a little later, that fourpence was now behind the bar.

Mary made her way home to the lodgings she shared with her friend, Emily Holland, at 18 Thrawl Street, but without her spent rent money, she was turned away.

'I'll soon earn it back,' she said to the landlord, 'with the help of this here new bonnet.'

Emily Holland saw her around half past two in the morning, standing at the corner of Osborn Street and Whitechapel Road. Emily asked her if she was coming home, but Mary told her she'd spent her rent money and more besides, claiming she'd earned and spent it three times over that night.

༺❦༻

'John!'

Agravain reached under the pillow for his knife and spun round before realising it was Nimuë shaking him awake.

'What is it?' he said, straining to see her in the dark.

'It's beginning, I can feel it!'

Agravain fumbled for a match in the dark and lit a lamp. He blinked in the new light and saw Nimuë kneeling on his bed, hands balled just above her crotch. Her face contorted, and when he touched her shoulder, she yelped.

'What's the matter?' he asked, almost shouting.

'I feel it in my womb, something's happening,' she said, doubling over.

'What? Where do I go?' asked Agravain, but she could not tell him.

Buck's Row, Whitechapel, London
3.40am August 31st 1888

As John Paul drove his cart along Buck's Row, he spied a man standing in the road, who turned and called him over, his tone urgent enough for Paul to ignore any concerns about being robbed. Something was amiss. The other man, Charles Allen Cross, pointed at the figure of a woman lying in front of the gated door to a stable. Together they approached and saw that her skirt was raised.

'She's dead,' said Cross, voice shaking as he peered down at her, the lack of light thwarting him.

'Could be knocked out,' said Paul. 'Let's get a copper, mate.'

They pulled down Mary Ann Nichols' skirt to once more cover her lower half then went in search of a policeman, eventually happening upon PC Jonas Mizen.

'She's either dead or drunk, but for my part, I believe she's dead,' reported Cross before he and Paul carried on their way, leaving Mizen to examine the body.

While PC Mizen was doing so, PC John Neale entered Buck's Row on his beat, and he summoned a third constable. They began to make their enquiries, but nobody had seen or heard anything amiss, not the constables patrolling the streets, the horse slaughterers working overnight nearby nor the residents of the street.

The police sent word for Dr Llewelyn, who arrived around 4am. He decided that the woman had been dead for some 30 minutes, her throat slit twice from left to right and with many other wounds to her abdomen.

Malagant, lying awake in bed, staring at the ceiling with eyes that were no longer there, replaced with a swirling red mist, began to breathe in.

Jack the Ripper, he thought, *it has a certain ring to it.*

Chapter Nineteen

Tuesday 12th of January 2021

'What are you looking for?' asked Arthur as he limped after Nimuë. She was circling the woods near the abandoned church while they waited for Bors and Dagonet to arrive in another car to take over waiting for Agravain.

She did not reply, laying hands on trees, stooping to take up handfuls of earth, closing her eyes as though concentrating. When she did so, Arthur felt as though he was passing through waves of energy, rippling towards him for a moment. Finally she found a narrow, shallow stream and fell on her knees before it. She placed both hands, fingers splayed, into the water, and hung her head so that her hair hung forward over her face and shoulders.

Arthur stood leaning on his cane with one hand and resting the other against the rough bark of a tree, marvelling as he watched the enchantress at work. A sleepiness came over him, and he had to blink to stay awake. He felt a pulling sensation on his heart, which seemed to skip a beat.

Nimuë's limbs stiffened, and just as Arthur thought his eyes would close, she gasped and pulled back from the water.

She knelt there, mud staining her dress, and Arthur saw her chest and back heaving as though she had just undergone a great trial.

'Nothing,' she whispered. 'I cannot find him.'

Arthur made his way to her side, and he leant down to help her up.

'Let's go back to the car,' he said, wondering at the nature of the woman whom he was supporting.

―――

'What's he playing at?' asked Tristan, pacing back and forth in Arthur's drawing-room.

'Perhaps he was caught?' said Gareth.

'I doubt it, they just put out a fresh appeal for him in the news. His picture is all over the internet,' said Kay.

'Something is wrong,' said Nimuë. 'I cannot sense him.'

Arthur's leg ached and so he settled in his wingback chair by the fire. He rubbed his temples and then his eyes, letting out a low, exhausted groan.

'I don't understand either,' said Nimuë, 'but Malagant must have something to do with it. He baited Agravain, drew him out and then he disappeared? It must be the Dread Knight.'

The four of them remained in silent thought for a few minutes, Tristan still pacing the room.

'Well, what do we know?' he asked eventually, almost shouting.

'He wanted out, he got out. He gave us a list of names and addresses. Was concerned for those people,' said Tristan.

'Our people,' said Nimuë. Arthur thought she sounded as though she were finally confessing after a long and arduous interrogation.

'Nimuë?' he said. Tristan and Gareth moved to stand behind him, flanking his chair.

The enchantress clasped her hands in her lap and looked down at them for a little while, breathing softly. She reached up and tucked loose strands of hair behind her ears.

'Agravain and I were married, long ago,' she said when she looked up to meet Arthur's gaze. 'We lived together, in London, for many years.'

Arthur said nothing, too surprised to respond, but Tristan spoke for all of them.

'Married? We knew you were..acquainted, but why has this been kept secret?'

'Not secret, but not spoken of,' she said. 'It pains me, and he cannot move past that time.'

'In what way?' asked Arthur, realisation a few seconds away.

'We had children together, John and I,' she said, 'Ariadne was our first, born in 1734. Henry followed, but he died when he was but a babe.' Her voice nearly broke, but she continued. 'We had another son who lived, Arthur, and three more daughters, Jemima, Alice and Caroline, but only Caroline survived.' Hearing Nimuë and Agravain had named their son after him caused Arthur to reel back in his chair. He covered his mouth with his hand as Nimuë continued, moving her feet together toe to toe, heel to heel and apart again, heel from heel, toe from toe, watching the movements.

'They are all gone now, of course. All died, long ago.'

She looked up, her body trembling, tears spilling from her eyes and rolling down her cheeks.

'You were at Waterloo? Bors spoke of it around the table earlier?' she said.

'We were,' said Arthur, choking as he spoke.

Nimuë nodded.

'1815. The year the last of my children died, and I left John. I could not bear to be in the company of ghosts, to see their faces every time I beheld his.'

She fell forward, elbows on knees, burying her face in her hands as, for the first time, she let her walls down and sobbed, crying for her lost loves, those she had found and those she birthed. The true reason she could not stay forever.

Arthur groaned as he stood, moving to her side with the aid of his cane. He reached down and rubbed the nape of her neck.

'I had no idea,' said Arthur.

'Excuse me,' said Tristan, his voice cracking. He swept out of the room, closing the door behind him. Gareth watched him go, stared at the door and then, frowning, exchanged a glance with Arthur, both men contemplating the ramifications of such losses, such a life.

Nimuë recovered herself, wiped away her tears and smiled up at Arthur, shrugging off his hand.

'I'm alright,' she said, smiling though her eyes were glassy. Arthur returned to his chair, and Gareth retreated to the far side of the room, Arthur noted.

'I left,' she said, matter-of-factly, 'when my children were all gone, and there were grandchildren and great-grandchildren to think about, when questions were beginning to be asked about why John and I never aged. John withdrew from the family, but stayed in London, keeping a watch over our brood, our children's children's children and so on down the years. He kept a book, recording every detail of their lives, helping those who became troubled as best he could. It was his way of honouring our girls and our boys, I think.'

Arthur tried to imagine their faces, feeling his brother's sorrow, as best he could, one who had fathered no children, quite forgetting Mordred.

'The names on the list I gave you are, I believe, our descendants. Malagant must have threatened them. It is the one thing that would drive John to escape.'

Arthur nodded.

'We have people watching them, but the list contained only a few names. There must be many, many more? Do you have more details?' He regretted asking, as Nimuë's composure lessened, a flash of pain visible in her eyes.

'No,' said Arthur, before she could reply. She had distanced herself, he could see that.

'We must put Malagant down, Arthur, the last of your sister's works. He is a hellish thing, unnatural, and though John . . . Agravain . . . has contested him over the centuries, he cannot defeat him alone. I was too weak when last he walked abroad, but I have studied hard these 13 decades past, and with your help, I believe we can stop him.'

'First we must find him,' said Gareth. 'We failed before.'

'We know he has threatened Agravain. If we can find him, we can find Malagant,' said Arthur.

'I fear Malagant already has him,' said Nimuë. 'Remember, I cannot sense him as I ought.'

They fell silent and then she stood suddenly.

'I know where we might start,' said Nimuë. 'Somewhere he would definitely go.'

⁕

Dark woods. A lone woman, scared, looking back over her shoulder. A creature moving low, hunting. A violin sounding urgent music. The tension began to build then . . . nothing . . . the violin stopped. The woman reached the door to her cabin, she was fumbling for her key, turning it in the lock and . . .

The creature pounced. The violin struck up. She screamed. The audience screamed.

Malagant, sitting alone in the back row of the cinema, laughed as hundreds of people in the seats before him jumped as one, some pretending they had not reacted at all, others clutching their partners and others chuckling, no doubt feeling foolish.

A greenish smoke, visible only to him, drifted from their bodies. He gripped the back of the empty chair in front of him, and extended his fingers. The smoke flowed towards him like oil carried on the tide, seeping into his fingertips, under the nails, soaking into the nail-beds. He felt their fear cascade through his body, coating his molecules, running through his veins. A momentary fright, but a cheap night out for the Dread Knight. The audience settled, but it would not be long before the violin started up again.

Perhaps tomorrow he would go to see The Woman in Black at The Fortune Theatre, he thought. *Jumpy, that one.*

Later that evening, Malagant returned to the hotel room he had taken in Brown's Hotel on Albemarle Street, London.

'Now,' he said, sitting at a desk and starting up his laptop. 'Shall we continue?'

Agravain looked on in terror, unable to move, powerless to stop the Dread Knight.

Malagant typed in a URL and logged on to an ancestry research site.

'An amazing tool. Technology has made so much so easy and so much so difficult,' said Malagant. 'Wouldn't you agree, Agravain? I mean, of all people, you should understand how things have come on. It was all pounding the streets, speaking to witnesses, cultivating contacts and knocking on doors when you were an investigator, back before electricity. You kept your entire legacy in a single journal and now, it's all right here at my fingertips!'

Agravain struggled, but he could not move, could not speak.

A few clicks of the mouse and a family tree appeared on the laptop screen.

'Ariadne, Henry, Arthur, Jemima, Alice, Caroline . . . they're all here. I barely had to do any work, so many people have shared their own research, helped me fill in the blanks.

I probably know more than you do, now,' he grinned, enjoying taunting the helpless knight.

'And here,' said Malagant, scrolling right down to the bottom of the page, 'are your living descendants. Living for now, at any rate.'

Agravain screamed objections, unable to stem the fear despite knowing how his adversary was relishing it. Malagant drank deep.

'There is nothing more potent than the terror of a powerful man,' he said, then continued his research, trawling social media, websites, online phone books and any other sources he could find to put addresses to the names.

Chapter Twenty

London
1st of September 1888

News of the murder spread through the East End all that morning, and, before the sun was up, one of Agravain's informers had brought word, in person no less, and in a carriage, so that his employer might be appraised of the situation straightaway.

Agravain thanked the man, paying him not only his fee, but the price of the return carriage journey.

'She did not die easily, it seems,' said Agravain, recounting the tale for Nimuë as they shared a pot of coffee over breakfast, but sparing her the details. 'Do you think this is the event that caused you such pain last night?'

'Oh, I am certain of it,' said Nimuë, into her cup, not raising her eyes to meet his.

'Why so?' asked Agravain. 'Murders are not such a rarity, Nimuë. I have investigated many brutal crimes these past years. Why should this lady's demise stand out among the rest of the victims?'

He lit a cigar and offered one to Nimuë, but she smiled at him as though he was an idiot and waved it away. She sighed, considering his question, and set down her cup before answering.

'It is not the murder itself that is remarkable,' she said, 'It is the anticipation I sense in Malagant and, something, I am not sure what, about the perpetrator. The death of this unfortunate is just the beginning.'

'Well, we must be about it, either way,' said Agravain. 'Assuming you are coming with me.'

Nimuë stood and snatched up her coat and bonnet.

'This time you will not work alone,' she smiled.

⁕

They hurried through the East End in a hired cab, telling the driver to pull up a short distance away from Hanbury Street so they could walk the distance to their destination. Agravain led Nimuë through the streets, already busy despite the early hour.

As they drew closer, Agravain halted.

'I do not know how you would be received at the scene of the murder,' he said. 'Being what you are?'

'A woman?' asked Nimuë, raising an eyebrow, and Agravain was glad to see that she was amused by the idiocy of the age rather than angry with him for voicing the truth.

'There would be questions,' he conceded.

'Well, which activities, pray tell, would be acceptable in the eyes of the Establishment for this mere woman?' asked Nimuë, folding her arms across her chest.

'There will be crowds as close by as the police will allow. If you could disappear among them, listen to the local talk, ideas and theories. Memorise their faces, in case the perpetrator is among them.'

'Cor blimey, I shan't have no problem fitting in, guv,' she said, and Agravain laughed.

'Nimuë . . . ' he said, but Nimuë simply winked and set off towards Buck's Row. Agravain shook his head, watching her walk away, amusement mingling with the great, steady weight of sadness he had felt since she returned, as though their reunion was but a dream. Too soon, he would surely wake, and Nimuë would be gone, and he would be alone again, as he had been for the better part of the century.

He took a deep breath and went in search of answers, left hand in his coat pocket and carrying his cane midway along its length in the right.

As predicted, people were crowded around, but a number of constables were keeping onlookers at bay. Agravain held back a minute and, taller than most, he scanned the faces of the officers, most of them familiar, until he found the right man. Only now did he sidle his way through the crowd.

'PC Wainthrop,' said Agravain. 'How's the family?'

'Oh, hello sir!' said the constable. 'Well, sir, well.'

'A busy morning already,' said Agravain.

'Yes, sir, you could say that,' Wainthrop gave a humourless laugh.

'Who's in charge?' asked Agravain.

'Inspector Helson is giving the area a once-over at the moment, I believe,' said Wainthrop.

'Joseph Helson,' said Agravain, snapping his fingers. 'Just the man. Alright to come through here, man?'

He shook the constable's hand in a particular way as he passed him by and although the constable spluttered as though about to object, he let Agravain through.

Agravain strode down the street, approaching the gate to the stableyard through which stepped Inspector Joseph Helson.

'Inspector!' said Agravain, lifting his cane to draw the officer's attention.

'John,' said Helson. 'News travels fast.'

The men shook hands, once more in that particular way.

'How are the children? Little Edith still as sweet as ever?' said Agravain.

The men exchanged niceties for a few moments more before a heavy silence fell.

'Well then,' said Agravain.

'I hope you've not had your breakfast yet,' said Inspector Helson. 'I just came from the mortuary. Two severe lacerations to the neck and multiple stab wounds to the abdomen, exposing the innards. Likely used a long sharp knife.'

'Witnesses?'

Helson gave a significant look to a sergeant who had ventured too close, and the man moved off.

'Nothing of note. We've searched the vicinity and found nothing left behind. Dr Llewelyn believes the lady died no more than thirty minutes before she was found, and that was around twenty to four this morning. Couple of men on their way to work stumbled across her. She was killed where she was found, I'd wager, judging from the blood.'

'Do you know who she is yet?' said Agravain.

'Not formally,' said Helson, 'but rumours are flying.'

'Polly,' said Nimuë. 'Stays at 18 Thrawl Street.'

Agravain felt his head spin, he blinked twice, and the reaction must have been noticeable as Nimuë gripped him around the shoulders, steadying him.

'What, John?'

'Polly at 18 Thrawl Street,' said Agravain. 'Mary Ann Nichols.'

'You know her?' asked Nimuë.

'She's one of ours,' he said, and a single tear rolled down his cheek.

― ∞§∞ ―

After a long day of making enquiries around the East End, Agravain and Nimuë travelled back home. Neither of them had an appetite despite walking for miles, and Agravain sat at his desk the moment he was inside, only pausing to remove his hat and coat. He began hauling journals from drawers and poring over the notes therein. He could sense her pacing quietly behind him, but she did not disturb him until she returned with two glasses of brandy.

He turned the pages of his journals.

'John,' said Nimuë.

'Hmm?'

'Do you believe Malagant is the murderer?' she asked.

Agravain shook his head and muttered to himself.

'John.'

'What?' he snapped, shifting in his seat so he could turn to face her.

'I can't hear you,' she said. 'And mind your tone.'

Agravain sighed.

'I have had Malagant under surveillance for decades. He never bloodies his own hands. He doesn't orchestrate these acts, he just holds court for those who do, or for those who encourage those who do. No, this will be one of his followers, a deranged individual. I may already have met the man,' he said, tapping the stack of journals.

'How so?' she said.

'Keeping London safe is my business, and though Lord knows I fail at it daily, I do keep myself appraised of its denizens. There are informers everywhere, and I have long-standing acquaintances within the Metropolitan Police. I try to travel in their circles, drink in their pubs, visit their churches, and I help them out from time to time in a private capacity. There *are* likely suspects abroad. I need quiet and solitude for a few hours. Let me check my notes, Nimuë, and I will see what I can put together.'

'Beyond that though, you must ponder the significance of Malagant's involvement. I do not come to London for every murder, John. There is more to this . . . something is beginning.'

'I will begin with the facts, Nimuë, I do not have your insight. Perhaps you can consider that aspect while I work.'

Nimuë refilled Agravain's brandy glass, put on her outer clothes and set out to take the evening air.

Agravain did not notice her leave, so engrossed was he in his journals, desperately trying to dismiss the memory of Polly Nichols' face from his mind.

※

They rendezvoused again that evening. Agravain was waiting in his chair by the fire drinking coffee and staring at a piece of paper he held up to the light when Nimuë returned.

She sat opposite him, and he handed her the list, which she read, frowning, as he fetched her some coffee.

'James Kelly/John Miller, Aaron Abrahams/Kosminski, Charles Cross . . . ' she read and then paused, looking up. 'Did not Charles Cross discover the cadaver?'

Agravain nodded.

'And another man encountered him approaching the body, but we do not know whether he was, in fact, the killer, disturbed after the act and forced into a lengthy subterfuge to distance himself from the crime,' said Agravain.

'I see,' said Nimuë. 'And the others?'

'These gentlemen have previously come to my attention, and I believe they may be in the area. I will reach out to my contacts around the city and have them put under surveillance.'

He was about to continue, when a thought struck him and he hurried over to his desk and retrieved a journal.

'There have been other murders this year. Martha Tabram was killed . . . when was it . . . back in . . . ' he stabbed a finger into the book. 'There! 7th of August. Stabbed some 39 times. Generally considered to have been the victim of one of the gangs that prey on the prostitutes of Whitechapel, but there was a suggestion that soldiers may have been involved, to the extent that officers attended the garrison at the Tower of London to see if they could identify the suspect.

'I must go over everything that has happened lately, and examine everything we know about everyone,' said Agravain.

'For my part, I have thought about Malagant,' said Nimuë. 'And I can only assume that the foreboding I feel now when I have not before is that there is a degree of conspiracy to this matter, plotting with the perpetrator, some scheme by which he can further his goals.'

'We can but watch and wait. We know one thing at least; his goal is to invoke terror where he can. There must be some new factor in play.'

⁂

That new factor became immediately apparent when Agravain sat down to read The Star, a newspaper that had yet to reach its first birthday. An article posited a link between the murder of Martha Tabram, Mary Ann Nichols and of another woman called Smith.

'This is how he will do it,' said Nimuë, after Agravain had handed her the article to read. 'He doesn't even need to print the news himself. A whiff of a sensational story, and the editors cover their front pages with the stuff of nightmares. And it has only just begun.'

Agravain pulled out the notebook from his coat pocket and seated himself by the fire.

'We must go through all of the children's children and so on,' he said, 'do what we can for those who live in the area.'

But Nimuë turned her back on him and would not look at the list, would not speak of their family, neither living nor dead.

⁂

London
5th of September 1888

Nimuë was correct, Agravain reflected, once more reading The Star. It had only just begun.

'Listen,' he said, spreading out the paper on his desk while Nimuë came to stand beside him.

'LEATHER APRON THE ONLY NAME LINKED WITH THE WHITECHAPEL MURDERS. THE STRANGE CHARACTER WHO PROWLS ABOUT AFTER MIDNIGHT. UNIVERSAL FEAR AMONG WOMEN - SLIPPERED FEET AND A SHARP LEATHER-KNIFE,' Agravain concluded as Nimuë began to read over his shoulder.

She frowned.

'What is it?' asked Agravain.

'The scapegoating begins,' she said, pointing at a particular line.

⁕

Spitalfields, London
8th of September 1888
Eight days after the murder of Mary Ann Nichols

Annie Chapman was spiralling. She had left her family after her youngest daughter died of meningitis, receiving an allowance of 10 shillings a week from her estranged husband until he had died two years before. Her son was disabled and in the care of a charitable institution, her other daughter travelling with a circus in France. She'd lived with a sieve maker in Whitechapel for a time, but when the allowance stopped, he left her. Annie made her living doing crochet work and selling flowers, and was an occasional prostitute. A friend would later say that she had given up on life and though she was civil and industrious when sober, she was often the worse for wear through drink.

The week had already not gone well. Annie had fought with Elize Cooper in their lodging house over a trivial matter. Of course she'd return the bloody soap, she'd just misplaced it, but Cooper wouldn't see reason. She'd thrown her a halfpenny to buy a new one, but that wasn't enough. It had come to blows, and Annie's face and chest still bore the bruises of that encounter.

Like Mary Ann Nichols before her, Annie found she hadn't the money to pay the lodging house, but she assured the watchman when he saw her just before 2am that she would head out and earn her rent.

Just before six in the morning, carman John Davis left 29 Hanbury Street and went into the yard at the rear. There he saw Annie Chapman's body between the steps to the building and lying alongside the fence. Annie lay on her back with her legs drawn up, knees turned outwards, clearly visible as her skirts were pulled up to her waist.

Her throat was cut and her face covered in blood.

Chapter Twenty-One

Wednesday 13th of January 2021
The West Cemetery, Highgate, London

Rain drummed against the pavements, pattering on the umbrellas handed to the tour participants by their elderly guide as they gathered just inside the gate of Highgate Cemetery.

'For you, sir,' said the tour guide, and Arthur thanked him as he put up an umbrella.

'And for you, miss,' said the guide.

'No, thank you,' said Nimuë, 'I like the rain in my hair.' She smiled and the guide, momentarily bemused, moved off, calling for the group to gather together. Dagonet and Bors moved up behind Arthur and Nimuë as the tour started while the others waited in the car, parked precariously on the terribly steep Swains Lane outside.

'Are we *really* going to have to take the tour?' asked Bors.

'It's the only way to get inside without breaking in, now that this place is disused,' whispered Arthur, and Bors gave a heavy sigh.

'You can wait in the car if you prefer?' said Arthur, and

Nimuë laughed, but waved the knights away when they turned to her looking quizzical.

As the tour started and the group stepped forward, Nimuë wrapped her fingers around Arthur's upper arm, moving in close.

'It's so different from the last time I was here,' said Nimuë, in a whisper, so as not to disturb their guide as he led them up a narrow path through woodland, lined with graves, pointing out particular graves, telling their occupant's tales, explaining the significance of the various features of the gravemarkers themselves.

'How long has it been?' asked Dagonet.

'Over a century,' said Nimuë. 'I came here only once, but never went into the mausoleum itself, only watched for John . . . for Agravain . . . through the gates, but even from there, well, this place was busy with gardeners and groundsmen, the paths well-maintained and the surrounds all landscaped and manicured, more reminiscent of a garden than a cemetery,' she said, releasing Arthur's arm and stepping away, looking up at the trees.

He too turned this way and that, examining the crowded rows of gravestones, which seemed to shamble from out of the cover of the trees like the unliving. He felt as if he had stumbled into a secret place, sequestered from the real world, a fey realm not quite fully protected from the insidious passage of time, as the wild undergrowth and creeping vines attested. The paths were uneven, the grounds overgrown and nobody was visiting any of the graves. Thick silence permeated the air between bursts of imparted knowledge from their guide, and it was not difficult to imagine a fairy sleep enchantment was at work as they pushed through the still air.

'Haunted,' declared Bors, and Arthur was about to rebuke him when he saw the sorrowful look on Nimuë's face.

'It is haunted. I can feel them all calling. No, not calling. Reaching out to us, silently shouting, tugging at our clothes,' she said. Arthur noticed the words caught in her throat.

'That isn't creepy at all,' said Dagonet.

'Are you alright?' Arthur asked Nimuë. He thought she wasn't going to reply for a few seconds, but then she spoke, not taking her eyes from her feet as they trod the broken, uneven path.

'How long before I sense somebody I recognise? Those with faces I can scarcely recall when I try, voices I cannot remember,' said Nimuë.

'How will you know the way if you've never been inside?' asked Dagonet.

'A mother knows,' she said, and Arthur saw she was turning an iron skeleton key over in her hand.

The group came to a stop outside a looming stone wall with an arch in the centre, flanked by stone columns. Arthur looked through the arch and could see a short, roofless passage through which plants were hanging down, with rows of doors on each side, leading to tombs, but reminiscent of a row of terraced houses, yet in a grand majestic fashion. Another gated stone arch stood at the other end of the passage. The group passed along the Egyptian Avenue and out into a space now seemingly sunken, a curving trench linked on both sides with tombs. As Arthur looked up, he could see a tree growing out of the central island of the Circle of Lebanon. The group moved up a staircase so that Arthur found himself walking on the same level as the tree, now looking down into the trench.

The tour guide led them to yet another gate, and while the old man unlocked it, Arthur realised that Nimuë's nails were digging into his arm and saw that she was looking off to the right, staring and trembling slightly.

The guide pushed the gate open, and with no time to react to Nimuë, Arthur steered her into the dark catacombs, where bats flapped overhead despite it being the late morning. Shelves of coffins covered the walls from the ground to the ceiling of the narrow brick passage, most barred by stone with inscribed epitaphs, but some exposed, the rotting wood of the coffins visible within. They made their way down the passageway, heeding their guide's warnings to mind their footing as his torch beam swept around them.

Back outside, the tour moved off, and Nimuë pulled Arthur back just before they rounded a bend. Arthur's company paused and watched the tour recede.

'This way,' said Nimuë, staring up at Arthur with dark circles under her eyes, the face of her skin pale and taut.

She looks drawn, thought Arthur, *as though she is wasting before my eyes.*

'We don't have much time,' said Arthur to Dagonet and Bors. 'Stay here in case the guide comes back?'

'And tell him what?' huffed Bors.

'Whatever works,' said Dagonet, as Nimuë pushed through a curtain of hanging vines to disappear into the trees. Arthur followed.

Ivy-covered trees barred their way, and as Arthur ducked beneath low branches, keeping Nimuë in her long coat just in view as she slipped through the woods, he was transported back to his youth, when he had a more profound belief in the magic of nature, or of its commonality; a sense that had faded as technology and science replaced wonder and faith. He remembered pushing through forests, close on Merlin's heels in a scenario all too similar to the present. They were off the established paths now, but broken gravestones and tumbledown tombs could be spied, obscured by plant growth every now and then. Nimuë forged ahead as though drawn with an increasing power. Arthur hurried to keep up, picking his way through the tangle of roots and stones, steadying himself on his cane and bracing himself against tree trunks.

Nimuë disappeared from view, and as Arthur drew closer, stepping out from behind a cedar, he saw that she was standing in front of a stone mausoleum, carved to a resemble a scaled-down London townhouse of the 18th century style, the entrance through a faux front door, appearing to be the height from the ground floor to the top of the first.

The doors stood open.

Arthur wanted to ask Nimuë if she was certain they were at the right building, but she clutched her throat with her hand, and when she turned to watch Arthur approach, he saw her eyes were brimming with tears.

'It's shaped like our house,' she said, 'our family home.'

Arthur frowned and examined the mausoleum for himself, wondering at how little he understood of Agravain's heart and soul, if he would choose such a burial place for his children.

Arthur drew his Colt revolver and pulled out a pocket torch.

'Come on,' he said, moving towards the entrance, but he saw Nimuë was hesitating. He paused, watching her struggle with her emotions, with her fortitude and courage, and then saw her swallow hard and step forward.

Nimuë stepped through the doors into the Marlow family mausoleum, and Arthur followed on behind her into the lit interior, a stone bench gracing the centre of the room. Arthur's eyes were drawn up to find the light source, and he saw a thick glass window in the roof.

He heard a sharp intake of breath and was in time to see Nimuë shrinking back against the wall beside one of the doors. Arthur followed her gaze and saw for the first time that each of the slabs covering the stone tombs around the room was cracked and partially destroyed, some more than others.

Arthur examined the room, first scanning it with his eyes

for potential hiding places, and once he was satisfied that the only places to hide were within the tombs himself, he stepped back beside Nimuë and whispered 'watch my back' to her.

Arthur readied himself with the revolver, moving to position himself so that he could check each of the tombs in turn, but nobody was hiding within.

'It's alright,' he said, and Nimuë pushed herself off the wall, stepping forward and never taking her eyes from the closest tomb. Arthur watched as she crossed the mausoleum and then, after a breath, laid her hands upon the stone edge and peered inside. He saw her whole body heave as she let out a single sob, he saw her arms shaking even as she braced herself against the stone.

Nimuë reached inside and, to Arthur's horror, when she straightened up and turned to him, she held out cupped hands before her, a mound of dust, bone shards and scraps of materials. Her eyes were wide, streaming and her whole body trembled as her look seemed to convey a question he could not guess.

'Nimuë, I . . . ' he started, but she cut him off.

'Leave,' she said quietly, with no anger in her voice. Flat, reserved, strung tight.

Arthur hesitated for only a moment then bowed his head to her and stepped back out into the cemetery, circling and taking in the architecture of the mausoleum exterior.

Minutes passed before Arthur saw Nimuë step through the door, closing and locking it behind her. Her face was red, her eyes puffy and bloodshot, but she smiled at him, weak yet somehow reassuring.

'I found this,' she said, handing Arthur an envelope. A modern envelope.

He ripped it open and slid out the contents.

A notecard read:

Arthur,
There is nothing more potent than the terror of a powerful man.
Malagant

Arthur frowned at the rhetoric, wondering what Malagant could be getting at, until, that is, he lifted the note and saw the photograph beneath.

A photograph of Caitlyn pushing through the gate of Hunter's Cottage.

Chapter Twenty-Two

London
8th of September 1888

'Mutilated,' said Agravain, walking away from the inspector and coming to stand before Nimuë. 'Worse than before.'

'Don't tell me the details,' said Nimuë. 'I can imagine.'

'Abberline feels the same man killed Polly Nichols last week. The same cuts to the neck,' said Agravain.

'Did anybody see anything?' asked Nimuë.

'Not that they're telling me,' said Agravain. He shivered and looked around. 'But I imagine there will be arrests even in the absence of evidence. Rumours are flying already. They found a leather apron back there, and there have already been headlines about a local man who goes by that name. I've already . . . '

Nimuë shuddered violently, and Agravain reached out to steady her.

'What's wrong?' he asked.

'Nothing,' she said. 'It's just, I can feel him all around, a tickling in the back of my neck, the sense of someone watching me.'

Even before she finished speaking, Agravain's mouth dropped open as, just for a few seconds, he could perceive red smoke drifting from her like breath on a chilly morning. A moment of insight that ended all too soon.

'He's feeding,' said Agravain. 'Getting fat on the milk of these atrocities.'

'Perhaps it is time to send word to Arthur,' said Nimuë quietly. Agravain did not reply.

Whitechapel, London
29th of September 1888
8.30pm

Catherine Eddowes was having a whale of a time, drunkenly making a very passable and very loud impression of a fire engine outside 29 Aldgate High Street until two police constables escorted her to the police station, stinking of alcohol.

'Name?' asked the sergeant on her arrival.

'Nothing,' said Eddowes, and she was led down to the cells to sober up.

Whitechapel, London
30th of September 1888
12.30am

PC William Smith walked slow and steady on the Berner Street beat, checking the doors of local businesses were locked, peering down alleys, looking up at the windows.

He drew close to the International Working Men's Educational Club, adjacent to Dutfield's Yard, and saw a couple standing on the opposite side of the street; the man, carrying a long package wrapped in newspaper, wore a black, diagonal cutaway coat and a hard felt hat, while the woman wore a red flower pinned to her jacket. He continued on his beat, slow and steady.

⁕

30th of September 1888
12.45am

Israel Schwarz passed the gateway to the International Working Men's Education Club, and as he did so, he saw a man in a peaked cap stop and speak to a woman with a flower pinned to her jacket at the entrance to Dutfield's Yard. He grabbed the woman and tried to pull her into the street, but instead pulled her down to the footway. The woman screamed three times, but not loud enough to draw much attention. Schwarz, not wanting to get involved, crossed the street and saw a second man standing in a doorway. The man wore a dark overcoat and a hard felt hat with a wide brim, and he stood smoking a pipe on the opposite side of the street.

'Lipski!' called the man in the peaked cap to the fellow on the other side of the street, and, thinking that the first man was shouting to his accomplice, Schwarz ran away up the street. He was not followed.

Around the same time, dock labourer James Brown passed the corner of Berner Street and Fairclough Street with his supper when he saw a man and a woman standing outside the Board School on Fairclough Street. The man said something, and Brown heard the woman reply,

'No. Not tonight. Some other night.'

Brown reached his home at 35 Fairclough Street, just a little way from the junction, and some fifteen minutes later he heard cries of 'Police!' and 'Murder!'

30th of September 1888
12.50am

Finally sober, Catherine Eddowes was brought up from the cells and enquired about the time.

'I'll get a damn fine hiding when I get home!' she exclaimed when she got her answer.

'And serve you right. You have no right to get drunk,' replied PC Hutt.

30th of September 1888
1.00am

PC Hutt led Eddowes down the passage out of the police station.

'Close the door behind you,' he said.

Eddowes grinned.

'Alright. Goodnight, old cock,' she said, and she closed the door as she left.

30th of September 1888
01.00am

Louis Diemschutz, steward of the working men's club, returned home, driving his horse and cart, from a day hawking jewellery. The wooden gates to Dutfield's Yard stood wide open, but as the horse entered the yard, it shied to the left. Diemschutz looked down and saw a black shape on the ground, which he prodded with the end of his whip then used it to try to lift the shape. Unable to do so, he jumped down and recognised that it was a woman lying by the brick wall on the right of the passage. Diemschutz ran into the club, looking for his wife. He found her in the company of others and told the gathering that there was a woman lying out in the yard, but that he did not know if she was drunk or dead. Returning with a lamp, it was soon apparent that the woman, Elizabeth Stride, although still bleeding, was indeed dead, her throat cut with blood on her hands and wrists.

The murderer escaped north up Berner Street and disappeared west down Commercial Road in the direction of Whitechapel High Street even as the first cries for help went up.

30th of September 1888
1.34am

Joseph Lawende, a commercial traveller, Harry Harris, a furniture dealer, and Joseph Levy, a butcher, passed into Mitre Square. It was surrounded by buildings, accessible at three points, perhaps an eight-minute walk from the police station where Catherine Eddowes had been held. They saw a man and a woman, who had her hand on his chest. He wore a pepper-and-salt loose jacket, a grey cloth cap with a peak and a red neckerchief.

'I do not like going home alone with those sort of characters about,' remarked Lawende to the other two men as they passed by.

30th of September 1888
1.45am

PC Watkins shone his light into the southwest corner of Mitre Square, a popular spot for prostitutes, and spied Catherine Eddowes lying on her back in a pool of blood. Her throat was cut, and she had been brutally mutilated, more so than Mary Ann Nichols, Annie Chapman and the recently killed Elizabeth Stride.

30th of September 1888
2.20am

PC Long passed down Goulston Street, a short distance north of Mitre Square, and saw nothing suspicious.

30th of September 1888
2.55am

PC Long's beat took him down Goulston Street again, but this time he spotted a piece of bloody material on a stairway. A piece of Catherine Eddowes's apron.

London
1st of October 1888

'What do you have?' asked Agravain, drawing on his cigar and sending out a puff of smoke. Inspector Abberline waved it away from his face and withdrew a folded piece of paper from his jacket's inside pocket.

'A letter, sent to the Central News Agency on the 25th. Just a copy. Can't let you get your hands on the original, old boy. Not yet, at any rate. What do you make of it?' said Abberline.

Agravain unfolded the paper and read:

Dear Boss,
I keep on hearing the police have caught me but they wont fix me just yet. I have laughed when they look so clever and talk about being on the <u>right</u> track. That joke about Leather Apron gave me real

fits. I am down on whores and I shant quit ripping them till I do get buckled. Grand work the last job was. I gave the lady no time to squeal. How can they catch me now. I love my work and want to start again. You will soon hear of me with my funny little games. I saved some of the proper <u>red</u> stuff in a ginger beer bottle over the last job to write with but it went thick like glue and I cant use it. Red ink is fit enough I hope <u>ha. ha.</u> The next job I do I shall clip the ladys ears off and send to the police officers just for jolly wouldn't you. Keep this letter back till I do a bit more work, then give it out straight. My knife's so nice and sharp I want to get to work right away if I get a chance. Good Luck. Yours truly

Jack the Ripper

Dont mind me giving the trade name

PS Wasnt good enough to post this before I got all the red ink off my hands curse it. No luck yet. They say I'm a doctor now. <u>ha ha</u>

'Hmmm,' said Agravain. 'Jack the Ripper.'

'Quite the moniker,' said Inspector Abberline, leaning across his desk.

'He makes a mockery of the theories that he is Leather Apron or perhaps a doctor,' said Agravain.

'Quite, but that could be a double bluff, easily,' said Abberline. 'Though the handwriting is suggestive of someone well-educated or at least, well able to form letters, even if the language itself is a little crude in places.'

'Do you consider it to be genuine?' asked Agravain.

'Well, here's the thing . . . ' said Abberline, and he produced another piece of folded paper, which he handed to Agravain.

'This arrived with the Central News Agency today. It was written in the same hand, but on a postcard, postmarked today.'

Agravain opened the paper and read aloud.

> *I was not codding dear old Boss when I gave you the tip, you'll hear about Saucy Jacky's work tomorrow double event this time number one squealed a bit couldn't finish straight off. Had not time to get ears off for police thanks for keeping last letter back till I got to work again.*
> *Jack the Ripper*

'This does little to prove its authenticity,' said Abberline. 'Postmarked today, but the whole of

London had heard of the 'double event' by the end of yesterday.'

'And yet, there is the mention of the ear clipping in the first letter, before the double event,' said Agravain. 'Was not the lobe of Catherine Eddowes's ear cut away, but left behind?'

'This is why I bring it to you, Marlow,' said Abberline. 'Perhaps something to consider when tasking your informants. We will be publishing these letters to see if a member of the public recognises the writer's hand.'

'I would advise against it,' said Agravain. 'You will be inundated.'

And so it proved to be true, with letters pouring into the newspapers and police.

Jack the Ripper sprang to life.

Chapter Twenty-Three

Wednesday 13th of January 2021

'Pick up the bloody phone,' Arthur said in a low growl, as he and Nimuë hurried back to join Bors and Dagonet on the path.

The call to Kay went to voicemail for the second time.

'Damn it,' he said, as they emerged from the trees.

'Back to the car,' Arthur barked, before his knights could say a word. 'Malagant is going after Caitlyn.'

'I'll call home,' said Dagonet, pulling out his mobile.

'I've already tried Kay, Tristan and the house. They aren't picking up,' said Arthur, his leg screaming at him to slow down as the four of them rushed back through the cemetery.

A man and a woman stepped into view from behind a mausoleum. They watched Arthur, Nimuë and the knights retreating, then the woman made a phone call.

⁓⁓⁓

Arthur's phone rang while they were on the motorway northbound, still some time away from home.

He looked down to check who the call had come from, expecting to see Tristan or Kay's name, but instead . . .

Caitlyn Calling

Arthur's stomach churned as he accepted the call.

'Hello?' said Arthur.

'Hello, Arthur,' said a familiar, male voice, but Arthur could not place it.

Dagonet's phone started ringing, and Arthur looked over as he struggled for a response.

'Tristan,' Dagonet mouthed, pointing at the screen.

'Who's that?' asked Arthur.

'It's me, Arthur,' said the voice. 'Agravain.'

Arthur's mind went blank, and he thought he might pass out as his vision began to narrow to a point. He didn't understand what was happening.

'Get over to Hunter's Cottage. Yes, straight away. I'll call you back,' he heard Dagonet tell Tristan.

'Agravain? You're with Caitlyn? How do . . . ' said Arthur, but Agravain interrupted.

'Malagant has us both,' said Agravain. 'He's given me a message to pass on.'

'Go on,' said Arthur, his tongue like a desert lizard lying limp in his mouth. He licked his lips.

'He's going to kill us,' said Agravain, 'then what's left of my family.'

Arthur said nothing.

'Are you there, Arthur?' said Agravain.

'How did he find you?' asked Arthur.

'He won't let me tell you anything else,' said Agravain.

'What does he want?' asked Arthur.

'Nothing,' said Agravain.

'Nothing?'

'It's all going to happen. He's not bargaining with you, Arthur. He just wants you to know,' said Agravain.

'There is nothing more potent than the terror of a powerful man,' said Arthur.

'Quite so,' said Agravain, and the line went dead.

Arthur looked down at his phone as the call screen disappeared and the light died, the screen fading to black.

'What's happening?' asked Nimuë.

'Malagant has Agravain and Caitlyn,' said Arthur.

'What do we do?' asked Dagonet.

'I don't know.' Arthur rubbed his right eye with his fingers, pressing down until he felt the pressure on the eyeball. He looked out of the window as the urban landscape gave way to fields and woods, Gareth speeding to get them home.

'I don't know,' Arthur said again, turning to look at both Nimuë and Dagonet.

'What can we do?'

⸎

'He called on Caitlyn's phone?' asked Dagonet, and Arthur nodded.

'That's a start. I need a pen,' said Dagonet. 'Pen! Who's got a pen?'

Bors rifled in the glove box and handed one back over his shoulder.

Dagonet asked for Caitlyn's number and scrawled it on the back of his hand before starting to dial. He paused and looked up.

'Someone call Tristan. He's going to Caitlyn's place,' said Dagonet. He finished dialling another number.

'On it,' said Bors, pulling out his own phone.

Arthur sat beside Nimuë, feeling totally helpless.

'What is this all about?' he said to her. 'He doesn't want anything from us?'

'He thrives on terror, you know that. It would be a reward in itself, but drawing strength from Agravain and from you? Meting out revenge for Morgana's demise? He has been waiting a long time for this,' said Nimuë.

'But why now?' said Arthur. 'He's had centuries! Where has Malagant been? What has he been doing?'

Nimuë took Arthur's hand in hers, sending a pleasant sensation across the surface of his skin and flying up his arm to tickle the base of his neck.

'I am beginning to suspect,' said Nimuë.

'Suspect what?' said Arthur, but she would say no more on it.

'I've been too passive,' she said aloud, but seemingly to herself. 'I learnt so much from Merlin about power and control, but eschewed it in favour of sowing harmony, understanding the world . . . with him gone . . . ' her words trailed off.

'You're going to have to step up,' said Arthur.

'As are you,' said Nimuë.

They locked eyes, combative for a moment, walls going up, but Arthur saw there was no malice behind the words, and they once more fell silent as Gareth ticked off the miles.

Arthur's phone rang. Tristan.

'It's not good news, Arthur,' said the knight, then recounted what he and Kay had found.

Arthur flinched as Nimuë gripped his knee.

'What?' he asked.

'You have been bouncing your leg up and down for the past 20 minutes. You're driving me mad,' she said.

'Hmmph,' said Arthur. 'I'm sorry.'

Nimuë smiled at him.

'Look,' she said, pointing across his face out of the passenger side rear window, 'we're here.'

The car bumped along the dirt path towards the monument then turned down off down the narrow drive to Hunter's Cottage.

'Stop the car,' said Arthur, and he was out and running, still limping, down the drive. He rounded a steep bank that obscured the cottage and slowed as he saw Kay standing by the open gate.

'Tristan's inside,' said the knight.

Arthur shambled down the short curving path to Caitlyn's door, careful not to trip on the lip of an uneven shard of flagstone. The front door had been forced, splintered around the lock. He stepped inside, noting a broken side plate by the mat just inside and peered round the door into the lounge. The fire was out, but still warm, the embers glowing. A half-full mug of tea sat on the coffee table.

No sign of Samson.

'Arthur?' Tristan's voice drifted in from the hall.

Please don't let them have hurt the dog, thought Arthur, as he hurried across the hall and into the kitchen.

He stopped in the doorway when he caught sight of the overturned chairs, the wooden table tipped on its side. And was that blood on the floor?

Arthur stepped close and, groaning, squatted as low as his leg would allow, his weight on his quavering cane.

Tristan's feet stepped into view on the other side of the small puddle as Arthur examined it. The former king looked up to see Tristan, solemn and grave.

He nodded.

'Blood, aye,' said the knight. 'Human or dog though? That's anyone's guess.'

'No sign of anyone? Is Samson hurt?' asked Arthur, gritting his teeth as he stood.

'Just this mess and the plate in the hall. Door and gate were open when we got here,' said Tristan.

Arthur stood to leave, but as he did so, he heard a whimper off to the left. He approached the pantry and, easing the door open, his eyes adjusted to the dark within, and he saw Samson cowering in the corner.

He opened the door and squatted down.

'Hello, boy,' he said, holding out a hand. The dog,

shaking, remained where it was at the back of the pantry for a few moments and then, gingerly, it approached, sniffed Arthur's hand and let him stroke him.

'That's it, it's alright,' he said.

Arthur found Samson's leash and took the dog with him when he left.

'No cameras covering the road for miles in every direction,' he said to himself.

'A few tyre tracks on the drive though,' said Tristan, 'much use they'll be.'

'Perhaps this will be . . . ' said Dagonet, trotting over from the direction of the car. 'I just got off the phone from Sam at Cordon Investigations. He's pulled some strings and we've tracker data from Caitlyn's phone.'

'Why would Malagant leave it on, knowing it could be tracked?' asked Arthur, as Bors joined them.

'The phone?' asked Bors. 'Because he's 2,000-year-old demon spawn who doesn't keep up with technology?'

'Fair point,' said Dagonet. 'Can't see the Dread Knight queueing for the latest iPhone!'

'We can't all be geeks like you though, Dag,' said Bors, and he shoved the slighter built knight, pushing him slightly off balance.

Dagonet widened his eyes, looking over Bors' shoulder, and as the big man began to turn, Dagonet slapped the back of his neck, hard.

'You little . . . ' growled Bors.

'Enough,' Arthur intoned. 'Is this a time for japes? Where's the phone pinging?'

'Not far from here. Seems to be stationary somewhere in Runbridge. Can't tell you more than that,' said Dagonet.

'Well done,' said Arthur. 'Let's move.'

'Runbridge?' asked Tristan. 'That rings a bell.'

He pulled out a notebook and began flicking back through the pages.

'We've got guys from both Cordon and Hektor Security there now,' he said.

'The list. Agravain's list,' said Nimuë, and Arthur jumped, only now realising she had joined them.

'Then we know where to start. Let's move,' said Arthur. Nimuë, Arthur and the knights ran to the cars. 'Tristan, get on to your people in Runbridge and warn them someone's coming.'

'Aye, sir,' said Tristan, hauling out his phone.

A few tense moments passed while Tristan spoke with the man on the other end, but Arthur saw the relief in his face as he puffed out his cheeks and expelled the air.

'They're all in order, but we should get there quick,' said Tristan.

'On it,' said Gareth. Arthur's car powered up the drive, followed by Tristan and Kay in the second vehicle.

'He may not know we're coming,' said Arthur. 'Time has outstripped his knowledge.'

'Perhaps, but I would not be so sure,' said Nimuë. 'Now hush while I think. Bullets and blades are not always enough, boy, don't you know that yet?'

She settled back, leaning into the headrest, her eyes closed and long hair over her shoulders, breathing slowly in and out as though meditating.

Arthur smiled, thinking of how much she had just sounded like Merlin.

He could feel the power thrumming the air around her, and he was comforted momentarily before turning his thoughts to Caitlyn.

Her safety was his paramount concern, but he could not help but wonder what she thought was going on, how much Malagant and even Agravain had told her. If she survived, was their relationship at an end? Surely it must be.

They pulled into Arthur's driveway and left Samson with Kay. The Rottweiler seemed content enough, especially when Bobbi, Nimuë's border collie, made him welcome. They hurried back to the car and set out once more.

Onward drove Arthur, Nimuë and the knights, seeking their ancient foe.

Chapter Twenty-Four

London
17th of October 1888

'You should most definitely give this to the police, Mr Lusk,' said Agravain, as Nimuë picked up the box and peered inside.

'It's definitely a human kidney,' said Nimuë, setting it back down. 'Didn't . . . ?'

'Yes, Catherine Eddowes's body was missing a kidney,' said Agravain.

He read the letter through again. The handwriting was very different to that on the Dear Boss letter and the Saucy Jack postcard. It appeared haphazard and manic. The writer was clearly less literate or affecting to be so.

From hell.
Mr Lusk,
Sor
   I send you half the Kidne I took from one women prasarved it for you tother

piece I fried and ate it was very nice. I may send you the bloody knife that took it out if you only wate a while longer
   signed
   Catch me when you can Mishter Lusk

George Lusk, a builder who led the lately formed Whitechapel Vigilance Committee, stood with his arms folded across his chest. The committee had been formed by local businessmen and organised men to patrol Whitechapel at night, hoping to catch the Ripper.

'I supposed it to be a hoax, Mr Marlow. It's a human kidney, like as not, but it is not beyond the realms of possibility that it has been acquired other than through murder,' said Lusk.

'No possibility should be ignored,' said Agravain, not taking his eyes from the letter. He had a feeling in his gut about it. There was something about the deranged nature of both the 'From hell' and the handwriting. The spellings intrigued him too. Sor instead of sir. Prasarved instead of preserved. Was the writer Irish, perhaps, writing as he spoke? Or perhaps that too was a ruse.

'I should hand it over immediately,' said

Marlow. 'Perhaps something can be done to ascertain the kidney's provenance.'

※

'Things are gathering apace,' said Nimuë, walking with her arm linked with Agravain's. They ascended the steps to his front door and there stopped while he fished in his pocket for the key.

Agravain merely grunted in response to her comment.

'Perhaps it is time to write to Arthur,' she asked.

'Where Arthur goes, Merlin follows,' Agravain reminded her.

'Perhaps he is needed,' Nimuë replied. 'I do not have the strength to dismiss Malagant myself, and you would surely be able to root him out together with your brother knights?'

'Perhaps,' said Agravain, unwilling to admit defeat. He was relieved when Nimuë let the matter lie.

Once settled, Agravain aired the thought that had been plaguing him since their exchange on the doorstep.

'I do not know how one defeats the Dread Knight,' he admitted. 'He cannot be injured, we know that.'

'I have some ideas, though I am not yet

strong enough. I believe Excalibur could finish him, if he could be bound to a body, but it is only theory. If anyone knows, Merlin does,' said Nimuë, once again bringing the conversation to a close.

'Are we any closer to identifying the Ripper?' she asked, to break the silence.

Agravain sucked his teeth and tapped at the arm of his chair with his index finger.

'There is too much of everything to go on, except consistent facts. He has left nothing behind except a scrap of bloodied apron. We know that he is targeting middle-aged female prostitutes of the East End. We know that in each case, the throat has been cut, but that the mutilations are escalating. Organs are removed.'

'All save for Liz Stride,' reminded Nimuë. 'She was not mutilated at all.'

'No, and perhaps it indicates that the killer was disturbed before he could complete his work. He certainly compensated less than an hour later with the unfortunate Catherine Eddowes,' said Agravain, taking a sip of his coffee. 'There is talk that Stride was not killed by the same man, that perhaps her jilted lover, Michael Kidney, may have killed her. It could account for the lack of mutilation, but so could the killer being disturbed.'

'Which brings us to the letters,' said Nimuë. 'The first Dear Boss letter mentioned sending the police his victim's ears and then less than a week later, Eddowes loses part of her ear. Did the Ripper send the letter?'

'No,' said Agravain. 'I have put that possibility to bed, I believe. That and the Saucy Jack postcard. Not directly from the killer, but certainly from someone with a vested interest in stirring up the mythology around the murders,' said Agravain.

'Malagant?' asked Nimuë.

'Perhaps. Or perhaps a member of the Press, either working for Malagant or trying to sell more newspapers,' said Agravain.

'Or both,' Nimuë concluded.

'Quite,' said Agravain. 'This latest letter to Mr Lusk, though, it is from quite a different animal. I have my suspicions we may be on to something there, and yet it does not lead me to a suspect.'

'At this rate, we will never find him, and Malagant grows stronger every day. He must be behind this, John,' said Nimuë. She jumped up from her chair and clutched the side of her head. 'It's so frustrating. How can we find him? How do we put him down?'

She turned on him suddenly.

'We must tell Arthur,' she said. 'You must send for Merlin.'

'I have you, what need have I for Merlin?' the knight countered.

'Our arts are different! I sense much and understand much of the world, but Merlin is that and more, he is a master of politics, of manipulation and combat.'

'And yet you bested him,' said Agravain.

'His ardour weakened him,' she admitted. 'It is ever man's folly.'

'I will not send for him if it means you must go,' said Agravain.

Nimuë threw up her arms and stomped out of the room, leaving him to brood.

Agravain was turning the pages of his journals, reading by lamplight when he came across the account of that earlier killing, of Martha Tabram on 7th of August, twenty-three days before the first of the Ripper murders. Once more he discounted the possibility that the same person was responsible, after all, she had been stabbed 39 times, and been found in a building, rather than having had her throat cut and being left to die in the street.

Agravain paused when he came to the mention of Tabram having spent the evening with soldiers, and the constable attending the garrison at the Tower of London.

He closed the book and held it in his hands, staring through the dying embers in the grate.

His eyelids felt heavy, and so he sought his bed, lying down beside Nimuë, but found he was unable to sleep despite how weary he felt. Something as yet unclear about Tabram's murder plagued him.

Before half an hour had passed, he carefully slipped out from under the blankets, took his clothes into the parlour, and he dressed in the dark. He pulled on his revolver in its holster, hiding it beneath a jacket and overcoat before pulling on his bowler hat.

Agravain opened his front door, locking it behind him ever so carefully, then set out into the night.

※

There were seven lamps in his street, providing adequate lighting in periodic pools through which Agravain walked, all too conscious of the shadows that surrounded them, especially those that hid the entrances to side alleys or to buildings.

Initially intending to walk the back streets until dawn, he found himself on Whitechapel High Street heading west, then turning down Minories and from there gradually making the 15-minute walk that left him standing before the Tower of London.

He looked south down Iron Gate to where Tower Bridge was gradually being constructed to connect the East End to the south side of the Thames. The view had changed much all around since the days of the Great Fire, when Agravain had last been with Arthur and the knights in the fortress just over the wall ahead of him.

A raven cawed within and, looking up, Agravain saw a dark shape pass overhead. He determined that tomorrow he would return with Nimuë, and get inside the Tower, suddenly unwilling to go alone. He turned back and started. Silent and tall, Daisy, one of Branok's raven familiars, was standing, hands on hips, less than a metre from him.

He took a step back on instinct as another raven cawed.

'We have wandered a little from our patch, haven't we?' she said, inflecting a cockney accent.

Agravain reached for his revolver, but a sharp blow to the back of his head sent him reeling. The last thing he perceived was the ground coming up to meet him.

───※───

Nimuë awoke before dawn, but she was not surprised to find she was alone in bed, knowing full well how Agravain would stalk the streets of Whitechapel until the sun was up, crossing paths with the men of the various vigilance committees as they attempted to apprehend Jack the Ripper. She grew more concerned as the morning progressed, and as lunchtime approached, she knelt on the parlour carpet, closing her eyes and reaching out to him, something she had often done over the years, even in their long separation.

She sensed he was alive and nearby.

Nimuë pulled on her outer clothes and spent the evening walking the beat Agravain had assigned himself, but she could see no sign of him as she walked it one, two, three times. She stopped in at his haunts, at the pubs, clubs, the businesses where he had acquaintances. She stopped informers she recognised in the street, though some of them feigned ignorance of John Marlow entirely, and, she realised, quite properly.

Morning gave way to afternoon, and evening threatened to arrive when Nimuë, panic rising, decided to take action herself.

―――※―――

The pain lancing into his skull was like repeated screams under his skin, and it eventually woke him. Agravain opened his eyes briefly and caught a glimpse of a luxurious room with hardwood furniture and other items, richly gilded. He reached up to touch the back of his head, and he realised he was not restrained. In the next second he remembered what had happened, and he snapped fully awake.

He was sprawled in a comfortable chair, just one among a circle of seats and sofas. Agravain sat up and, feeling something cold on his cheek, he wiped away a line of drool with the handkerchief protruding from his jacket's breast pocket. He rubbed the back of his head as he looked around. Colourful carpets, gold-framed portraits and landscape paintings, a chandelier, tall windows with a view of the river. Agravain stood and moved to the window, attempted to open it, but could not see how.

Wooden double doors opened and a butler stepped into the room, standing to attention by the entrance.

Malagant swept in, and the butler stepped back out, pulling both doors closed behind him. The Dread Knight was dressed in a long black coat and cape, white gloves and a top hat. He began to remove his outer garments, throwing them on to a chaise longue without a care.

'How is your head?' he asked, sticking out his lower lip in an expression reminiscent of a child about to cry.

'I'll live,' said Agravain. He scanned the room for other windows or doors. No doors, two more tall windows.

'Oh, possibly, John, possibly. Much depends on our impending conversation.'

Agravain folded his arms across his chest, careful not to inhibit his movement by tucking his hand under his arm. He needed to be ready to fight.

Malagant crossed the room, and as he did so, he reached inside his jacket pocket. Agravain reacted immediately, moving to draw his revolver, and only then did he realise that his holster was empty.

A little laugh, and Malagant withdrew a cigarette case. He snapped it open and offered one to Agravain, who reluctantly accepted. Malagant withdrew a silver and enamel vesta case and lit the cigarette for him.

The Dread Knight waved a hand at the chair in which Agravain had so recently been sprawled, and when Malagant took the sofa opposite him, crossing his legs and leaning back to smoke, Agravain also sat, leaning forward so that his weight was on his feet, ready to spring forward.

'Why have you brought me here?' asked Agravain.

'Haven't you been looking for me?' said Malagant.

'I intend to put a stop to the Whitechapel Murders,' said Agravain.

'I can't allow that,' said Malagant. 'You know how well they nourish me.' As he said this, he blinked and when his eyes reopened, the sockets were visible, filled with an intense blood-coloured swirling smoke. Malagant breathed in and more seemed to form from the air to be drawn into his nostrils.

'Besides,' said Malagant, turning an upturned palm towards Agravain, causing the knight's body to emit that familiar red vapour, 'it's all going so well! The city is in a crazed panic.'

'Enough,' Agravain growled, jumping to his feet. 'Enough of your parlour tricks and devilry. You are killing innocent people. Terrifying the whole city.'

Malagant grinned, his eyes like red ink swirling in black water.

'I have killed nobody. I would not lower myself to such barbarity,' he said.

'But you encourage the perpetrator,' said Agravain. He readied himself to fight, eyes darting here and there, searching for his weapons, for *anything* that could be used as a weapon.

'Would you like to meet Jack the Ripper?' said Malagant, his eyeballs suddenly reappearing as he stood. He turned his back to Agravain and crossed the room to a table that stood between the middle and right-hand window. He poured brandy from a decanter into two glasses and brought them over to Agravain, but this time the knight refused his offer.

'Suit yourself,' said Malagant. He set down one of the glasses and, plucking the cigarette from his lips, he drank the contents of the glass in his hand without pause, then reached down to retrieve the other.

'There are some people I would like you to meet,' he said, and led Agravain towards the double doors.

The two men passed down a wide corridor with footmen lining the way and then Malagant took a sharp right into what Agravain had thought to be just an alcove. A small door led to a tight spiral staircase. Malagant stood back and indicated he wished Agravain to go first. He hesitated momentarily, but deciding he had few options, Agravain set off up the stairs. They led to a small landing and another door, painted black, with both a red eye painted in the left corner and a green eye in the right, both gazing down upon the shape of a man, arms outstretched, wrought in silver. Malagant joined him on the landing and pushed the door open.

Agravain stepped through into a long dark room, lit only with candles in sconces.

Rows of pews faced the far end of the room, divided by a central aisle. The far wall was covered with crimson drapes and just before it was a raised stage upon which stood an ornate throne. Beside it stood another throne, smaller and less audacious. Daisy was perched upon it in her human form, but she squatted on the seat of the throne itself, arms tucked behind her back, black feathers protruding from her shoulders and along the backs of her arms. Her human face stretched into a long grey beak. A mass of black hair and feathers cascaded down, framing her face.

On the left-hand side of the stage, looking down over the corresponding pews, was a tall marble statue of a man in the Greek style, but with a single ruby for an eye. On the right-hand side of the stage, looking over its pews, was another statue, identical but for its eye, which was a large green emerald.

Malagant strode down the central aisle, steering Agravain with an arm wrapped around his shoulders, which the knight tried to shrug off, only to find that the Dread Knight was too strong.

As they stepped past the first row of the high-backed pews, Agravain heard a laugh from his left. He looked in the direction of the sound and saw a familiar face seated next to others, some that he knew, some that he didn't.

Agravain jumped as the door behind them slammed shut. Malagant waved a hand at the central throne.

'Sit, John, sit,' he said. Agravain did as he was bid, walking amidst a cloud of green vapour that now rose from his body, green with a hint of red amongst it.

From his position he could now clearly see the men sitting on the first pew under the gaze of the red eye.

Malagant stood on the stage beneath the statue and addressed the gathering.

'Thank you all for joining me here tonight,' he said. 'We have an honoured guest.'

The Dread Knight turned to look at Agravain, biting his lip. He looked as though he was trying to restrain himself, but the effort was too much, and once more his eyes disappeared and the now mostly red mist around Agravain hurled itself towards Malagant, swirling all around him.

'John Marlow, let me introduce you to the newest recruits to the Order of Deimos, Daisy's chosen few. James Kelly, who dispatched Mary Ann Nichols. Aaron Kosminski, who ended poor Annie Chapman's suffering. Michael Kidney, who killed his lover, Elizabeth Stride, and the notorious Dr Tumblety, who got rather carried away with the unfortunate Catherine Eddowes.'

Agravain shifted forward in his seat, eyeing Kelly in particular, rage growing inside him.

'And finally,' said Malagant in a raised voice, 'though you have met before, let me reintroduce you to the architect of the Whitechapel Murders, Daisy, chief amongst Branok's familiars, and, no doubt, she is the reason we found you lurking outside the Tower.'

'You killed Martha Tabram,' said Agravain, turning to the half-woman, half-raven who was perched before him. It bowed its head and then said, in a creaking, cracking caw of a voice,

'Not in person, but there were those amongst the Tower garrison who were easily . . . influenced.'

Agravain tried to rise, intending to grapple with the familiar, but he could not move his limbs more than an inch.

'That wouldn't be polite, John,' said Malagant, who walked slowly in front of him, smiling, his hand outstretched, exerting control.

'Tabram's killing was messy. Frenzied. Put down to criminal gangs. We had to put our heads together and come up with a more distinctive method,' said Malagant, as he came to stand beside Daisy's throne. He reached down and ruffled her mane of locks and feathers.

'Why have you brought me here? Why are you telling me all of this?' said Agravain.

'My motives are two-fold, John. Do you have it, my dear?' said Malagant, and Agravain looked on in horror as Daisy reached into her short jacket and withdrew his own journal, the one that contained all of the pertinent information about his descendants. She handed it to Malagant.

'First, to gain some insurance,' the Dread Knight smiled, 'and secondly, to ensure you have a vested interest.'

With that, he tucked the book back into Agravain's pocket, then stood before him, his arms up and fingers outstretched.

The Dread Knight's face contorted, and stretched as he began to moan and draw the red mist from Agravain. The knight struggled, feeling energy draining from him as the terror rose, panic overwhelming him, unable to take his eyes from the demon before him as one of the men on the pew below called and laughed.

Malagant's skin drained of all colour and black veins rose to the surface of his face as his eyes disappeared, the sockets spilling red vapour. As Agravain watched, his heart beating so fast that he thought it would give out on him any moment, the flesh of Malagant's latest host began to disintegrate before him, his features growing more and more emaciated until only his bones were visible. A swirling cloud of red and green mist formed the outline of a man, ghostlike before him, and it joined with the vapour being drawn from Agravain, intensifying in colour, turning to scarlet as Malagant's body entirely disappeared. The cloud before Agravain stretched out two insubstantial hands and cupped his face. There was a momentary pause, and a hush fell over the chamber, as even the monsters who witnessed the act fell silent.

Malagant drew back, hung in the air before Agravain and then rushed forward, entering the knight's body, soaking through exposed skin and into his pores, rushing into his nostrils, through his open, screaming mouth until the Dread Knight had been utterly consumed.

Daisy hopped down from her throne and as she landed she took on her full human form. She drew Agravain's revolver from her coat pocket and aimed it at him.

Agravain slumped unconscious in the throne, his chin against his chest.

Chapter Twenty-Five

Runbridge, England
January 2021

'Muuum. Mum!'

Kayleigh Turner sighed, dipping her rubber-gloved hands into the soapsuds filling the kitchen sink.

'What is it?' she called back.

'Muuum,' called her ten-year-old from upstairs.

'Give me strength,' said Kayleigh and resumed washing up. 'You come to me,' she said to herself.

'Muuhuuuum,' called Simon again.

Another sigh from Kayleigh. She peeled off the gloves and, taking a towel with her, she dried her hands as she set off towards the stairs.

'Mum!'

'I'm coming!' said Kayleigh.

She stepped from the landing into Simon's bedroom, ducking under a suspended model Spitfire and stepping around a collection of action figures scattered on the floor. Simon's legs were protruding from under his stars and moons curtains which were drawn across the window despite it being the middle of the day. He knelt on his bed and was peering outside.

'What's up, buddy?' Kayleigh asked. Simon ducked down to look out at her.

'There's a man standing in the back garden,' he said.

Kayleigh's tongue felt as though it had suddenly inflated.

'What?' she said, not moving for a moment, then kneeling on the bed and pulling back the curtain.

The garden was empty save for the shed, the swingset and a lone football sitting on the neatly trimmed grass.

Glass smashed downstairs.

'What is that?' wailed Simon as Kayleigh swore. She looked around frantically for a moment, but heard a voice downstairs.

'Under the bed!' she hissed to Simon. 'Quickly.'

He clung to her and wouldn't let go. Kayleigh peeled him off and, quite forcefully, causing him to cry out - a sound she would always regret - she pushed him until he clambered under the bed.

Kayleigh got to her feet just as the bottom stair creaked. She bit her lower lip, and, hands shaking, she swung Simon's window open, hoping whoever was coming up the stairs would think he had climbed out.

The stairs creaked as someone climbed them.

Kayleigh dashed out onto the landing, leaving Simon's door open.

She reached the top of the stairs just as a strange man stepped into view.

'Get out of my house!' she roared, and as she did so the

air around her seemed to first tense and then contract. Unaware she was doing so, Kayleigh unleashed a wave of power against the intruder. The man staggered, falling back against the wall. Kayleigh flew forward, digging her nails into his face and throwing her meagre bodyweight into him.

She caught him off guard, and the man grunted as he tried to regain his balance. He gripped Kayleigh's arms and as Simon began to scream, the man fell backwards down the stairs, taking Kayleigh with him.

'Park here,' said Tristan. He dialled Arthur's number on his mobile.

'Leave the line open, and I'll call if I need you,' he said then got out of the car and walked round the corner into the next street.

They waited. Thirty seconds. Forty. Fifty. Arthur put Tristan's call on speakerphone.

'Two of the Hektor Security guys are dead in the van. There's screaming coming from the house,' Tristan's voice blared out suddenly. 'I'm going in.'

'Get round there!' said Arthur, but Gareth didn't need telling. The car leapt forward from a standing start and tore into the next street. Arthur could see the plain white Hektor Security van up ahead and the garden gate leading to the house diagonally opposite was standing open. Tristan was running up the path.

Arthur, Nimuë and the knights burst out of the car and ran towards the house.

'I'll go round the back,' said Gareth as he passed through the gate and peeled off towards the gate which led down the side of the house to the rear garden.

'With Gareth,' said Bors.

Arthur carried on up the path as he watched Tristan throw his shoulder against the front door. The knight started kicking it.

The sound of grunts, screams and a commotion came from the other side of the door.

'I won't get through it like this,' said Tristan.

The knight ran to the nearest window and, picking up a rock from the garden, he smashed the glass.

Arthur heard sirens in the distance as he crouched and lifted the metal flap of the letterbox to see into the house beyond. The sound of the screaming intensified immediately.

Arthur could see a muscular man all in black, wearing a ski mask and black leather gloves, wrestling with a young woman. Arthur caught a glimpse of the blood-sodden back of the ski mask. Seconds later, Gareth and Bors ran through the kitchen at the rear of the house, down the hall and they grabbed hold of the man just as Tristan appeared from the living room.

'Are you alright?' he heard Tristan say, stooping to check on the woman. She pushed him off, screaming, blood dripping along the side of her nose. She tried to stand, but it looked as though her leg was broken. Gareth and Bors were dragging the man towards the front door. Arthur straightened up as he heard both the door being unlocked and the sirens drawing closer.

'We have to go!' said Arthur. 'Now!' he bellowed at Tristan, who was managing to calm Kayleigh.

His knight hesitated then ran for the open door. The four of them hurried back to the street. As Gareth and Bors bundled the man in the ski mask into the rear of the car, Tristan opened the driver's door of the van and shoved one of the dead men out of the way as best he could, leaning in to bend the man's legs.

'Call once you're clear,' said Arthur, and Tristan nodded as Dagonet climbed into the passenger seat. He started the van and drove out of the street.

Arthur hurried back to the car, sliding into the driving seat. Gareth and Bors were struggling in the back even as Arthur drove off in the same direction as Tristan.

Where was Caitlyn? And Agravain? Was it Malagant they struggled with in the back seat or just one of his cultists?

Arthur's mind raced as he drove, forcing himself to keep his speed low. At a junction, Tristan turned left and so Arthur turned right so they could take alternative routes towards home.

But could they return home now? Surely someone would have seen them? Identified the cars?

'Stay down!' roared Bors from behind him, but Arthur couldn't spare a glance in the rear-view mirror. He had to concentrate on getting them out of the area without drawing any more attention.

A thumping noise, the sound of a punch, and then a strange laugh. One more thumping noise, more laughter and then a third punch and all fell silent.

'What's the plan?' asked Gareth, leaning between the front seats.

'Get a safe distance away and regroup. Any update on Caitlyn's phone?' asked Arthur.

Gareth pulled out his mobile and placed a call.

'It's still active and in the area,' said Gareth.

'That's something,' said Arthur. 'Can we narrow it down any further?'

'I'll see if anyone answers,' said Gareth, dialling Caitlyn's number.

Arthur let out a gasp and braked involuntarily as a familiar song began playing from the back seat. He pulled over at the side of the road and turned in his seat to look into the back.

Bors dug in the man's jacket pockets and withdrew Caitlyn's phone, still ringing.

'Damn,' breathed Arthur. 'Get his mask off and wake him up,' he said.

Gareth sat the man up in the middle seat and pulled off the bloody ski mask.

They sat in stunned silence. Nimuë recovered first.

'John,' she said, barely louder than a whisper.

Arthur and the knights exchanged glances.

There, unconscious in the backseat, the back of his head bloodied, sat Agravain.

'What the . . . ' started Bors.

'Malagant must have Caitlyn elsewhere?' said Gareth.

Nimuë shoved Bors aside and knelt on the seat beside

Agravain, cupping his face in her hands. Arthur saw her bow her head, and once more he felt that thrumming, pulsating power emanating from her.

Agravain sat up, his eyes flew open and a throttled, gargled sound burst from his throat. Sweat poured down his forehead, and he looked about him, jittery and flinching to the touch. He saw Arthur first, then Bors, barely registering Gareth as he turned and saw Nimuë beside him.

'Nimuë?' he said. 'I . . . ' He reached up and touched the back of his head.

'Where?' He blinked twice, scrunching his eyelids closed and then opening them wide as though trying to stay awake. 'What's happening? Have you dismissed Malagant?' he stared at Nimuë, eyes wide.

'We just caught you trying to beat your descendant to death,' said Bors. 'So quit playing innocent and get talking.'

Agravain closed his eyes suddenly, as though an unbearable migraine had just ignited.

'No . . . ' he said. 'Nimuë, kill me.'

But Arthur saw that Nimuë was far from receptive to Agravain's pleas. She was sitting back once more, frowning, no, scowling at her former lover, Arthur decided.

'Nimuë?' he said.

'There is something amiss,' she said in a cold, stern voice. She felt Agravain's forehead as though checking for a fever, closing her eyes and bowing her head once more.

Arthur gasped as blood-red smoke began to rise from the enchantress's body, and a second later, he realised that he too was emitting vapour.

Agravain's eyelids shot open, but there were no eyeballs beneath, just empty sockets filled with red swirling mist. Gareth and Bors dived forward, seizing his arms.

Agravain began to speak.

'Hello, Arthur,' said Malagant, and he grinned with Agravain's mouth.

Chapter Twenty-Six

Minories, London
20th of October 1888

'Here now, you can't sleep here.' A gruff voice. Stern.

Agravain woke on cold ground, his face against a wall and with a boot pressing on his side. He rolled over, head swimming as though badly hungover, his hands shielding his eyes.

'Wha . . . ' he said, barely able to form words, his mouth was so dry.

A uniformed police constable stood over him, scowling, that is, until he saw who it was he was nudging with his boot.

'Mr Marlow!' the constable extended a hand to help Agravain to his feet. 'Do beg my pardon, sir, but well, we can't have folk sleeping on Minories, can we, sir?'

Agravain squinted, examining the constable's face, unable to place him, his head was so foggy.

He reached round to the back of his head from where the almighty ache was still emanating.

'I . . . I apologise, Constable,' was all Agravain could think of to say.

'None of that, sir, but we'd best get you home. Have you been robbed, sir?' the constable frowned again, looking at the matted blood-drenched hair on the back of Agravain's head. Agravain stooped to pick up his bowler hat and patted himself down. His journal was where it should be, and so was his revolver. His billfold was also in its secret pocket.

'Not robbed, it seems,' he said groggily. 'I have all my possessions, but I have been struck.'

He fought to remember the previous night's events, but a haze hung over them, and he was forced to consider the possibility that he had indeed got drunk and perhaps ended up in a fight. It was true, he did ache all over, as though every molecule in his body was under strain. He remembered standing before the Tower, resolving to return with Nimuë, remembered that moment of inspiration about Martha Tabram and the garrison.

The ravens, he thought.

'Shall we cut along to the station, sir? I can take a statement,' said the constable. Randall, Agravain remembered the officer's name, Peter Randall.

'Perhaps I will come along later, Pete,' he said. 'I think it best I head home and rest. Perhaps see a doctor.'

'Alright, Mr Marlow, if you say so, but let me see you as far as the end of Whitechapel High Street, just so I know you can walk unaided,' said the younger man.

'You're a credit to the uniform, Pete,' said Agravain and fell in beside the police officer as they walked towards his home.

From a doorway on the other side of the street, Daisy watched him go. She waited for the appropriate moment then leapt into the air, bursting from the doorway in her raven form. She wheeled higher and higher, cawing, then set off back to the Tower.

⁕

His front door was ajar. Agravain climbed the steps, holding on to the railings for support, peering through the gap. He steadied himself on the top step and reached for his revolver as he pushed open the door.

'Nimuë?' he called, and he heard her reply, the sound of his name echoing, faint, but reassuring from within. She stepped into the hall, visibly relieved, but after a second, her expression turned to one of concern.

'What happened to you? You're white as

snow and you can barely stand!' she said, clasping his arm and ushering him inside.

'I don't know,' he answered, 'but I need to rest. Bump on the back of my head, but nothing else amiss, I think. I was found lying by a wall down on Minories,' he told her.

'You don't remember anything?'

'Not a thing,' he said, yawning and closing his eyes.

'You've a concussion. Don't fall asleep,' said Nimuë.

As she busied about fetching him a glass of water and something to eat, Agravain noticed that she kept watching the clock.

'Are you expecting someone, or perhaps you have somewhere to be?' he said, remembering how the front door was ajar and realising for the first time she was dressed for outside, even down to a bonnet.

She stopped a few yards from his chair then continued towards him, handing him the glass.

'I have a train to catch. The time has come again, John,' she said softly. 'When you didn't come home, well, I reached out to Merlin. He'll be here very soon.'

She put a hand across his forehead.

'You're feverish,' she said, then winced, drawing back her hand. 'Something isn't at all right here.'

'I'll be fine,' he assured her, staring at the floor, his words barely audible as he dwelled on losing her once more.

'Oh, John. I can't dwell here, away from clean waters, walking streets with memories I cannot face. You've known that for a long, long time. I am bound to you, but I cannot remain in London. There is a great wide world out there, beyond these streets, up the great river. There could be for you too, you know? You've done enough here. Work with Arthur, bring this latest spree to a close. Deal with Malagant.' As she said the word a pain incised through his brain. 'And then put all this behind you. Don't be a martyr,' she concluded and leant down to kiss him on the head. 'Now, I must finish packing what little I have. I want to be away before Merlin arrives.'

―⁂―

He wanted to stand, to embrace her before she left, but he felt too weak, too nauseous to move, his guts churned, and he felt so chill that he shivered.

'Don't get up,' Nimuë said, as he attempted it. She leaned down and let him wrap his arms around her, her hands on his ribs. She planted a long, loving kiss on his lips.

'Come and find me, John, when this is done.

Perhaps we can roam together, if you can leave London behind you.'

'I will,' he said, knowing that he couldn't. There were the children to watch over. 'Send me word.'

Nimuë nodded. 'Goodbye for now, my love,' she said, and left the house, closing the door behind her. Agravain looked up at the many ink drawings that hung on the walls, his gaze lingering longest on an old portrait he had drawn of Nimuë.

He took them down one by one and stowed them out of sight.

───※───

It had been more than 200 years since Arthur and Merlin had locked Branok away within the White Tower, leaving his raven familiars to watch over him; that meant it had been more than two centuries since Arthur had seen Agravain. For the most part, he had avoided London during that time, coming into the city only once, to receive the Victoria Cross from Queen Victoria herself for his conduct during a disastrous action in the Crimean War. The London of 1888 was a world away from the London of 1666, and yet Arthur felt immediately on edge as he stepped down from the train on to the platform at King's Cross station. The air felt heavy, redolent of industry and grime, at least to his nose, one who had always dwelled in the countryside whenever there was a choice. Merlin stepped down beside him, as did Tristan, Kay, Percival and the other knights.

They hailed cabs outside the station and gave them the address Nimuë had provided in the short and simple letter. Agravain was missing. Malagant was abroad and likely the force behind the murders Arthur had been reading about in The Times.

―∞§∞―

They turned into Agravain's street just as Nimuë was approaching the junction. She looked up, saw Merlin and smiled. The wizard turned without a word and walked back the way he had come. Tristan set off after him.

Nimuë raised her eyebrows and sighed, but as she laid eyes on Arthur for the first time, she bowed her head slightly, and curtsied.

'Sire,' she said, before recovering herself.

'Nimuë, I presume?' said Arthur.

'You presume correctly,' she said, forcing herself not to look at the faces of the other knights, feeling their glares and stares like white-hot sunlight on her skin. Her cheeks began to flush.

'I will not linger, for Merlin's sake. Agravain returned this morning, but he has been attacked, though he has no memory of it, and he is quite unwell. I will trust you, sire, to ensure he is treated,' she said.

'We will look after Agravain. He is our brother, after all,' said Arthur.

'Perhaps it is time you acted as though that were true,' she said, raising her chin. 'Look after him.'

Nimuë nodded to Arthur, crossed the street and disappeared into a side alley.

Arthur looked to see if Merlin was still walking away, and saw Tristan had halted him farther up the road. The knight pointed back towards Arthur, and after a moment, Merlin came back to join them.

'What business does she have here?' the wizard muttered. 'No good can come of it.'

'Agravain has returned, but is unwell,' said Arthur, ignoring the comments.

'Likely that woman put a hex on him,' said Merlin.

Arthur made no reply, disliking the petulance in the wizard's voice.

⁓⁓⁓

The bell rang, and it was with considerable effort that Agravain levered himself up out of his chair and made the journey down the hall. He leant heavily on the door as he opened it, and all the more so when he saw Arthur standing on his mat.

He tried to speak, to give greeting, but the words stuck in his throat as eyes brimmed. He swallowed, and steadied himself, as Arthur's smile grew.

'It has been far too long, brother,' said Arthur.

'Sire,' was all Agravain could manage.

'Arthur will suffice, or sir if you cannot stomach my name. Can we come in?'

Arthur stepped to the side, revealing Merlin, Tristan and the others arrayed on the steps down to the street. Agravain clasped his hand to his mouth and moved away from the doorway, allowing them entrance. Arthur took him in an embrace as he stepped inside the building, Merlin muttered greeting, it might have been 'my boy' and his brother knights shook his hand or clapped him on the shoulder. For a moment, any bitterness over his long absence was forgotten, and warm greetings were exchanged until the tears rolled down his cheeks. He had not realised until then just how isolated he had been.

'Nimuë reached out to Merlin,' said Arthur, who had taken up her chair across from Agravain. The wizard stood beside him, leaning on it, while the knights spread out through the room.

'She said that Malagant is back. Is it true?' asked Tristan.

'Aye, it is true. He has been in London for a century or two now,' said Agravain, feeling quite faint. He wrapped his arms around his torso and shivered. Clearly still furious, from his expression, Merlin took out a pouch from within his robes, and sprinkled a herb into the glass of water on the table by Agravain's chair.

'Drink. It will fortify you,' said the wizard.

'You will not poison me, I hope,' said Agravain, sweat forming on his brow, his body shaking. 'Now that you know about Nimuë and I.'

'Do not speak her name,' snapped the wizard.

'Merlin . . . ' chided Arthur softly, but the wizard held up his hand.

'No, boy, no,' and he slunk away to the window, wringing his hands together behind his back.

'Why did you not send word?' asked Arthur, and Agravain pointed at Merlin's back. Arthur nodded.

'Very well,' he said under his breath, 'but

now it has come to a point where you require aid?'

'I did not seek it, sire. Sir. Arthur,' said Agravain, 'but I have been missing for a time, and other parties grew concerned. In truth, perhaps I should have requested Merlin's aid before now, but the situation has been complicated.'

Agravain explained all he knew of Malagant, of how he had dwelled in the city, had no direct hand in the evils he revelled in, but evil-doers flocked to him and of how the cult had sprang up. He told of the rise of the newspapers and how first Malagant had stirred public fear, before the industry gained its own momentum, and he was no longer required to involve himself to the same extent.

'I have had him stand before me on more than one occasion, but I know full well that my weapons would cause him little harm.'

Arthur made no reply, and Agravain wondered if the former king wished he had come to assist him when his knight first told him that Malagant was in London so long ago.

'I have kept watch, and I have not seen that Malagant has had a direct hand in most matters, but the murders in Whitechapel. They are different, they have been orchestrated, designed to cause terror, to feed the presses, to create panic. The whole of the East End, nay, the city, is afeared,' said Agravain. 'I have been digging. Tristan, hand me that journal. No, under that one. Thank you.'

He flipped the pages to where he had cut out articles relating to the stabbing of Martha Tabram.

'I missed this in the first instance. She was killed after spending the evening with soldiers from the Tower of London.'

'Branok?' said Arthur.

'He slumbers still,' said Merlin, 'but I sense that the enchantment I placed over him, sealing him in, has been weakened somewhat.'

'I suspect Malagant is in league with Branok's followers. Perhaps Branok and Malagant were working together at the time of the plague and of the Great Fire, who knows?' said Agravain. 'I had meant to return to the Tower, but the last I remember is standing before it in the early hours, and a raven's call, then waking on the street days later.'

'We have long neglected Branok, and it seems his ravens may have not been as idle as he,' said Arthur.

'They cannot be killed, Arthur,' said Merlin, returning to the former king's side. 'They are naught but spirits in the form of flesh. They are bound to Branok.'

'What of Malagant?' said Arthur.

'A demon. Parasitic. Drawn up from the hells by your sister, perhaps?' said Merlin. 'Who can say? I have banished such creatures before, but he has been abroad longer than any of us, and if what Agravain says is true, he is feeding now. I do not know whether I can dismiss a creature of his power.'

'Nimuë believed that although she did not have the strength, you could bind him to a body and that Excalibur might dismiss him,' said Agravain, and the wizard scowled.

'We will find out,' said Arthur. 'Agravain, sleep while you can. Tonight we will pay Branok and his familiars a visit. At the very least, we will put a stop to the murders.'

―⁂―

Agravain led the way to the Tower, being the one to know the streets. He felt better for resting, the nausea had subsided and although his head still ached, he no longer felt feverish. He put the improvement down to Merlin's herbs, quite unaware that inside him, Malagant now lay dormant, quietly feeding, but less ravenously while he watched his plans unfurl, allowing him only the memories he wished the knight to recall.

Once they reached the Tower, Merlin did as

he had before, muttering arcane words and waving his hand so that the guards, seeming half-asleep, let the party enter unopposed.

Through the passages and down walkways they moved, until finally they stood before the White Tower.

'Show yourselves,' called Arthur, as Merlin closed his eyes and extended the fingers of one hand towards the Tower.

'The enchantment has significantly weakened,' said Merlin. 'It will not hold him as long as I had anticipated.'

A raven cawed above them, and the six familiars assembled on the South Lawn, each shifting into human form as they landed.

'We have come for Malagant,' said Arthur.

One of the ravens hopped forward, then, in a transformation so fast that it could barely be perceived, there was a young woman with jet-black hair, in a long, crimson dress, standing before them.

'The Dread Knight is not here,' Daisy cawed. 'Hello, Agravain.'

'We know of the murders,' said Agravain.

'Agravain, Agravain,' the assembled ravens cawed together. The knights shivered.

'What of them?' said Daisy.

'You had a hand in them?' asked Arthur.

'Perhaps,' she grinned. 'Watching and

waiting is so . . . dull, and Malagant asked so sweetly.'

'Be silent, foul spirit,' said Merlin, shouldering Arthur and Agravain aside. The wizard, shorter than the familiar, came to stand beneath her, and shook his staff under her nose.

'You cannot kill me, wizard,' said Daisy. 'I am already dead. Long dead. Dead and gone. Am I even here?'

She cawed, and while Agravain jumped, he saw that Merlin was unperturbed.

'I cannot kill you, but do not think that we will hesitate to kill your master. He was granted clemency out of pity, but I will dash that Tower to rocks so that Branok dies beneath them if it stops your mischief.'

Daisy tilted her head, her lips pouting and extending slightly into a beak then reforming as human lips. She cawed.

Merlin raised his staff, and Agravain felt the earth shudder beneath his feet. A cracking sound filled the air.

Daisy cawed again.

Behind her, the other five ravens took their human forms.

'Stop,' said Joseph.

'Enough,' said Martha.

'She does not do the master's bidding in this

matter. We will contain her if she will not agree to desist,' said Nathaniel. 'We will watch for the Ravenmaster's return as is our duty. No more. We will restrain our sister. The murders will stop.'

Daisy looked back over her shoulder, eyes entirely black. She turned to Merlin, then to Arthur and, finally, to Agravain.

To Agravain, she bowed.

'I suppose it was inevitable,' she cawed. 'I will remain here, but you may not stop Malagant so easily. The Order of Phobos and Deimos is everywhere. Still, at least I was entertained for a while, and it will not be so long until my master wakes.'

Before anyone could reply, she took a step backwards, wheeled and hurled herself skyward, transforming into a raven once more. Daisy flew up to the roof of the White Tower and perched there, looking down upon the assembled crowd, cawing incessantly.

'You will be true to your word?' asked Arthur.

'We will,' the familiars replied as one.

'Then our business is concluded,' said Arthur. The ravens hopped and flew away, dispersing about the Tower, leaving Arthur's company standing in the moonlight.

'It's done,' said Arthur.

'Not yet,' said Agravain. 'What of Malagant?'

Chapter Twenty-Seven

London
18th of October - 8th of November 1888

In the days after they gave Branok's familiars their ultimatum, Agravain, Arthur and Merlin worked to establish Malagant's whereabouts, debating how best to deal with him. In that time there were no more murders, and it seemed to Agravain that Arthur was growing restless and keen to leave the city. Agravain sent out tasks to informers, but they came back with less news than ever. It seemed that the Whitechapel Murders had concluded or, at least, they were in hiatus.

Tension grew as the days ticked on. One morning they were discussing the situation in the parlour when matters came to a head. Agravain had been suffering from a persistent migraine for several days and was feeling steadily more foolish because of Malagant's absence. Their discussion was interrupted by the doorbell. A baker from Whitechapel High Street had brought a report, but after Agravain's hopes were raised, they were quickly dashed. The report was as disappointing as they all had been of late. Agravain handed the man a shilling and sent him on his way.

'You've built quite the network here,' said Arthur. 'Butchers, bakers . . . '

'Candle-stick makers,' finished Tristan.

Agravain felt the criticism, and his patience was ragged, his vision blurry and his head aching thanks to the migraine.

'I've built quite a network, but?' he said.

'But to what end, Agravain? You stay informed of people's coming and goings, prevent many crimes, but far from all of them. Could your time not be better spent elsewhere?' asked Arthur.

'Better spent? Better than looking after the neglected and the needy? Your people?' asked Agravain, his voice rising in anger.

Arthur held up a hand.

'I do not mean to belittle your work, but it is on such a small scale, Agravain. While you have been gone we have served in many wars, influenced the fate of the nation, your brothers and I fought in the Revolutionary Wars, we fought Napoleon at Waterloo, took part in the Charge of the Light Brigade. We are fulfilling our destiny as warriors, serving England,' said Arthur. 'I would have had you at my right hand, brother,' said Arthur.

'I can hear the disdain in your voice,' said Agravain. 'You think nothing of my work here.'

'What have your works amounted to? You have nothing to show for any of it!' said Arthur. 'Come back with us and ride out again.'

'I cannot. I owe it to my people,' said Agravain.

'Your people? Londoners?' asked Arthur. 'You take the capital as your own fiefdom, is that correct?'

'You speak treason,' said Tristan. 'You have a duty to Arthur and to the rest of us.'

'I have a duty to those who cannot protect themselves. I watch over them as best I can with the resources I have available to me. Perhaps I could do it all the better if you concerned yourselves with the actual lives of the people you claim to care about, but you are too concerned with the broad strokes, Arthur! You are playing at king in the shadows, when you could be making a tangible difference to the lives of the people on the lowest rung of society's ladder.'

No sooner had the words 'playing at king' left Agravain's lips than Tristan strode towards him. He struck out with his right hand, but

Agravain caught his wrist, ducked under his arm and drove his elbow into Tristan's solar plexus. His brother knight's lungs emptied and as Tristan doubled over, Agravain stepped behind his right leg, wrapped his left hand around Tristan's throat and hurled him backwards. Tristan fell over Agravain's leg and crashed on to his back.

'True warriors you must be, if you can be bested by a street dweller like me!' shouted Agravain, and he lashed out with his right elbow as he felt a hand upon his shoulder. He felt it connect and turned to see Arthur reel backwards, clutching his broken nose.

His stomach swirled and the anger flowed through him, a red mist obscured his vision, an imperceptible laugh echoing inside his mind, and he staggered back as Tristan leapt to his feet.

Agravain reached into his jacket and levelled his revolver at Tristan's chest.

'Stay back,' he said, pulling back the hammer.

Arthur, still clutching his nose with one hand, stepped forward and pushed back on Tristan's chest.

'Enough. We have outstayed our welcome, it seems,' he said, and he walked out into the hall.

Tristan stood panting, head lowered, scowling, looking as though he would pounce at any moment, but when Arthur called his name from the hall, he straightened up, shook his head and followed.

Agravain holstered the revolver, crossed the room and slammed the parlour door, panic rising in him.

What have I done?

Inside him, Malagant fed.

Agravain leant with both hands against the back of the door for a minute, listening to the commotion of the knights arguing and moving things on the other side. He was gripped with a sudden terror that he had betrayed his king, committed treason and was now to be forever exiled, utterly sundered from Arthur's company.

He dashed out into the hall to find Arthur still standing there, holding a handkerchief to his bloody nose as the knights busied past him, carrying bags out into the street.

'Sire, I . . . '

But Arthur held up his hand.

'We have both spoken with little thought and less compassion. Rash action indeed,' he said. 'It is for the best that we go, Agravain. We are on different paths, but you may call on me again, if you are in great need,' he said. 'I trust you will come if summoned.'

Agravain nodded and watched as his brothers, unwilling to look him in the eye, departed his home and life.

He would not see any of them again for decades.

London
8th of November 1888
4.00am

There is nothing more potent than the terror of a powerful man.

Agravain started awake, drawing in a sharp breath as he sat up in bed, Malagant's words still ringing in his ears.

He cradled the elbow that had broken Arthur's nose, running his fingertips across his knuckles then reaching to the other side of the bed, running his hand over the vacant spot where Nimuë had lain.

And should lie still, he thought.

His bedroom was dark and cold, like his life, Agravain thought in that moment.

He lay back down, turning on his side, closed his eyes and attempted to sleep.

It begins today, said Malagant from inside his head, but Agravain did not register the thought as he drifted away. His eyelids fluttered, but he did not wake.

He did not wake for many, many hours, and when he finally did, the sun was already high in the sky. He could barely open his eyes, although only a sliver of daylight was shining across his pillow. He poured himself a glass of water from the jug on his bedside table, and, after opening the curtains, his headache began to fade. He began to feel more himself again.

Agravain grabbed his upper arm where the muscles ached. His whole arm felt stiff, and even after massaging it up and down for several minutes, it did not loosen up.

He readied himself some coffee and, too nauseous to eat, he put on his hat, coat and boots and went out to fetch a newspaper.

Agravain yawned frequently on the way to the news stand, where the seller tipped his hat upon seeing him.

'Ello Mr Marlow, sir. I missed you yesterday!' he said, reaching down and bringing up two parcels of newspapers, both tied with string. 'Today's and yesterday's as well, sir. Unless you bought yesterday's elsewhere?' he said, not quite able to sustain eye contact, attempting to look as though he did not feel betrayed.

'I bought my usual bundle on this very spot yesterday morning!' said Agravain.

The seller frowned.

'Why, here's the bundle here, Mr Marlow? I

remember saying to myself, 'this ain't like Mr Marlow, missing his morning reading!' Perhaps you forgot though, sir. Comes with age, that sort of thing,' he concluded.

Agravain paid the man his due for both bundles despite feeling he had quite lost his mind, mostly as he liked the fellow, and he did not wish to call him a liar.

The mystery deepened, however, when he got home and saw that he did not recognise the headlines on the top of the second bundle, and yet he was sure he had been to get the newspapers. He used a small knife to cut the string binding the newspapers and found to his surprise that all of the news articles were quite unfamiliar. He did the same with the second bundle just in case he had muddled them, but no. Frowning, unable to understand, he scanned the dates of the newspapers. The 8th and 9th of November 1888. But yesterday was the 7th? He fetched the top newspaper from the stack on his desk and sure enough, there was the newspaper from the 7th, its front page filled with articles Agravain remembered reading.

He sat down in his wingback chair, utterly confused. Yesterday was the 7th. He had bought newspapers and read them. That was evident from their presence on his desk. Allegedly, though, he had missed buying his bundle on the 8th. But today was the 8th! And yet it couldn't be, for here were the newspapers dated the 9th.

Agravain felt as though he was going quite mad, and his headache returned with a vengeance. Dark spots danced before his eyes, so he closed them and tried to ignore the whooshing of blood in his ears. Once he had calmed himself a little, still feeling out of sorts, he picked up the newspapers and, feeling quite alien to himself, a stranger in a strange land, he began to read.

Before an hour had passed, quite exhausted, he fell asleep in his chair.

◆

Banging at the door. Agravain woke with a start and dashed to answer in his confused state.

A policeman was standing on his doorstep, a man in his 30s with a prodigious handlebar moustache. PC Davis.

'Good afternoon, sir,' he said. 'Sorry to trouble you, but Inspector Abberline wanted a message passed.'

Agravain glanced at his pocket watch. Four in the afternoon. Impossible. He had slept most of the day away.

'What message is that, William?' he asked.

'There's been another, sir. One Mary Jane

Kelly of . . . ' he paused to consult his notebook, ' . . . of 13 Millers Court in Spitalfields. Off Dorset Street. D'you know it, sir?'

Agravain nodded. He knew Millers Court. One of his informers, Liz Prater, lived upstairs.

'Thank you for taking the time to come and see me, William. Can you tell me anything else?'

'Not me, sir. Just the errand boy. Any message in return, sir?' asked the constable.

'Only that I will be there directly,' said Agravain, and bade the policeman farewell.

The Ripper had struck again. Not one of the raven familiars nor under their influence, surely, with Branok under threat?

A stabbing pain in his head developed as he thought about it. Agravain rubbed his temple and went to fetch his things.

His arm being so stiff, he struggled to pull on his coat, but in just a few minutes, he had set off towards Millers Court.

Abberline and Agravain shook hands as they walked towards the scene. It seemed that 13 Millers Court was on the ground floor, just below Liz Prater's room as it turned out. It had a single window, partly broken, and a door to the street. Agravain felt a chill creeping over him as he walked, and he blinked as a light-headed feeling came over him. He felt somehow drawn to the room, a physical pull on his body, no more than a light tug, but it was there, even if he did not quite perceive it as such.

'Another resident of this damned place saw Kelly just before midnight, bidding her goodnight,' said Abberline. 'She says she was in the company of a stout, ginger-haired man in a bowler hat when she went in. She was heard singing after midnight, but the lady upstairs, Elizabeth Prater, says she had stopped by one in the morning. She heard a cry of 'Murder' around four in the morning, but thought nothing of it. You hear that a lot around these parts, as you know. She did nothing about it and went out herself at around half past five.'

Abberline pulled out a notebook and consulted before continuing.

'The landlord's assistant, Thomas Bowyer, put in a knock about quarter to eleven this morning, but got no answer so he reached through the broken window to pull the coat she used as a curtain aside, and he saw her, poor soul. He was quite put out.'

'She died between one and quarter to eleven this morning then?' said Agravain.

'Near as it can be pinned down, doctor thinks about half past four. Prater thought she heard someone leaving about quarter to six this morning. Presumably after she got back from her bit of rum.'

'Same method?' asked Agravain.

'Far worse,' said Abberline. 'I shall never forget the sight.'

He recounted the details and a rising horror grew in Agravain until he felt as though he must ask the inspector for a moment, but the narrative drew to a close and the policeman offered to show him inside the room.

As soon as he stepped through the door, Agravain began to suffer a panic attack, his eyes wide, his breathing rapid and sweat dripping off his forehead. He thought he might pass out and was turning to leave when he caught sight of the fireplace. A sudden image of a fire in the now-empty grate filled his mind, a fire fuelled by a bloody shirt and trousers. A fire that burned so hot that it melted the solder securing the kettle's spout. The damaged article lay there still.

Agravain massaged the muscles of his stiff arm as he ducked back out into the street.

'Are you alright?' asked Abberline.

'I have not been well these past few days,' said Agravain, 'Do excuse me for a moment.'

'Of course, Marlow,' said the inspector.

Agravain walked away from Millers Court and headed to the Ten Bells on the corner of

Commercial Street and Fournier Street with the intention of getting a drink to steady his nerves.

He ordered a brandy at the bar and had just set down his empty glass and ordered another when he saw Elizabeth Prater eyeing him from a table on the far side of the room.

When she realised she was caught, Prater leapt up and hurried towards the door. Agravain darted after her and caught her before she could leave.

'Liz?'

She turned to face him, but backed away a step, not allowing him to come too close.

'Good day, sir,' she said.

'What's the matter?' he asked.

'Nothing at all, Mr Marlow,' said Prater. 'You've always been a friend to me, sir.'

'What are you talking about, Liz?' asked Agravain, frowning. 'Come and have a rum with me? You look frightened half to death.'

It took some cajoling, but the promise of a drink or two eventually lured Prater back to the table.

'I'm sorry about Mary,' said Agravain once they were settled at a table.

Prater took a swig of her drink, not meeting his eye.

'You told the police you went to bed at half past one, but were out by half past five, and heard someone leave about quarter to six, is that right? Is there anything else you can tell me, Liz, that might help us find the man responsible?'

'Who would know better than you?' she said, seemingly finding the courage to lock eyes with him, 'seeing as I more than heard who left just before six this morning.'

She lifted her glass in a trembling hand to drain her glass.

'And now I'm a dead woman,' she said, setting it down again and biting her lower lip as she met his eye.

'I don't understand,' he said, but he was beginning to, in his heart.

She leaned in.

'I won't say a word to the police. I didn't yet, did I?' she said. 'You've been good to me. I won't tell no-one it was you who left Mary's place this morning, you have my word.'

Agravain sat back so fast his chair tipped on two legs. His head swam and vision blurred. He rocked back down and massaged his right arm once more.

'You saw me this morning,' he whispered.

'I didn't see nothing,' she assured him.

'Liz, tell me,' he said, but it took a few more minutes of sipping and denials before she finally relented, nodding when he asked again.

'Aye, I saw you as I came back from me morning tot in this place,' she said.

'Did we speak?' he asked.

'Don't you remember?' she asked, and he shook his head.

'No, sir. You were right stern and off with me, but your eyes, they was blood-red, not a hint of white, and you had this macabre grin on your lips, Mr Marlow. For a minute, I thought you was a devil. And then I heard about poor Mary. To think what she went through right under me as I slept,' said Prater, beginning to weep.

Agravain looked around, unable to process the information.

Would you like to remember, John? asked Malagant from inside his head.

And Agravain remembered.

Everything.

Chapter Twenty-Eight

*London
1888*

'Mr Marlow?' said Liz Prater, as Agravain stood then staggered, forcing him to steady himself by leaning on the table with one hand as he clutched his head with another. He said nothing to Liz, blinking and massaging his temples, and when he looked up, he saw Prater had slid along the bench.

'I won't say a word,' she said, people closing in behind her, drawn by the commotion.

Agravain tried to concentrate, but images of his own hands butchering Mary Jane Kelly the previous night, the blood, the gore, the entrails, intruded into his waking thoughts. He remembered throwing some of her organs into the fire, as well as his outer clothes, which had acted as a disguise. He held up a hand, wincing as though struck by a terrible migraine, signalling for Prater to stay, but as soon as she was off the bench, she hurried through the assembling crowd to the door.

Agravain started to shout after her, but once more the image of Kelly on the bed intruded, the blood on his hands, and he vomited, bent double over the table. Ignoring the angry shouts of the landlord, Agravain barged his way to the door and out into the street. His entire body shook, wracked with fear, and he wandered aimlessly, sweat pouring from his brow.

Delicious, said Malagant inside Agravain's mind, *but perhaps that's enough for now, John.*

One moment, Agravain was a wreck, looking every inch the drunken madman, breathing hard, sweating and mumbling incoherently, the traumatic memories dominating and overrunning his mind, the next his mind was clear. He turned on the spot, halfway across Whitechapel High Street, then had to dart aside to avoid a horse and cart, the carman shouting a warning.

He remembered being in the pub with Liz Prater, but how had he got out into the street?

Agravain started back towards the pub, thinking perhaps Liz was still there. There were many outstanding enquiries regarding the murder of Mary Jane Kelly.

No, you're done with this particular investigation, John, said Malagant directly to

Agravain's subconscious. *You have other business now.*

Agravain came to a standstill. The Ripper killings seemed to no longer hold his interest. He turned and began walking back towards home, disturbed by the taste of vomit in his mouth.

You've spent so long hunting me, John, and now you've found me, it's time we got away together. You've spent far too long haunting the streets of London. We're going to travel, John, expand your education as I did before returning to London. We're going to take the Grand Tour of Europe! And then beyond. And unlike my previous hosts, you do not age or die! We can stay together forever if fate dictates it, and in time, we'll go after Arthur, when he once again has something he cares about enough to fear losing. Until then, we'll go wherever terror reigns, and I will ride you into battle, John, my trusty steed. But first . . .

Agravain whistled as he passed out of the East End and returned home, where he began to pack up his belongings, taking special care to load his journals into their own case.

He settled in his chair and turned the pages of the latest journal, perusing the names, addresses and details of his many descendants, at least, those that he had managed to track down.

But suddenly he could no longer control his hands. Agravain watched as they continued turning the pages, he tried to move, to stand, to look around, but all he could do was watch through his own eyes like a ghost trapped in a jar.

Then he was in Mary Jane Kelly's room once more, murdering her, tearing at her organs. He couldn't react with his body. Couldn't cry out. Couldn't close his eyes or shove the images aside, as Malagant allowed him access to his own memories.

'Remember their names, John,' said Malagant with Agravain's voice as he inspected the journal, 'they'll all be dead before long, and there is nothing, nothing, that you can do to stop it.'

Agravain watched, helpless, the long descent to madness beginning, unable to sob, or feel what emotion does to a body. Some posit that when a body feels pain, it is processed in the brain, but diverted back to the site of the injury, both to warn of the danger to the area and to protect the brain from feeling the sensation itself. Agravain's mind could not help but process everything it was seeing, feeling and fearing, unable to cry, shake or sweat. He lived within his emotion.

Malagant sat back in the chair, savouring

the torment and terror.

Later that afternoon, there was a knock at the door, and Agravain was carried with Malagant to answer it.

John Kelly and Dr Francis Tumblety were at the door.

'Gentlemen!' said Malagant. 'I have a gift for you.'

The Dread Knight handed Agravain's journal to Kelly.

'Make copies and distribute them to all existing members of the Order. Give them out to all new recruits. Let it be known that I will pay handsomely for every name I can erase from this book. Make them suffer,' he said.

No, thought Agravain, *I'll kill you, Malagant. Do not touch them.*

Malagant ignored him and continued to speak with the men on the doorstep.

Agravain fought to exert his will, straining to move his limbs, but there was a disconnect he could not overcome.

'Quiet down, John,' said Malagant after bidding Kelly and Tumblety goodbye, closing the door behind them. 'You are in no position to . . . ' but Malagant stumbled and nearly fell as Agravain's concentration won through for a moment.

He straightened up, and Agravain, profoundly

relieved that he had some measure of control and for a moment, without fear, felt Malagant scowl.

'Goodbye, John. I'll let you know when I need you,' said Malagant.

The light began to dim, and Agravain's fear soared once more as Malagant shoved him deeper into his own mind, his field of vision narrowing, as though dropped into a dark pit until finally, he saw nothing, he heard nothing and all he could do was think, worry and feel.

'There is nothing more potent than the terror of a powerful man,' said Malagant.

The next morning, two of the Order arrived and loaded his luggage on to a carriage. Malagant climbed inside. After a few hours, he brought Agravain closer to the surface so he was able to see and hear once more, his memories intact.

Malagant turned his head to look through the window, and Agravain could see fields all around, that London was already far behind them. Malagant fished the journal from his pocket.

'I thought you should see this,' he said, turning the pages. 'My people brought news this morning.'

He found the right page, and to Agravain's horror, he saw that three of the names there had fresh lines drawn through them, a young mother and her sons.

Sorrow, anger and terror raged within him, and as he struggled, he heard his own laugh filling the carriage.

'Until we meet again,' said Malagant, and for Agravain, the world faded away once again.

⸻

Over the coming years, Malagant allowed Agravain to perceive the world only when it suited him or if he needed to feed on the knight's emotions. He remained in the dark as the world changed, and, in his own arena of investigation, he missed such developments as iodine fuming, which allowed fingerprint lifts to be transferred to paper so that crime scene lifts and suspect fingerprints could be compared. For the most part, when he was allowed to see, Agravain was only permitted to see the pages of his own journal as Malagant crossed off another name. He had no concept of where he was or how he got there.

On occasion, Malagant would force Agravain to watch as he committed some horrible crime using his hands, feeding on not only the victim, but on his host as he did so. He glimpsed strange streets, clothing he did not recognise, heard languages he did not understand.

He felt the heat of southern climes, saw starvation in dusty lands and took part in foreign wars, sometimes allowed full control of his body in the midst of a battle after a period of sensory deprivation, leaving him disorientated, panicking and fighting for his life while Malagant enjoyed him. On one such occasion, Agravain attempted to turn his gun on himself, but Malagant wrested back control, and the last thing Agravain heard was the Dread Knight scolding him before he was thrown back into the dark, wondering whether his body would survive, and if not, whom Malagant would move on to next.

※

England
August 1916 - One month after the Battle of the Somme.
Arthur has been sent back to England, his leg injured on the same day that Gaheris, Galahad and Lamorak were killed.

A garden. Sweet scent in the air. Blossoming trees. Agravain pinched the bridge of his nose, feeling momentarily faint. He looked up to find a path before his feet, leading to the door of a cottage he did not recognise. Where was he? How had he got here? He tried to remember.

That doesn't matter, said Malagant directly to his subconscious, slamming up the defensive walls. *I thought you might like to see something. Focus, John.*

Agravain felt his limbs moving unbidden and, dazed, he watched as a bystander while Malagant knocked on the cottage door. It swung open, and a young woman stepped into view. It appeared she recognised him, as she bowed her head and let him pass.

Agravain continued to observe, absorbing details as Malagant took him up the stairs before coming to a stop before a door. Malagant knocked once and, not waiting for an answer, he pushed the door open.

Agravain's mind cried out as he saw Arthur, pale and with black circles under his eyes, lying in a bed, covered with a blanket despite the summer heat, his injured leg elevated. Arthur looked towards him, and Agravain saw the former king's eyes immediately fill with tears.

Arthur tried to speak, but his voice broke, and he covered his eyes with his forearm as he began to sob. Malagant made Agravain watch, saying nothing, while Arthur composed himself.

'I'm sorry. Just to see you here, at this time, I . . . '

Malagant stepped up to the bedside, and Agravain could feel the Dread Knight's glee as he feigned compassion.

'I came as soon as I heard about you and our

brothers, sire,' said Malagant, with Agravain's voice.

Arthur reached up and gripped his hand, but as he did so, Malagant pushed Agravain under, down into the dark where he saw and heard nothing, bereft to see Arthur injured, not understanding what had happened or which of the knights had been lost. He quailed, and he heard Malagant's distant laugh.

He awoke some time later and saw he was standing at the open door of Arthur's bedroom. The former king thrashed and turned in bed, speaking in his sleep. Malagant grinned and drew red smoke from Arthur's body.

Perhaps we'll stay a while, said Malagant, *while his knights are still abroad.*

It was the last Agravain heard before he was denied his senses one more. He sank into unknowing, filled with dread and sadness, with only Malagant for company.

◈

Sussex, England
1941

'I knew trusting you was a mistake,' Tristan said in a low growl as he massaged his jaw.

Agravain stumbled forward, and his brother knight reacted without hesitation. Tristan's fist caught him under his chin, and Agravain's head snapped back. He crashed into the dirt. Branches swayed above him.

'Why did you come back if you think so little of our king?' asked Tristan, looming over him. He was dressed in Home Guard uniform and carrying a Sten gun.

'He's a coward,' Agravain heard Malagant say with his voice. 'Too afraid to fight. The King of the Britons, an air raid warden?' The Dread Knight laughed.

Tristan aimed the gun at Agravain's chest.

'Say it again,' said Tristan, and Agravain saw that his brother's anger was barely contained. He fought to assert control, but Malagant suppressed him once more.

⁂

Agravain awoke to see the Nazis in Paris, and again while working in a concentration camp.

He walked beside a mass grave on one occasion, watched children separated from their families as they stepped down from trains on arrival at the camps. He smelled the burning flesh and saw the smoke pouring from the camp chimneys.

⁂

Omaha Beach, Normandy, France
6th of June 1944 - D-Day

Agravain found himself in hell, or so he thought until he recovered his senses. Shouts and explosions, the rattle of the machine-gun he was manning from his high position as he fired at soldiers running up a sandy beach, steel warships visible in the distance in the sea beyond. He stopped firing and looked around him, unable to understand his German colleagues. Agravain dashed out of the bunker, could hear the rounds zipping through the air all around, and he charged towards the beach, hoping to be cut down.

No, John, said Malagant, and Agravain slowed to a jog, then a walk, he ducked behind a sandbank as Malagant took back control of his body. Agravain fought back, struggling with the Dread Knight. He pushed back against the bank and was on his feet once more. He took one step, two steps, before Malagant struck his mind a savage blow that sent him hurtling back into the void.

⁂

The glimpses at the journal became less frequent as the years passed by, and although the killings continued, exposing the knight to all manner of trauma, compounding his own fears, he was seldom allowed control of his body again after his successful attempt at resisting on Omaha Beach.

Malagant took him to Vietnam in 1957 and on into China as millions died in Mao Tse Tung's Great Leap Forward. The tour continued.

༺═══════════༻

Tuesday 28th of January 1986

Agravain came back to consciousness to find he was sitting on a comfortable sofa in the living-room of a strangely decorated house with toys strewn across the floor. His arm was around the shoulders of a blonde woman in her thirties. Disorientated, Agravain tried to pull away, but only managed to twitch, and the woman looked up at him, tears streaming down her cheeks.

'It's awful,' she said, and looked back across the room at a wood-cased television, which was showing a news report. A vehicle Agravain did not recognise, could scarcely comprehend, the space shuttle Challenger, was rocketing through the sky towards space before a sudden explosion filled the screen. The coverage switched to photographs of the astronauts who had been aboard. Agravain ceased struggling, wondering where he was as he watched the coverage of the disaster, as the woman beside him spoke of the poor families. When Agravain attempted to stand, Malagant pushed him under the dark waters once more.

The next time he was allowed to see, that same television was covering the Chernobyl disaster in April of the same year. This time the blonde woman was standing, hands on her hips, pausing as she went about some task to watch the coverage.

She's one of yours, by the way, John, whispered Malagant in Agravain's mind, *in more ways than one now. If that seems wrong, there is no cause for concern, I'll be done with her before long.*

Agravain struggled against Malagant as the Dread Knight tried to suppress him, but his own revulsion at the revelation, his own fear empowered his foe, and he felt his control beginning to dwindle. He concentrated as hard as he was able, and managed a certain degree of control.

Agravain stood and hurried across the room to the only door he could see. He ignored the shout of the woman behind him and ran out into the street, where cars rushed by. Agravain ran for the road, unable to choose his time carefully, he hurled himself out, hoping to be hit by one of the vehicles. Brakes screeched and there was a scream, but as Agravain felt the skin of his arms and legs tear on the road surface, he saw a car had swerved round him. The wind went out of him, and Malagant took hold once more.

―――

Agravain remained trapped, hidden, while the world moved on; as the first man was convicted in the UK on the basis of DNA evidence in 1988 and as technology advanced. He fell behind, outdated, though he didn't know it.

―――

New York
October 2001

Agravain was sitting in a car the next time his senses returned. He was in the rear seat and the driver was chattering away about something in a familiar, but unexpected, American accent.

Good morning, thought Malagant. *We've taken a little trip across the pond, John, and I thought you might like to see our latest hunting ground. We might not stay long, given how well-armed the local constabulary are, but since the Twin Towers were brought down, the Americans have engaged in a War on Terror. How delightful! I can taste it in the air.*

<hr>

Agravain witnessed more murders, more killings, perceived with no agency as in a dream. He managed the briefest moments of control, but Malagant had learnt from his rebellions, and only allowed Agravain out when the deed was almost done, and once he no longer had a weapon to hand. He adapted his methods, reducing the risk should Agravain regain control.

It had been over a century since Malagant had possessed Agravain's body, spending that time fully awake, but hidden in a locked room deep within his own mind, the door guarded. He dwelt in his memories, the viewings of countless killings, so many wars, so much fear, panic and terror as Malagant made his way through the world. He tried to think back on his fond memories, to remember the faces of his children, Nimuë's touch, his years of service to Arthur, the brotherhood of his fellow knights, but the flashbacks came to dominate his mind, as he constantly relived his trauma, until he visualised himself as nearly naked save for bare rags, clutching his knees and rocking back and forth within a locked cell, eyes wide in the pitch black.

But a thought took hold, the tiniest chinks of light in the door, the most occluded of views through the broad bars in his window. Agravain worked away in silence as a man might dig at the floor of his cell.

July 2009

Agravain opened his eyes. He lay on his side, under a blanket on a comfortable bed, with a painted wall a few inches from his face. He made no attempt to move, listening for Malagant.

Nothing.

He concentrated and his lips parted. Emboldened, but cautious, Agravain stretched his fingers out then curled them into fists. He started to roll onto his back, but he sensed Malagant stir, so he ceased the attempt and enjoyed being in control of his own body for however short a time.

I cannot take back control when he has summoned me out, but I can slip out from my prison while he thinks me suppressed, Agravain realised.

From time to time, between glimpses of

Malagant's crimes, views of gloved hands, of his own eyes peering out from behind a balaclava caught in reflective surfaces, Agravain would once more sneak back into his body, finding that if he kept his thoughts under control, he could ride along with Malagant without him knowing.

*

1st of February 2010

Skulking, sidling, formless and with his mind as clear as his constant meditation would allow, Agravain drifted to the surface unnoticed, a drop of water moving through water.

The light grew brighter and muffled sounds audible.

Agravain was walking down a busy street, a man at his side with whom Malagant was conversing.

At first, Agravain could make no sense of their talk, and he tried not to think at all, simply watching and listening, eager to learn all he could.

The pair were passing through a crowd of people, and Agravain recognised the accent.

London, he thought. Malagant frowned and stopped briefly.

Agravain shrank back into the mental shadows.

'Sir?' said the man beside him.

Malagant looked around him, moving to the side of the pavement, putting his back to the wall of a shop.

'I feel as though we are being watched,' said Malagant.

'No worries there, sir,' said the man, grinning. He opened his coat, and Agravain saw the handle of a knife, its pommel adorned with a red eye.

Now! Agravain decided, leaping into full control of his body, taking Malagant by surprise. He thrust his hand forward, snatching the knife from its sheath in a reverse grip before the cultist could react.

Malagant roared inside Agravain's mind, but the knight held his resolve, driven by fury at all he had been subjected to, all he had been made to do, all the losses he had been forced to endure.

Agravain buried the knife deep in the man's throat again and again and again, as people screamed all around. Malagant surged back toward the surface himself, and Agravain could feel himself being dragged back down, but he fought the Dread Knight off mentally, even as he threw the dying cultist to the ground.

Someone rushed forward and seized him by the wrist. Agravain kept hold of the knife, but made no attempt to attack his assailant.

'He deserved it,' Agravain shouted as a large man rugby-tackled him to the ground. The breath rushed out of him, and as more people piled onto him, Agravain struggled to breathe. As sirens grew louder, Agravain lay still and passed out while those atop him shouted at him not to move.

He came back to consciousness only briefly as steel handcuffs secured his hands together behind his back.

'You'll regret that,' said Malagant to him aloud. 'I'll make sure of it.'

And as two police officers dragged him to his feet, Malagant pushed Agravain back under.

⁂

They took Malagant before the custody sergeant, and the Dread Knight smiled, meek as a lamb, as he listened to the arresting officer give the circumstances. He quietly accepted it when the sergeant authorised his detention and provided his name as John Marlow.

He co-operated fully while in custody, happily giving Agravain's fingerprints and DNA when required, which would, as the investigation progressed, connect him to a series of unsolved murders in the UK. Agravain remained hidden, determined to give as little away to Malagant as possible until the moment presented itself.

It was only once the matter had gone to trial and Agravain had been convicted on eleven counts of murder, that Malagant brought Agravain to the surface.

The knight awoke in the cell that would be his home for years to come.

'You put us here,' Malagant said with Agravain's voice. 'So you can enjoy it.'

'Happily,' said Agravain, seeming to talk to himself, 'if it keeps you off the streets.'

'I can bide my time, John,' said Malagant. 'I have my people on the outside, working away. Ticking the names off your list. I'm sure there is enough fear within a prison's walls to sustain me, never mind that which you emanate whenever you think of our adventures together. And you do not age, John. One day they will release you.'

Agravain said nothing.

'There will be a reckoning,' said Malagant. 'With you and with Arthur, once you have suffered enough.'

'Count on it,' said Agravain.

Malagant fell silent, leaving the knight alone in his cell. Agravain let out a sigh and began to pace the cell, happy to be in control of his body once more.

Twenty years, thought Agravain. *Perhaps they'll let me have a book?*

He sat on the edge of his bed, preparing to make the best of it, but his memories began to plague him. Suddenly he was back in Mary Jane Kelly's room. He could feel her skin on his fingertips. Then he was watching the corpses of the innocent tumble into the mass graves at Belsen. His body shook, he sweated and he cried out, clutching his knees.

You'll be here for decades, thought Malagant. *Ask for a book if you think it will help you.*

Chapter Twenty-Nine

Runbridge, England
2021

In the rear of the car, Bors and Gareth leapt forward to take hold of Agravain's body, pinning him back, but Arthur could see that Malagant was offering no resistance. Nimuë sat as far away from him as she could.

'Where is she?' asked Arthur, caught between fury, shock, concern for Caitlyn and concern for Agravain as a thousand realisations dawned.

Malagant rested his head back against the seat and closed his eyes.

'Are you asking for a chance to save her?' asked Malagant.

'Of course,' said Arthur.

'The same chance you gave me to save Morgana?' His eyes shot open, and it was as though he had gripped Arthur by the back of the neck, hauling him forward without moving a muscle.

Bors crunched his left elbow into Agravain's throat, but Malagant did not react at all, just turned to look at Bors.

'I always wondered why Arthur thought you deserved to sit at the Round Table when your mind is so feeble,' he sneered as he spoke. 'I don't feel his pain, you idiot. Agravain will though. See?'

Agravain lurched, his throat in spasm as his senses came back to him. He coughed, struggling to breath, eyes wide as he looked frantically between first Gareth, then Bors and then Arthur.

'Kill me, Arthur,' he managed to say between coughs as his gaze came to rest on Nimuë. His voice was ragged and hoarse, rising to a shout. 'You don't know what I've done!'

Fear rose in Arthur.

'Where's Caitlyn? What's he done with her?' he asked.

'He won't let me remember,' said Agravain. He turned to Nimuë once more. 'Please, if it's in your power, destroy him,' he pleaded, and a tear escaped the corner of his eye.

'John,' she whispered, and she closed her eyes, extending her hand towards him.

'Where is she?' demanded Bors.

'I don't . . . ' Agravain started to say, but he stopped mid-sentence and the smile crept back. He tilted his head to one side, considering Nimuë.

'Is it in your power?' he asked. 'Did Merlin teach you well enough, enchantress?' The Dread Knight stuck out his lower lip in a pout. 'I don't think he did, you poor thing. Helplessly watching as I devour your lover from the inside out, manipulating his every waking moment. Do you know how many children your children had? How many children's children's children there should have been? Have you any idea just how many John has managed to kill with his meticulous record-keeping? I've all but eradicated your legacy,' said Malagant. 'Though there is still work to do.'

Arthur saw Nimuë's cheeks reddening as she scowled. She was trembling, clenching and unclenching her fists.

'Caitlyn is an innocent, Malagant, as Morgana never was,' said Arthur, trying to keep his voice level in an attempt to sound calm. 'We were at war a very, very long time ago. Tell me where she is and put an end to this.'

'And then what? I'm required to relinquish Agravain, leaving him in your tender care? The king who forsook him, the knights who resent him and the woman who abandoned him? I'm the only one who stayed, Arthur,' Malagant laughed. 'He already told you to kill him! And somehow, I don't think you'll want me wandering around in his body. Are you going to let me occupy another host? No, there is literally nothing you can do for me,' Malagant concluded. 'Your woman will die at a time of my choosing and until then, I will harvest you, King Arthur, and make you pay for what you and what this one,' he prodded his chest, 'did to my mistress and the child in her belly.'

'I don't understand why you are doing this now, after all this time,' said Arthur.

Malagant laughed.

'I have been quite content torturing John, taking him to see all the sights over the years and then, thanks to his petulant nature, watching him waste years in a cell, but since Merlin died and his enchantment ended, poor old John has begun aging, and so have you, and that means we are on the clock, so to speak. Ticking down towards the end. We had to get out,' said Malagant.

'You sent the letter, imitating the Ripper?' said Nimuë, then frowned as Malagant started chuckling.

'Which Ripper?' he said. 'Daisy? Tumblety? Kelly? Kosminski? Kidney? Or perhaps, John himself?'

They stared at him, saying nothing, not knowing what to say, and Malagant filled the silence.

'I had the letter sent, yes, and withheld poor John's memories long enough for him to seek escape and to draw Arthur's attention. To draw you. To bring us all together,' he said. 'I could have escaped on my own, of course, but I gave him just enough control that he escaped himself, so that he would be responsible for all that followed. The irony is the Order and I have already killed a great many of his descendants. The list I gave him were just a few of those who remain, though they too will be erased.'

'And now you plan on sitting there, gleeful at the thought of my fear and an innocent woman's suffering?' asked Arthur.

'That,' said Malagant, 'is what I do. So yes, keep scheming and planning, thinking of some way you can turn this in your favour, but the reality is, if you kill John, I'll simply possess one of you, unless the good lady here seriously surpasses any expectation I have of her, and if you attempt to, how do you say, exorcise me, there's every chance John will crumble away to nothing as did my previous host. If you let me live as I am? You condemn John to a lifetime of servitude and trauma, locked away in here, and I will never, never, tell you where your girlfriend is stowed,' said Malagant. 'She will die, Arthur.'

'If you will let them go, I will surrender to you, Malagant. I will be your new host, and you may do with me what you will. Just let her go, and do not harm Agravain or his kin,' said Arthur.

'Such a noble gesture,' Malagant nodded, but Arthur could see he was being mocked as the skin around the Dread Knight's eyes crinkled. 'I might be persuaded.'

Nimuë hurled herself forward, gripping Agravain's head in both hands, crying out as she did so, and Arthur saw the pain and fury in her eyes. She brought her head down so that her forehead and Agravain's smashed together with a cracking sound that made the others wince. The thrumming power hit Arthur like a series of waves, each one sending him closer and closer to sleep, but he fought the impulse, blinking it away, readying himself.

'Hold him,' he hissed as Malagant cried out, Agravain's eyes once more hollow sockets, but this time the red smoke poured from them in a billowing plume. It wreathed up around Nimuë's arms until they were completely obscured, she began to groan and cry out.

'She's ripping him out,' said Bors. 'What do we do?'

Agravain flung out his hand and gripped Bors by the wrist so hard that the burly knight let out a gasp as the bone slightly fractured.

Nimuë's groans escalated into a scream as she disappeared in a haze of red smoke which filled the car, energy crackling around her and the pounding, thrumming growing in intensity, each wave coming faster.

Agravain kicked and thrashed, his skin draining of all

colour, veins turning black as Nimuë drew Malagant out of his body.

'She's killing him,' said Gareth.

'It's what he wanted,' said Bors, looking down at the hand gripping his wrist and then up at Arthur.

'Agravain!' Arthur shouted. 'Can you hear me?'

Agravain reached out with his other hand, and Arthur saw him caress Nimuë's cheek, even as the flesh turned white.

'Where is she?' Arthur was forced to shout over Nimuë's screams.

Nimuë pushed with all of her might with both hands, driving Agravain's head back against the headrest, the red smoke rushed back towards his body, disappearing into it through his skin, his eyes and his mouth, and Agravain's head fell to one side as colour returned to his skin. Nimuë slumped over him, remaining prone for an instant then raised her head and shook Agravain by both shoulders.

'John! Wake up, you have to wake up,' she said.

Agravain's eyelids fluttered then opened wide, and he gasped, chest rising and falling.

'Is he gone?' he asked.

'No, and we must be quick,' said Nimuë. 'He is locked away in your mind as you have been, but I do not know for how long. You must bind him within for as long as you can! Hold him under! Arthur, get us back to the house now!'

'We must know where he is keeping Caitlyn!' said Arthur.

'Arthur, drive!' shouted Nimuë. 'Trust me.'

'I will not risk her, Nimuë! Agravain, where is she?' he demanded.

'I don't know,' Agravain coughed. 'I couldn't see. I didn't see any of it.'

'Arthur, if you do not drive, all will be lost,' said Nimuë. 'We cannot hold him for long.'

Agravain braced himself against the seat in front, scrunching his eyes closed and beginning to scream.

'He's fighting me!' he said.

Arthur started the car and began to drive, breathing hard.

'Suggestions,' he demanded, but there was no answer from Bors or from Gareth.

'We must get to the house,' said Nimuë.

Never had a car journey taken so fast seemed to last so long. Arthur pulled into the drive of the house, practically jumping up and down in his seat, his nerves shot from the screaming behind him.

He rushed to open the door, but Kay, alerted by a call from Gareth, was there before him.

Gareth and Bors dragged Agravain from the car, carrying him between them so that his feet dragged against the floor as they took him inside, Nimuë carrying on behind, head bowed, water now pouring from her eyes, her hair sodden, one hand outstretched, fist clenched and shaking as she held Malagant in place, working with Agravain to secure the Dread Knight within.

'Into the drawing-room, quickly,' she screamed, and

Arthur was glad the nearest neighbouring house was some distance away.

Arthur led them in, and the two knights tried to lie Agravain on his back, but he curled into a foetal position, bringing his knees up to his chest as he continued to groan and scream. Arthur watched Nimuë move to stand over Agravain as his knight shifted on to his knees, still writhing, his palms forced into his own eyes.

Nimuë placed her hand on his head, concentrating hard, but managed to speak.

'Fetch Excalibur,' she intoned.

Arthur hesitated momentarily, but moved to fetch his sword, feeling its power as he took it from his desk.

'What are you doing, Nimuë?' he asked, standing a little way distant.

'We don't have much time,' she said. 'So speak quickly.'

She closed her eyes, and it seemed as though all the water drained from her body. Her skin shrivelled and crinkled as she poured her elemental magic into Agravain.

She dropped to her knees beside him as he stopped contorting and took her in his arms.

'Agravain?' said Arthur.

His knight looked up and saw his former king standing before him, armed with Excalibur.

Panting, he fought to gather his breath.

'Finish it, Arthur, kill me and kill Malagant,' he said.

'I cannot,' said Arthur. 'You may yet be saved.'

But Agravain shook his head.

'We are one now, the Dread Knight and I. He has used

me to do great evil, Arthur, and he must not be allowed to take a new host.'

'And what of Caitlyn?' Arthur whispered.

'He cannot tell you, Arthur!' Nimuë screamed as she fought to keep the Dread Knight suppressed. 'He is wearing me down. You must do it now!' As she spoke her hair washed away in a flow of foaming water, steam rising from her body. Cascading waterfalls fell from her outstretched arms as she flung them around Agravain's neck.

Arthur stepped forward, still not raising the sword. Agravain looked up from his knees.

'My king,' said Agravain, pleading, 'my hunt is at an end. Your enemy kneels before you, ready for his sentence to be carried out.' His voice dropped to a whisper. 'Help me escape my torment.'

Arthur paused, considering all that had passed between them, all that needed to be rectified or unsaid, which could not be if he did as his knight asked.

He lifted Excalibur, imbued with the power of the lands that formed the isles over which he had been king. Agravain nodded and turned to Nimuë. Arthur realised Agravain recognised the decision had been made even if *he* did not.

His knight leaned in close to Nimuë.

'I love you,' he whispered and, for a moment, she ceased her efforts, looking into his eyes.

'And ... I ... you, though,' she leant her forehead against his, 'I cannot stay forever.'

Red smoke seeped from around Agravain's eyes, drifted up from his body and began to coalesce above their heads.

AGRAVAIN'S ESCAPE

Nimuë cried out and a blast of energy sent Arthur staggering. The red smoke was sucked back into Agravain's body, which shuddered, forcing him to release his grip on Nimuë. Nimuë shook violently as the power thrummed and the water of her body chased the smoke back round Agravain's eyeballs, coursing into his nostrils and mouth, filling his lungs until her entire form had poured into him, her body a rushing torrent that disappeared within her husband, contesting the Dread Knight and holding him within his host.

All fell still and silent, leaving Arthur standing before his kneeling knight.

Agravain looked up and water streamed from his eyes.

'Do it,' he whispered.

Arthur stepped forward and as Agravain bowed his head, he held Excalibur aloft and brought the sword down, severing Agravain's head at the neck.

White light burst from the wound, blinding Arthur, and the other knights. He staggered backwards and shielded his eyes as water dripped from Excalibur's blade.

He lowered his arm and saw Agravain's decapitated body lying before him, a pool of water rushing out from his neck to soak the floors.

Silence fell, and Arthur felt his legs go out from under him.

He dropped to his knees beside Agravain, water soaking into his trousers.

He closed his eyes and leant forward, placing his hand on Agravain's shoulder.

'I'll find the rest of your family and look after them if it takes up the rest of my days,' whispered Arthur.

He groaned as Bors helped him to his feet, and he threw Excalibur to the floor, sending it clattering across the hardwood.

Arthur and the knights were gathered around the table when Tristan and Dagonet got back to the house. Arthur leant down to scratch behind Samson's ears, the big Rottweiler whining whenever he stopped. Bobbi lay quiet by the fire, seeming to know that his mistress was gone.

'What's happened?' asked Tristan, and Arthur took up the tale.

When he was done, the company sat in silence, mourning their fallen brother, Arthur knew. He spared a thought for Nimuë in the midst of his own grief, but before long had passed, he composed himself. There would be time to grieve later.

'We must find Caitlyn,' he said, closing his eyes and pinching the bridge of his nose. He heard Tristan sigh, and when he looked at his knight, he saw his friend's head was bowed.

'We must honour Agravain when we can,' he said, his voice breaking.

'And Nimuë too,' said Bors.

Arthur nodded.

'Never has there been a couple so misunderstood and maligned by those who should have known better. I regret the years we have lost, and I mourn their passing,' said Arthur.

They all fell silent once more.

'When did you last have contact with Caitlyn?' asked Dagonet.

Arthur sighed and pulled out his phone.

'She sent me a message just after ten,' said Arthur.

'And we have the time of the call Malagant made on her phone,' said Dagonet. 'That gives us a narrow time window in which she can have been snatched.'

'And we know that Malagant had that phone in his possession when he made the call. That suggests either he snatched her himself or met up with those who did,' said Tristan.

'They could be anywhere by now,' said Bors. '*She* could be anywhere.'

'Even buried in the woods,' admitted Arthur to himself as well as the company.

'We should go back to the house, have a proper look around,' said Tristan. 'Get a forensics team from Cordon Investigations in there? A dog too.'

'Agreed,' said Arthur. 'Kay, you and Dagonet work from here. See if there are any police reports that might give us a lead, take a look at the phone data, have a look at vehicle movements. Bors and Gareth, you're with me. I'm going back to Hunter's Cottage. Tristan . . . ' said Arthur.

'I've spoken with our guys watching over the rest of the addresses on Agravain's list. They know what happened in Runbridge. Back-up is on the way.'

'Good. If the Order attempt to get to Agravain's family, perhaps we can secure a prisoner with knowledge of

Caitlyn's whereabouts,' said Arthur.

He stood, drew his Colt and checked the action.

'Let's get out there and find her.'

※

As Arthur and his knights walked through the woods to Caitlyn's house, he could not help but contemplate the fate of Agravain and Nimuë, considering their choices, all that both of them must have gone through, seeing their family live and die as the centuries passed. He remembered that last tender moment between them, despairing that he would never know their true tale, that of the lady of the lake and the boldest of his knights, who watched over London in her infancy, a man who honoured justice above all else, and made the ultimate sacrifice.

※

In Highgate Cemetery, off the path, hidden amongst the trees, a mausoleum stands, surrounded by tall grasses. The ghosts of children play before the doors, which the cemetery volunteers often find standing unaccountably open. Birds sing overhead, but otherwise, the cemetery is silent.

Two spectres stand unseen upon the steps, a smiling woman, and behind, his arms wrapped around her, is a towering man in a bowler hat and coat. He holds her close, and, together, they watch their children play.

Thank you for reading **Agravain's Escape.**
I hope you enjoyed it!
If so, please leave a review!

The story concludes in **Tristan's Regret: The Return of King Arthur.**

If you haven't already, sign up to the Jacob Sannox Readers' Club newsletter, and I will keep you updated about its release, other releases, giveaways and discounts. It will not cost you anything, you won't receive any spam, and you can unsubscribe at any time -
www.jacobsannox.com/readersclub.html

Why not try **Dark Oak**, a semi-finalist in the 2018 SPFBO competition, the first book of my dark epic fantasy series,
The Dark Oak Chronicles?
www.jacobsannox.com/dark-oak.html

Humanity has finally defeated the Dark Lord, but Morrick fought on the wrong side . . .

Though he was a slave, he is branded a traitor and must earn the trust of new lords in order to return to his family - if they are still alive.

Now that their common enemy is dead, the nobles begin to forget old loyalties, and Queen Cathryn's realm looks set to plunge into war once more. But there are older and more terrible powers dwelling within the forest, and when they are awakened, Morrick will decide who lives or dies.

Printed in Great Britain
by Amazon